IN THE BEGINNING
WAS GARY, INDIANA

Gwyn McGee

BEYOND MAYA PRESS
IN THE BEGINNING WAS GARY, INDIANA
Cover Design: Steve L. Patterson
ISBN: 978-0-9834270-6-3

For my protective dad,
Willie Williams. East Chicago born.
Gary, Indiana raised. Hardened by the 1950's
Gary steel mill blast furnaces
and the life of a man of color in the USA.

Prologue

2003

The important events of my life were determined the moment I was born in Gary, Indiana. That precise moment. Yes, I'm talking astrology and you may not believe in it. You may not believe my story either...and that's your right. But there is one thing we can agree on; even if reluctantly. Birth ensures death. Most of us don't want to consider that truth, but that doesn't change it. Death quietly waits for us all. Now, consider how you would feel when the possibility of death is clear and present for someone you love. If you've already experienced this life altering moment you'll naturally embrace what I'm about to say. At that time no matter how much you may believe in a spiritual after-life, a particular kind of fear takes hold inside; a fear that can not be expressed in words. I was in that kind of space when I got off the Methodist Hospital elevator in Gary.

I kept repeating five-zero-four, five-zero-four; the

number the downstairs receptionist had given me; the number of my father's hospital room. I didn't want to think about something my good friend, Stephanie, an excellent astrologist, hesitantly told me. But I couldn't help it. Stephanie said there was a cosmic door in my father's astrology chart which made the situation ripe for his transition. For his death. You can imagine how grateful I was when she explained the door was an opening my father *could* go through, but it was not definite. I must say, at this point, I don't believe the future is absolutely fixed. If it is, what is the point of free will? So I held firm in my belief, door or no door, if my father had the will to live, even after a massive heart attack, life for him was still possible.

So much was going on inside my head and heart, my thinking was totally jumbled. Simple things didn't make sense, especially the set of numbers on the hospital wall in front of me, with arrows pointing in two different directions. I stopped, closed my eyes, slowed my breath and chose the direction I should take. With much apprehension, I proceeded up the hall.

Some of the rooms were closed; others were open and I could see patients hooked up to all kinds of tubes and machines. The sight of a particular skeleton-thin man seemed to drain me. By the time I arrived at the following closed-door, I couldn't think at all. So I simply stopped and stood outside. Five-zero-three. Was that the room number? Five-zero-three? I couldn't remember so I convinced myself it was.

I opened the door slowly, and went inside. There was a short hallway with a bathroom to the right, and the only thing I could see inside the room was the foot of the bed. I walked a few more paces and emerged into the small space. The woman who lay in the bed was not my father.

"Oh. I'm sorry. I've got the wrong room," I was embarrassed but probably not as embarrassed as the saggy, minute woman in the thin hospital gown. I turned to leave.

"Hello." Her weak voice stopped me.

I looked at her half bandaged face. I wanted to go to my father but here was another unfortunate soul serving time in the hospital. Someone's mother or sister, perhaps. Daughter for certain. I couldn't just walk away. "Hello." I offered a weak smile. "How are you doing today?"

She didn't answer.

"Come here." She motioned.

Her request caught me off guard. At first I hesitated, but then did as she asked.

"We've been waiting on you, Daughter of Mabel." Her one eye looked straight into mine.

I was shocked, to say the least. Since I did not know the woman, to hear her say she had been waiting for me was surprising enough. But to hear her say 'we have been waiting for you' sent an uncomfortable feeling through me. I started to tell her my name wasn't Mabel just as she placed a cool hand on my arm.

"You'll find a way to do what you must," she said with a labored yet gripping voice.

It was all too much. I withdrew my arm. I didn't know what she was talking about. I didn't want to know. I wanted to see my father. "I must go," I said, nervously looking around her room. There wasn't a single card. No plants or balloons. "What's your name?" I asked out of guilt.

My question seemed to surprise her. "I'm Sally Newman." Her eye penetrated both of mine. "I know you."

I suspected it, but her last statement confirmed her mental instability. Still my heart went out to this woman who looked to be my grandmother's age. I wondered if her confused state was the result of medication or if her delusions were caused by what ever landed her in the hospital.

"We have three more years before the 100th year begins." A strange brightness entered her eyes. "It's all rather exciting, isn't it? That we are all a part of this puzzle. We have our roles to play, you know."

The excitement that beamed from her face was tangible in a non-threatening way and I thought, anything that could make her feel so good could not be all bad.

I smiled at her as a nurse entered the room and walked over to one of the machines. "So you've got a visitor, Miss Newman ." She looked at me. "Are you a relative?"

"No." I stepped back from the bed. "Actually, I was looking for my father's room. I came in here by mistake."

She glanced at Sally Newman then focused her attention on the liquid inside of one of the tubes. "What's your father's name?"

"Benjamin Collins."

"He's next door." She motioned with her head. "What's your name?"

"Rossi Collins."

"Well, Ms. Collins, you should go on and see your father because I'll be coming to his room shortly." The nurse looked at Sally. "Are you ready for your sponge bath, Miss Newman?"

Sally gently nodded her permission, but she continued to look at me.

I felt something from this woman. There was a definite connection between us. I didn't know how to explain it. It's funny how life puts someone special in your path when you least expect it as if a master astrologist has planned it all. I felt as if I was to do more with Sally. What? I had no clue. So I left the room in search of my father.

CHAPTER 1

2006

I had no idea how important Charles Pulaski's visit that night to my aunt's house would be. For certain, the vengeful blizzard may have been a sign. Anyone who has lived through one winter season in Lake County, Indiana would know to remain inside if they had a choice, and eighty-two year-old Pulaski was born there. Storm aside, a feeble, old, white man driving the streets of Gary, Indiana near midnight just didn't happen, unless he was out of his mind. At the time, Aunt Tee and I thought that was Pulaski's case. But I should have known there was more.

I mean, I pride myself on being aware of the messages from The Universe, Spirit, God or whatever you prefer to call it, but Pulaski's claims that night sounded more like the ravings of a conspiracy theorist or an outright crazy man. Me, with my open mind, (such an ironic thing to say under the circumstance) couldn't fathom my purpose for being born was unfolding that night. You see, I believe we are all born with a particular purpose, but sometimes it is difficult to understand because the purpose is much vaster than we can ever imagine.

When my aunt opened the door after Pulaski rang the doorbell with jarring persistence, and there he stood barely keeping his balance in the furious wind and snow, I should have known the elements foretold something massive. I witnessed it all from the kitchen, and I was puzzled by his presence. Aunt Tee was at a complete loss.

"Mr. Charles! What are you doing out in this storm at this time of night? Does your son know where you are?" She asked, talking over an Etta James record that played in the front room.

"I had to come over here tonight, Teresa. I couldn't wait any longer. Tomorrow might be too late."

"What might be too late?" Aunt Tee used her shoulder to force the screen door open. "You come on inside here. I can't believe you've driven all the way over here in this weather."

A stooped Pulaski stepped inside. His gaze focused on my aunt's face as his thin hair clung to his wet scalp. "I thought about it all day; especially after reading that big article in the Post Tribune today about the possibility of Gary being chosen as a Brownfields Property site. This thing that's been going on has got to change. It must," he said through super thin lips. That's when Pulaski produced a brown envelop from a protected place inside his coat. "I came to give you this." He paused. "As collectors we've bargained and shared things about this town through the years. Despite everything that goes on here, I know you love Gary. I do too...even though I moved to Porter County." Pulaski looked down. "After some long hard consideration, I believe you're the best person to give these to." He offered the sealed envelope to my aunt with a steady hand.

For balance, I placed my hand against the faded green wall as Aunt Tee accepted the package. She studied the envelope for a moment then looked up at Pulaski as he continued to talk.

"You're a librarian, Teresa. You're a logical woman. But there's one special thing about you, you've got spunk and an open mind. That's mighty important in this situation." Pulaski stepped toward her. "You see my father was there." His voice lowered. "They chose him to dig the hole before the ritual. He told me the men who had him do it were big shots. The men who came out to the site that night were *very* important. He said he believed they picked him because he didn't understand English very well and he could barely speak it. At that time, my father hadn't long come here from Poland." Pulaski wiped away the melting snow that ran down the side of his face. He took a deep breath. "He said they did some awful things on that site."

"What are you talking about, Mr. Charles?' My aunt's voice was placating but she sounded confused. "What site?"

"U.S. Steel. Gary Works. They did a ritual on that spot before they built the steel mill."

Aunt Tee stepped back and I leaned against the kitchen wall; my antenna on full alert.

"A ritual?" She repeated.

"My father said he'd never seen anything like it in his life." Pulaski's eyes beamed. "Scared him almost to death, he said. But I believe he never told a soul about it until he knew he was dying and then he told me." His lips transformed into a wrinkled line. "I could cuss him for that."

When I heard Pulaski's death bed claim I came

out of the kitchen. Pulaski jumped as if he had been surprised by a ghost.

"Who is that?" He asked, eyeing me suspiciously.

"That's my niece, Rossi. You've seen her before, but I guess she was just a girl back then. She's my brother, Benjamin's child. You remember my brother, Benjamin, Mr. Charles. He came to a couple of our historical society meetings with his wife, Pearl, right before he died."

Pulaski looked as if he were trying to remember before he lowered his voice again. "Those are important photographs in that envelope, Teresa. There's proof there if you know what to look for." His face took on a resigned look. "It's all about power, you see. Gary is known as the murder capital of the United States. Have you ever thought about how that is possible? How did that come to be? I know some folks would just love to think you black people are crazy and no good, but I know it's not as simple as that." He drew another deep breath. "Gary had the first black mayor of a major city in the whole United States, Richard Gordon Hatcher. And there has been some world-class talent born in this town. Emory Tate, the most feared chess master in this country grew up here. It's like something is crying out to the world to take a deeper look." Pulaski turned his back to me and stepped closer to Aunt Tee. "There were forces laid down by those behind U.S. Steel when Gary was planned," he rasped. "They built that mill on land that was special to the Indians."

Pulaski glanced over at me, so I picked up an old Life magazine from one of numerous piles. I didn't want to appear too interested in what he was saying.

"My father was a self starter and somehow, through the years, he managed to get ahead. Back then we weren't nothing but dumb Pollacks to the white folks born in this country, but regardless of what they might have thought about him, my father was a smart man. After he learned English, he learned to read, if he wasn't working he had his head in a book." He paused. "My father claimed major contributors to this country knew about things besides business. Occult things. That they wanted to harness the power created on the land where the steel mill sits now, and control the destiny of the people associated with it."

Pulaski walked over to the front door. He placed his hand on the door knob.

"I'm going to stop talking while I can. I've already said more than I meant to say." He swallowed. "It took a lot for me to tell you about my father, Teresa, but the truth is, I didn't want to die before I told someone." He looked down then up again. "My son would just think I'm crazy. But I'm not." He looked at me then back at Aunt Tee. "I'm not. The founders of U.S. Steel were deep into the occult. And they used that knowledge, knowing what the future might hold."

"I don't know what to say," Aunt Tee said.

"I don't need you to say anything, but I do need you to take me seriously. If that Brownfields Property talk materializes, nearly the whole southeast side of Gary will be demolished and rebuilt. That includes your house, Teresa." Pulaski looked stern. "It might sound good on the surface, but what will it really mean for the people who have lived here for generations? Are they going to give everyone of you new houses on that newly developed land? I don't think so." Pulaski shook

5

his head. "It doesn't feel right to me. Maybe I'm just an old man who knows he's going to die sooner than later, and who wants to do something that might make a difference. Whatever my reasons, I'm sharing this information with you." Pulaski pushed the door open and some of Aunt Tee's papers blew from the cocktail table onto the floor. He stepped out into the snow. "Look for the Great Horned One in those photographs." The wind took possession of his words.

Aunt Tee shrugged at me as she took hold of the screen door. "You be careful, Mr. Charles. I'm going to call you tomorrow."

Pulaski didn't look back. We watched him trudge toward his car. He almost fell before he reached it. Finally, he climbed inside and drove away.

CHAPTER 2

Aunt Tee closed the door, turned, and looked at me.

"What in the world was all that about?" I asked.

"I don't know," she replied. "I don't know what to make of any of it."

"Is he crazy? I mean, do you know if he has a history of mental problems?"

Aunt Tee shook her head. "From the last time I saw Mr. Charles until now I have to say no more than I do."

"Really?" I said, not knowing what to think.

"That's right," she replied. "But all that stuff about U.S. Steel and a ritual makes me wonder. Maybe he is having some problems."

I walked over to the window and pushed the curtain aside. The houses across the street were barely visible through the snow. "I hope he makes it home okay. He looks too old to be driving, period. Let alone driving at night in this weather." I couldn't believe how fast the snow was coming down. "It's been a long time since I've been in Gary during the winter. It's snowing so heavy out there it's almost scary." I let the curtain fall back into place. "The truth is he wasn't rambling or anything. It's just that what he was saying wasn't logical. Did you see the article in the Post Tribune that he mentioned?"

"No. I've been running around so much I didn't have time to read the paper this morning." Aunt Tee stepped over a stack of magazines and reached for a neatly folded newspaper.

"While you're looking for the article can I open the envelope?" I sat on the couch.

She handed me the package and sat down beside me with the paper. "I hope they're not talking about making this area a Brownfields Property project."

"What is that? What's a Brownfields project?" I asked as I removed the photos from the envelope. I examined one of them. It was a slew of attached rectangles and squares.

"Basically it means major redevelopment," she said.

"But isn't that good?"

"Not if they're redeveloping your neighborhood and your house is not a part of the plan. What it boils down to, Rossi, is, it's an environmental cleanup that could possibly replace a bunch of our homes with new businesses and maybe even homes we probably couldn't afford."

I gawked at her. "How can they take your personal property to do that? Do they pay you a lot of money?"

Aunt Tee shrugged. "I only know a little bit about it because something like this happened in another city." She turned another newspaper page. "There's this thing called 'eminent domain'."

"Ohhh." I looked at her. "I remember seeing a news story about that on television. There was this couple standing there saying, you would never think your home could just be taken from you in the United States, but it was happening to them."

"I don't recall anything like that," Aunt Tee replied. "But I remember this group of people in Connecticut who ended up in the same situation. Some redevelopment was taking place in their community and in order to do it, their property was taken."

"That's crazy." I pressed a loose, covered button on Aunt Tee's couch back into place.

"It is." Aunt Tee turned the page. "They took their case to court, but the property developer won because the court basically said the redevelopment was for the betterment of the city as a whole." She turned another page. "I hope they're not planning to do that in Gary. Because you know me, Rossi, I won't stop until I've contacted everybody I know here and all across this country. And you know I know some folks."

"Yes, you do." I looked at what I called Aunt Tee's Wall of Fame; photographs of her with people ranging from President Carter to a young Michael Jackson.

"I will." Her eyes narrowed with determination. "I don't normally use my contacts for personal reasons but I surely would do it in this case. They'll have a fight on their hands if they want to take my house. Folks around here will be protesting from here to Kingdom Come if that's what they're planning to do. I don't know if it will do any good but look… here's the article."

I put the photographs on the table and got closer to Aunt Tee. I glanced over the article as she read and talked.

"They say it is only in the talking stage right now. But I don't even like that," she said. "I don't like that a bit, and you can believe I'm going to invite somebody from this Brown- fields idea to speak at one of our historical society meetings. I want to get to them before it is too late, if it's not already." She scanned more of the article. "The targeted area includes your mother's house too. My-y goodness. I tell you, you work all your life for something and here comes somebody who finds a way to take it." The lines in Aunt Tee's face deepened. "Like you said it's only in the talking stage. It may never happen." There was nothing we could do that night and I didn't want her to worry.

I watched Aunt Tee squint in a particular fashion and suddenly, she reminded me of my father. Don't get me wrong, now, Aunt Tee was anything but masculine. At sixty-seven she still loved her Estee Lauder and high heels.

"For it to be in the newspaper they are already talking very seriously about this." She glanced at me. "And you can believe I'm going to look into it. If we don't keep our eyes open, one day we black folks here in Gary are going to wake up and we won't have a place to lay our heads. It's really a shame."

"Don't talk like that, Aunt Tee," I said. "It's not worth getting yourself worked up about. Let's just see what happens."

Aunt Tee looked at me. "You think I'm worked up. I wonder if your mother has seen this. We haven't seen worked up until they start talking about taking her house."

I sighed. "I can't imagine."

"Once," Aunt Tee smiled softly, "not long after they purchased that house, your father told me it was your mother's dream house. It's obvious she puts a lot of care into it. That's for sure. She's got some beautiful flowers and things in the yard."

I crossed my arms. "Do you know they bought that house more than twenty-five years ago and you have never been inside?"

"Nope, I haven't," Aunt Tee said. "Your mother doesn't want me over there and she has made it very clear how she feels about me."

"What happened?" I asked, something I had wanted to ask for a long time.

Aunt Tee shook her head. "I don't know."

"You don't even have a clue?"

"Nope."

"I would ask her if I was you."

"After all these years?" Aunt Tee folded the newspaper. "If she can still hold on to it and I never knew what it was, I say it's your mother's problem." She looked at me. "You know your mother. Pearl can be one hard to get along with woman when she wants to be."

"Boy do I know it. That's why I'm over here right now. I decided I wanted to spend my last night in Gary right here. I couldn't take any more of her bossing me around. I am forty-four years old. You would think by now she would treat me like an adult. But there's nothing further from the truth." I hung my head. "I don't think she ever will."

Aunt Tee shrugged again. "When you get to be our age, Rossi, it's hard to change. And Pearl has been the same way for a long time."

"I'm not trying to make her change who she is, but I want her to change how she treats me." I sat back. "I don't know how Grandma Anna Lee stands it. She bosses her around like she's a little child too, and she's her mother."

Aunt Tee folded her hands. "Does she have a choice?"

I looked down. "I guess not."

"Well, that's that." She looked at the stack of photos. "You see anything?"

I shrugged. "They don't look like anything to me." I picked them up and passed Aunt Tee one photo at a time.

"What is this?" She turned a photograph upside down.

"I guess they are aerial shots of U.S. Steel, and the only reason I know that is because it's written on the back," I replied.

Aunt Tee turned a particularly blurry photograph over. "Gary Works. 1959". She shook her head as she looked at a few more. "I can't make heads or tails of these. Poor Mr. Charles. He drove all the way out here for this." She put them back into the envelope. "Well, I'm tired." Aunt Tee stood up. "I'm going to call him tomorrow but right now I'm going to bed."

I watched her walk toward the hall and I felt a familiar knot in my stomach. It had tightened a little more each day with my stay in Gary. "Why do you think Mama is so mean, Aunt Tee?" It just came out of me, and I wanted to add the words, especially mean to me. With all my constant pursuit of spiritual truths, I had not found the nerve to address this painful real-life issue. No matter how much I understood auras, karma and multiple lives, I could not find the tiniest opening for healing my relationship with my mother.

My aunt looked back at me. "Now that's a subject we surely won't get to the bottom of tonight." She paused. "Maybe it had to do with her upbringing in Alabama. There wasn't a lot of money and life wasn't easy. It couldn't have been."

I felt somewhat guilty for asking a question that had plagued me for a long time. "Yeah, I'm sure it wasn't."

"But those aren't excuses to mistreat anybody." Aunt Tee added.

I nodded.

"What time do you leave tomorrow?"

"Around five in the evening. I've got to leave here early, though. Grandma Anna Lee has a doctor's appointment in the morning and I promised to drive."

"All right then. I'll see you in the morning."

"Good night," I said, before Aunt Tee disappeared into a bedroom off the hall.

CHAPTER 3

I forgot about Pulaski. I returned to my home in Salt Lake City where I lived a good life. No one special to share it, but still a good life. Don't get me wrong. I've had my share of relationships, but the truth is now that I am ready for a committed relationship; I seem to be a magnet for men who have trouble with commitment. They either don't want it, or already committed to someone else. Karmic retribution? Perhaps. I only know I'm sick of it and by now, somewhat tired of trying. But back to Salt Lake, male relationships aside, my life was good there. You might not think being a multilevel marketer of natural healthcare products would be that exciting. But with the motivational meetings and conventions, it really was. A high school teacher I respected once told me I was a driven human being; so I discovered the multilevel marketing world was a good place for a person like me. Actually, it was through the healings and uplifting personal stories that I witnessed during my work that my spiritual life blossomed. There was an energy in those meetings that was amazing, and the walls burgeoned with the belief that we could do anything. I began to live my life on that premise. Most of my friends and acquaintances knew me for that, but my family was another matter.

Three months after I left Gary and returned to

Utah, a sad occasion precipitated my next visit to my hometown. In a brief telephone conversation, my mother told me, earlier that day, my Grandma Anna Lee had died. That was a Monday and my mother, being my mother, scheduled my grandmother's funeral that following Wednesday. Why? I had no clue, but I quickly made arrangements to fly to Gary. It was a whirlwind time typical of the cyclone of death that tosses you about in ways you can't prepare for, before it spits you out in unfamiliar territory.

I remember sitting through the funeral ceremony thinking about my grandmother, a quiet woman who I knew so little about, yet, I loved her. Once in awhile she'd offer me a sad smile or a gentle pat on the back, but the majority of my memories around Grandma Anna Lee involved ironing. She would iron for long periods of time early in the morning, late in the afternoon, and even in the wee hours of the night, producing crisp, flawless clothes. These cardboard clothes were the gifts Grandma Anna Lee gave to me along with a steady gaze that I believed missed nothing. But I wanted more from my grandmother. I didn't know why I did, and I didn't know how to get it. So I settled for her presence. My tears at her funeral testified to that.

I sat in the church beside my mother, who was the only surviving child of my grandmother's six children, and I listened to what the preacher had to say. Some of the things he said about Grandma Anna Lee I knew as truth; others were totally foreign to me. "Always there when you needed her... forever giving of herself". Perhaps he was right. I hoped so, but the truth is, that had not been my experience. Still I understood quite possibly she was that way. Sometimes what we are able to give to others, we can not give to our family because they have already determined who we are, and are reluctant to accept change in us. There is no place to share the most recent authentic self.

So I did what I was supposed to do in that church. I sat and listened. I sang the songs when it was necessary, and I tried to hold back my tears. I thought about how I believed everyone was born with a purpose. I wondered if my Grandma Anna Lee had fulfilled hers.

Finally, the service was almost over. The choir struck up the last spiritual and everyone stood and sang. Within myself, I invoked the short, sweet prayer on the back of my grandmother's funeral program; I then went on to read the words beneath it. I couldn't believe what they said. Grandma Anna Lee's burial would take place in Hurtsboro, Alabama.

I looked at my mother, who stared straight ahead. If she knew I was beside her, she did not show it. I knew my mother was determined to hold herself together. She was a master of holding and concealing things. Even now she gave a stellar performance; not one tear had fallen during the entire service.

I read the notification again before I looked at Aunt Tee, who sat to my right. Sensing something, she reached out and caressed my hand. I squeezed her hand, hard, before I pointed to the announcement. Aunt Tee picked up her program and began to read. In spite of her profile, I saw the surprise on her face when what it said hit home.

I had to close my eyes then. I had to. I had not been told about my own grandmother's burial place. It hurt me, but I was also baffled. Why was Grandma Anna Lee being buried in Hurtsboro? And why hadn't I been told? I burned to ask my mother right then and there. It took everything in me to hold back.

The gospel song ended and I opened my eyes when cued ushers came and stood beside our pew. Mama had one escort. I had another. Silently, I watched my mother's stiff frame as they walked ahead of us, and through moist eyes I looked at the faces that had gathered on both sides of the aisle. Some I knew. Others I did not. Still something inside of me felt obligated to give a smile, no matter how weak. They had come to honor the dead, my dead, and I wanted to thank them for that. By the time we reached the door my tears increased as my thoughts returned to my grandmother and the distance that had always plagued our family.

The ushers stayed with us, assisting us down the stairs into the basement of the church. When we reached the bottom, right away my mother left and headed toward the bathroom. I caught up with her and took her arm.

"Are you okay?" I asked, as I opened the swinging door.

She glanced briefly, into my eyes. "I'm okay," she said before she disappeared into the stall.

I went in the stall next to hers. I could hear her blow her nose, and I wondered if she was crying. By the time my mother emerged I was washing my hands. How she looked still remains branded in my mind. She appeared smaller to me; not that she was a big woman by any means, but her entire being seemed to have withered. It was obvious the last year and a half had taken a toll on her. During that time, my father, Benjamin, had died. They had been married forty-seven years. And now, Grandma Anna Lee, her mother, was gone. My mother's very body proclaimed how it had weakened her, even if she could not share how she felt.

In that instant, it was clear to me that that kind of loss holds pain I'm sure I didn't understand. Mama had been through a lot. We had been through a lot.

I dried my hands, wishing we could find comfort in each other, but it was extremely difficult. There was a block between us; invisible but strong. Yet, I could not, not hug my mother. I had to share my pain. So I hugged her, but she never folded her arms around me. Still I held on as I weighed her pain against my own and I realized that was something I had done all my life, weighing the pain of others against my pain. It was a suffocating habit; particularly so at that moment because despite everything, I needed to ask why Grandma Anna Lee was being buried in Alabama and not in Gary. Finally, my mother's body stiffened and I let go.

"Mama, I've got to ask you something."

She just looked at me and my heart quickened.

"On the program it says Grandma Anna Lee is going to be buried in Hurtsboro."

"She is." Her eyes never left mine. "I made arrangements for the burial to take place tomorrow."

"So you're flying to Alabama tomorrow?" I couldn't believe it.

"No. This evening."

A dam broke inside me and the tears rushed down my face. "Why didn't you tell me about this?"

My mother looked down. "I know you've got your business and all, and I didn't want to bother or worry you."

"Bother me...." I couldn't understand it. "She's

my grandmother, Mama. There's no business in the world that's more important."

"Well, I didn't know if you had a conference or a seminar. And I knew you were already coming here for the funeral and you'd have to take more time off from work and make all the arrangements, and I—"

"I'm self employed, Mama." I took hold of her forearms. "Mama, she's my grandmother too." My voice vibrated and so did the silence that followed. "Why is she being buried in Hurtsboro?"

Her back stiffened. "That's what she wanted." My mother's eyes glistened with the tears she would not shed in front of me. "My daddy had his ways and his beliefs. He never lived in Gary and he surely didn't want to be buried here. And he made Mama promise she wouldn't be buried here either; that she would be buried beside him in Hurtsboro."

I tell you, I felt like a total outsider, a stranger, although the reflection of my mother and me in the mirror stated otherwise. A loose genetic resemblance was unmistakable. But for some reason I suddenly recalled when my mother was my age she was much more attractive. I don't know why that popped into my mind, and despite my father's heavy-handed disciplinarian approach to all things, there's no doubt he took good care of her; sheltered my mother from the world in a way that, as an adult female, I have never been protected. The wear and tear of attempting to overcome the burden of everyday life decisions weren't etched in her face. They were in mine.

"Hurtsboro? Why is it I've never heard any of this stuff."

"You moved away years ago," she said. "You

missed a lot."

My mother's words were darts and I saw the accusation of betrayal in her eyes. I saw that she believed I had betrayed her. Betrayed the family by leaving. But you know something strange? My mother always discouraged my visits home. She made excuses time and time again whenever I tried to come. And of course when I didn't come I was damned for not coming. If I did come, I was damned. Damned if I didn't. Damned if I did. But at that moment, I refused to allow her to shift the focus of the conversation. "What time is your flight?"

"Four o'clock." She smoothed her skirt with her hand.

"And the airline?"

My mother examined my face. She knew what I was thinking. "It's too late for you to get a flight out now, Rossi."

I thought I had been stunned by Grandma Anna Lee being buried in Hurtsboro. But this! I couldn't believe my mother didn't want me there. My mother hadn't told me because she didn't want me at my grandmother's burial!

CHAPTER 4

The bathroom door opened. It was Aunt Tee. From the look on her face I could tell she knew she had walked into something.

"I knew you had to be in here." She looked at me, then my mother. "Just about everybody has come down from the service. I think they're waiting on you two." She paused. I believe she was weighing the situation. "Miss Bass is standing at the front of the room. I guess she's going to say a few words, and then, after that, everybody can eat."

"We were just on our way out," my mother said. She started toward the door.

"Mama." I was not giving in.

"What?" She looked back at me.

"What airline is it?"

Our eyes locked.

"Delta," she said before she walked out.

Aunt Tee and I looked at each other before we followed her.

Aunt Tee remained by my side as Miss Bass said what she had to say. Afterwards my mother was systematically approached by various people while my aunt and I stood to the side.

"You doing okay?" Aunt Tee asked.

"I guess," I replied.

"I could tell something was going on in there. You asked her about Anna Lee's burial, didn't you?"

"I had to."

"What did she say?"

"She said Grandma Anna Lee promised my grandfather that she would be buried there." I shrugged. "Something about his beliefs. How he would never live in Gary, and he surely wouldn't be buried here. I don't know." I bit my bottom lip to keep from crying. "Then, because I said I'd never heard anything about this, she threw up in my face how I left here so I don't know about my own family." A hot tear escaped. I hated being blamed, and I hated why I was crying.

Aunt Tee took hold of my hand again. "Oh, Rossi. Don't now. Don't. There's enough pain to go around already. Don't let how your mother's handling her grief add to yours." She patted my back. "I'm about your mama's age and I never heard about it either. Your father had a decent relationship with Anna Lee and I think Ben would have said something to me if it was this huge thing that everybody knew about. And you know our parents were born in Hurtsboro too so seems like I would have heard something."

Because of the lump in my throat I could only nod.

"Now I did hear your Grandpa Eli was kind of different. I think he had some Native American in him just like most of the folks from that area. My dad, your grandfather, Richard, knew him, and I distinctly remember him saying Eli's mama was definitely African, and she kept him real close to her while she was alive. But you know, back then a lot of mixing between races went on in Alabama. So your family and my family were no different, and they believed in stuff that folks nowadays would say was a little crazy." Aunt Tee's bottom lip protruded. "But when I think about it, if your Grandpa Eli was into that kind of thinking more than the common folks, there's no telling what he believed."

"That's probably true." I looked down as my thoughts swirled around my mother. "But I got to say it really hurt me when she tossed my leaving Gary in my face. Because from the way she has acted and the things she has said, and still says, I never knew it mattered to her." There was a fresh batch of tears.

Aunt Tee pulled me toward a private corner. "Look here. Your mother left home when she was eighteen years old and she hasn't lived in Hurtsboro since. So this is not about your leaving home. Trust me. By now, Rossi, you know your mother."

I could barely see her through the tears. "Not really."

"Yes you do. I'm not saying you know everything, because she's not an easy woman to understand. But don't let this all be about her. Anna Lee was your grandmother too."

I could see Aunt Tee was getting upset so I gave her a hug. "You're right. We'll get through this." I wiped my face. "But life is so strange."

"I am right," Aunt Tee said.

I was glad to see the stress lines all but disappear from my favorite aunt's face.

"And it is strange. Do you want to know how strange?" She continued, before I could answer. "I was going to call you a couple of days ago, and then Anna Lee passed away." She moved in a little closer. "There might be some truth to some of the things Mr. Charles said."

"Mr. Charles?"

"The man that came to my house that night with the photographs."

"Oh yeah." I watched people line up and fill their plates. I was trying to be present for Aunt Tee but it was difficult. I guess celebrating after a funeral is a good idea. It's supposed to be a happy time; the soul returning to its source and all of that. What I realized was, the activity and conversation were a distraction from the sorrow that accompanied the funeral service.

Aunt Tee continued to talk. "I went to a Gary Historical Society meeting this past weekend. There is a young man who's been coming to the meetings for quite awhile. His name is Thomas Bates. He's a really bright young man. He does a lot of pro bono work for young men here in Gary who he thinks might be able to straighten up their lives if they got a second chance." She glanced at the crowd. "Thomas is rather militant though. And he can be out there a little bit, but that's exactly why I showed the pictures to him; the photographs Mr. Charles gave to me. Plus, he knows his stuff when it comes to Gary."

Suddenly, what Aunt Tee was saying sunk in. I looked at her. "Don't tell me he saw something in them."

"No, he didn't." She shook her head. "But we didn't have a lot of time. He simply glanced over them." Her eyes brightened. "But I gave him a couple of photos to take with him. And Rossi, when I told him some of the things Mr. Charles said, Thomas didn't think they were crazy at all. As a matter of fact he started telling me some interesting things."

"Really?" I said, but my gaze strayed.

"Absolutely. Thomas said— Wait a minute." Aunt Tee stopped. "Is that Dr. Sparks?"

I followed her gaze. "Yes, it is. He's a member of this church."

"Un-huh." Aunt Tee touched my arm. " Look, I'll talk to you about what Thomas told me later. You go on and get you something to eat."

"Come with me." I felt guilty for not being able to give her my full attention. "Aren't you hungry?"

"I am," she said. "But I want to ask Dr. Sparks how he feels about this Brownfields Project initiative. I bet he knows the inside scoop. He's got all kinds of politician friends and getting his take on this will give me a deeper view of the situation." She patted my arm. "So you go ahead. I'll get me something to eat in a minute." Aunt Tee started to walk away. "Are you planning to go to Alabama?"

I nodded.

"Good. Good." She looked directly into my eyes. "Because no matter what your mother thinks she needs you right now. And you need her."

CHAPTER 5

I was able to get a flight on the same plane as my mother. I sat at the very back and was glad the flight from Chicago to Atlanta was relatively short. My mother had made arrangements to ride a van from Atlanta to Columbus, Georgia, where her cousin would pick her up and to drive her to Hurtsboro. But since I was there, I simply rented a car.

The introductions or should I say re-introductions in Columbus were rather subdued. Some of the folks in the neat brick house said they remembered me from when we visited when I was a child, but I didn't recognize a single face. I must say I felt a little out of place with these people who were relatives of mine but felt like complete strangers. Since we had a car I tried to convince my mother to call and tell them we would meet them at the cemetery in Hurtsboro. But she insisted Grandma Anna Lee's body would not arrive for another hour, and besides, her cousins would be disappointed if she didn't come.

I could definitely relate to that. Since I left home at eighteen years of age, my mother had called me a total of seven times on the telephone. And no matter how many times I invited her, pleaded, cajoled; I even wrote a letter, I could not get her to come and visit me. I knew what disappointment was when it came to my mother. So forgive me if I felt a tinge of resentment when she was so concerned about the feelings of what I considered to be strangers.

When we arrived at the house my mother's relatives... my relatives, and there were quite a few of them, offered us something to drink before they sat down and began to talk about life in the country in the old days. They sat on the arms of a well used couch, an old love seat, and folding chairs. They even leaned against the walls and crowded in the doorway between the kitchen and the living room. At first the conversation was slow, but eventually it built to a harmonious clamor of talk and laughter. There were minor confrontations when one person's memories did not match another. But they were always resolved with each one dismissing the other's point of view, and another round of laughter.

Still, what I noticed most was how alive my mother became in this setting. Not having seen these people in ever so many years, she bopped about talking and being helpful to anyone who appeared to need it. And it wasn't an act either. It was if the very air, the very soil of the South fed some nurturing space inside her. I watched as they snickered and gossiped and brought up names that meant nothing to me, and I longed to know who these people were. I couldn't remember my mother ever mentioning them when I was coming up, but maybe she had. Maybe at the time I was too young to care. Now I did care. I wanted to know my roots. But I didn't dare ask because it would have stopped the flow. Anyway, I was comfortable observing this new image of my mother. I liked her this way.

Self-conscious, I looked down when a thought

slipped into my mind. Perhaps it was because I could not share the memories of her younger days that brought such life to my mother, perhaps because I could not share the woman she was then, that she could not share the woman she was now, with me. Although I knew that was not my fault, it saddened me. It saddened me because if it were true, I would never be able to share life with the vibrant woman I observed in Columbus.

The hour passed so quickly, and only one of my easy-going relatives, Cousin Shank, joined us when we had to continue on our mission to bury Grandma Anna Lee. He said he would follow us in his large, blue Dodge truck. Still there were plenty of sincere goodbyes and open invitations for us to visit in the future. I didn't know if I would come back, but I felt if I did, I would be welcomed.

After a jaunt on the highway and a string of country roads, we arrived in Hurtsboro. The downtown was quiet enough, and then we drove up a road where my mother pointed to a house that she said was the oldest in town. Although the structure could only be a dilapidated building to most eyes, there was the definite presence of pride in her voice.

After driving for some distance, we arrived at the graveyard. We got out and we walked through a variety of wildflowers and tall grasses that reminded me of the dried floral arrangements available at Pier 1. Nature was the only one who provided flowers in that cemetery. Most of the small headstones, which included a few stone crosses and praying hands, were tilted with time and neglect. But what did I expect from a little country graveyard just off a dusty, gravel road, beside an old, white church with weathered paint and a small plain steeple?

A couple of men, one in blue jeans; the other in overalls stood near Grandma Anna Lee's casket. They watched us make our way through the headstones. When I was close enough, I saw ropes draped around my grandmother's ornate casket which looked out of place in the modest setting.

"Watch your step now." The man in overalls said, moving his arm to the left. "The grave is right in front of you by a few yards. Don't want nobody to step in it on accident."

I realized a patch of tall, spindly purple flowers had all but hidden the fresh dirt.

The sound of the slow approaching car caused everyone to look toward the road. It stopped. Three women and an elderly man, who needed assistance getting out of the vehicle, made their way toward the gravesite.

A genuine smile lit my mother's face when they reached us. "Hello, Aunt Ida."

"Hey there, Sweet Pea." She wrapped her ample arms around my mother's small body. "My my my, it's been a mighty long time. Mighty long." She looked at me. "And who is this you got with you?"

"You remember Rossi, don't you?"

Her mouth dropped open. "Lawwwd, I haven't seen you child in so long. I never would have recognized you. Come here and give your Great Aunt Ida a hug."

I did what the woman asked. She was vaguely familiar not so much as a memory but, perhaps, as a photograph.

"You don't see nobody but Ida, Sweet Pea?" One of the women put her hand on her slim hip.

My mother wrapped her arm around her shoulders. "Daisy." Then she addressed the others. "Martha, and Uncle Henry. Good to see everybody."

I addressed them too by shaking their hands. Cousin Shank followed with his greetings.

"Well, Baby Anne has finally decided to come home," Uncle Henry said as he held onto my hand and leaned on his cane with the other.

"Yes, yes," Daisy echoed.

Baby Anne? It was strange hearing my grandmother being called Baby Anne, but not as peculiar as hearing my mother being called Sweet Pea.

Finally, Uncle Henry released me and took some steps toward the fresh grave. "I know Eli must be glad." His voice ribald the sound the car made driving over the gravel roads.

"Where is Eli's grave?" Aunt Ida looked around.

"It's right here," Martha said. "I came out here right after Pearl called me and told me Anna Lee had passed." She pointed to a minute headstone that was all but covered by the dirt from the newly dug grave. "I wanted to make sure I marked the right spot so when the grave diggers came they wouldn't make a mistake."

"I'm glad you did, baby," Aunt Ida said. "Somebody's got to take care of these things. Daisy, Henry and I just can't get about like we used to."

"That's understandable, Aunt Ida," my mother said. "We are all getting up in age."

I looked at my mother. Lately, she made those kinds of statements more and more.

"I know that's right," Martha said. "Time waits for

no one."

"It sure doesn't. So I guess we best be getting on with it." Aunt Ida signaled and the men picked up the ropes.

"Do we want to sing anything? Say a prayer or something." My mother looked around.

"I want to say something," Uncle Henry said.

"Go-ahead, Henry," Aunt Ida said. "You're the man around here. And you knew both Eli and Anna Lee better than any of us."

Henry bowed his head. Seconds ticked by before he spoke. "Lord. We thank you for allowing Pearl to have the means to bring Anna Lee back home. I know, Lord, how important it was to my big brother, Eli. He wanted his wife to be buried here in the land of our ancestors. It meant a lot to him," Henry choked up, "and it means a lot to me."

From the nods and the words of agreement, it was obvious everybody felt the same.

For a moment, we stood listening to the wind blow through the wildflowers and grasses that had grown too tall.

"I guess that's all." Aunt Ida looked at each of us.

I saw my mother fight back tears. "I guess so."

The men with the ropes took that as their cue and they began to lower Grandma Anna Lee's casket into the grave. We stood in silence and watched. It was touching but rather austere until Cousin Shank began to sing, Soon I Will Be Done With The Troubles Of The World. His deep strongly accented voice conjured up pictures in my mind of the Southern black experience; its woes and its strengths. It made me think about how we as black folks left the South in droves. I didn't doubt that it was a good thing at that time, but with my grandmother's return in death to the land, it made me wonder if we should have kept a closer, conscious connection to our roots there.

Once the casket was in the grave, tearfully I threw the flowers I held in my hand on top of it, and I heard my mother say, "I guess this is it, Mama. I guess this is it." At that moment I didn't care about the wedge between us, I simply slipped my hand inside of hers.

Before we left the gravesite I walked over to Grandpa Eli's marker. Beneath his name was the word 'Seer' and I wondered if my family, the ones who knew him, really believed that to be true. Obviously, he still held power over their lives. He was powerful enough to bring Grandma Anna Lee back home to be buried, and powerful enough for his surviving relatives to celebrate the fulfillment of his wishes some thirty-three years later.

CHAPTER 6

Cousin Shank drove back to Columbus and mother and I trailed Martha to Daisy and Henry's house. Daisy insisted we come in and visit for awhile, and that we eat some of the food she had prepared with us in mind. At first Aunt Ida put up a fuss because she had also prepared food. But when Daisy announced she had cooked an entire meal Aunt Ida gave in, acknowledging that she had been out done and she knew it.

As we entered, the rectangular house was pungent with the smell of old age, memories and a general cessation of time. The ample picture window was covered by cream colored sheers and heavy, sun faded, green drapes. Although the house was basically neat; there was an abundance of knickknacks and photographs.

"Y'all have a seat where ever you want to," Daisy invited as she switched on an overhead light. "We love having company, and since Henry and I don't get around that well anymore, most of our folks come to our house."

"Especially on Sundays and during holidays," Martha said. "But it's for selfish reasons now, because up to this day, there is nobody in Hurtsboro that can cook a turkey and collard greens like Daisy." She looked at Aunt Ida. "Of course, you run a close second, Ida."

"I ain't stud'n you." Aunt Ida waved her hand. "My collard greens are awful and I know it. I stopped trying to prepare them for myself and anybody else years ago. You don't have to butter me up, Martha. Now, if you're talking about sweet potato pie, I can give anybody a run for their money with some sweet potato pie."

"Well, I got chicken instead of turkey today," Daisy said, "but I did fix some greens and a sweet potato pie. I hope that'll do."

"You didn't have to go through the trouble of cooking for us," my mother said as she followed Daisy into the kitchen.

"Wasn't no trouble at all. I've always loved to cook, and as I get older I find cooking for others gives me something special to do."

As all my female relatives gathered in the kitchen, I sat down in a chair that was a color somewhere between a green and black olive. I must confess I felt rather guilty for what I had been thinking. The truth is, Daisy's dinner invitation wasn't that appealing to me. I had it in my mind that she was too old to cook, and a distinct queasy feeling had come over me at the thought of her preparing food she could barely see. But as I watched her move around her kitchen with the ease of a fish in water, I knew I was totally wrong. I also realized although Daisy said she and Henry couldn't get around as well as they used to, it was Henry who had a problem getting around. Perhaps when you've been with a man as long as it appeared Daisy had been with Henry, and you still loved him, and of course from my history I'm only guessing, you might tend to claim his weaknesses and his strengths as your own. But I was certain to have someone in your old age had to be comforting.

I looked at Uncle Henry who had finally settled comfortably on the couch across the room from me. "How long have you and Aunt Daisy been married?"

"It's been about twenty years, hasn't it, Daisy?" He looked down as he listened for her response.

"Twenty years my eye. I married you when I was twenty years old, and that was fifty-eight years ago."

I shook my head. I couldn't imagine being with a man that long.

"That's longer than you've been in this world, isn't it?" Henry rested against the back of the couch, looking at me.

I nodded.

"You married?"

"Don't be asking her that, Henry." Daisy shouted.

I could tell from Daisy's out-of-the-blue reprimand that at some time my mother had already shared her opinion about my being single at forty-four, and it wasn't a very positive one. To me, my mother seemed to think finding a husband was as easy as buying a loaf of bread from the grocery store.

"I didn't mean any harm, we *were* talking about marriage." Henry's blue rimmed pupils searched my face.

"No, it's okay," I said. I could hear whispering in the kitchen. "No, I'm not married yet."

"So, I guess from the 'yet' in your answer you want to be," Uncle Henry said.

He was so forthright I couldn't help but be the same. "I do, if I find the right man. I don't want to get with somebody just to be with somebody." It was as if Henry's steady life knowing eyes drew the truth out of me.

"That's wise, because there's no hell like living with somebody you don't want to be with. I remember I decided to marry Daisy after Eli told me I had found the woman I wanted, but if I kept messin' around I was going to lose her."

"You never told me that." Daisy said.

"Yes, I have. You just like hearing me say it." He smiled at me. "Eli and Anna Lee had been married for twelve years by the time Daisy and I got married. Now, Eli was the one that had waited around a long time to get married." Henry's eyes narrowed. "I think he was twenty-eight when they got married and Anna Lee was eighteen." His expression lightened. "Eli had had his share of women. My brother was a really good looking man. Tall with this reddish-brown skin, and he wore his wavy hair to the back where it just about touched his shoulders even after it turned gray. So I guess he knew women pretty well, and I know he knew me."

I'd only seen one photograph of Grandpa Eli, but I thought I could see his face in Henry's face. "Grandma Anna Lee was only eighteen when she got married?"

My mother came and stood just inside the living room. "That's all she was," my mother said.

"Wasn't she eighteen, Pearl?" Uncle Henry addressed her.

"That's right." My mother looked as if she was arguing an important issue, instead of answering a simple question. "But that was common back then."

"What are you talking about?" Martha stood in the doorway between the living room and the kitchen. "Girls were getting married off as early as fifteen in those days."

"Ain't that the truth," Daisy added from the kitchen. "Some folks were looking at me as if I was already an old maid because I married Henry at twenty. Seems stupid now, but that's the way it was back then."

"Things were different," my mother said. "When I look back to when we were little, Mama and Daddy had us doing some things most people wouldn't dare do today. Especially Daddy. He believed in his herbs and everything else. And that bag he used to make... he made us wear it around our necks no matter what the sickness was. I know you remember that, don't you Martha?"

Martha's nose turned up. "And would threaten any of us if we tried to take it off before it fell off." She rolled her eyes. "There I was liking Billy Harper, but didn't want to get near him because of that stinky thing." She started laughing and my mother did too. They laughed so hard it was contagious. I laughed a little too, but Henry kept a straight face.

"Now you all can laugh at Eli if you want to, but he was thinking deeper than just a cold or a cough. He always said there was some kind of spirit behind the disease, behind the sickness."

"He did say that." My mother nodded. "Daddy really believed in all that stuff, and I have to admit many a time when there was sickness sweeping the school, most of the other kids got sick, but we didn't."

"That's because nobody else got near you." Aunt Ida turned her head. "Eli was obsessed with that stuff, and when Anna Lee was young, he used to scare her half to death with it."

I rubbed a knee that had been giving me trouble. I wanted to fold that leg beneath me; that always seemed to help. But I knew my mother would consider putting my foot on another person's couch bad manners, no matter how old Aunt Daisy and Uncle Henry's couch was. So I didn't, uncertain if the others held the same opinion.

"I think Mama was a little scared," my mother agreed. "I remember she used to tell him not to talk about it around us children."

Aunt Ida crossed her arms. "I'm telling you I know for a fact when they first got married Anna Lee was scared of Eli and all those things he used to do. She almost didn't marry him because of it."

"Well, if she was afraid she was afraid because she knew it was real." Uncle Henry defended his brother.

Daisy stepped into the living room. "Now don't y'all get Henry started, he says he still— ". She changed what she was about to say in mid sentence. "I'll just say this, Henry used to come back home and tell me some of the things Eli shared with him through the years. Now in the beginning I wasn't too comfortable with it either, but I have to say, I got used to it just as Anna Lee had to have gotten used to it; she lived with the man for nearly thirty years. It's not Eli's fault. It's that African and Indian blood mixing and boiling in the Jenkins veins."

"Just about all the folks in this area have both African and Indian blood," Uncle Henry said. "That's not why Eli was how he was." He locked his fingers together. "Our father was full-blooded Cherokee Indian and a medicine man. Now, he was the one who taught Eli, but my mother shared quite a bit of her knowledge with us boys too. Her mama was African and her father was mixed, but he didn't know his parents. My mama always said if she had had a girl there would have been quite a bit she could've taught her. I think that is one reason she took such a liking to Anna Lee. From the way they were when Eli and Anna Lee first got married, you would have thought Mama had birthed her. I know she taught her a thing or two, I'm sure of it. But it wasn't like my brother. Eli's understanding was Native American and African. So you all can say what you want to," Henry looked at each and every one of us, "Eli knew what he was doing and what he was talking about."

"We didn't say he didn't know," Martha said. "But that doesn't mean folks weren't talking about us for miles and miles around." She made a face. "I don't care what you say, Uncle Henry, Uncle Eli was strange. At least to me he was."

"And to most folks in this town," Aunt Ida said.

Needless to say all the talk about tribal knowledge and herbs intrigued me, and to talk about them so openly with my mother present, extremely satisfying. Once in awhile my mother and I would have a conversation about life after death, at least what she thought about life after death. Those talks always dealt with the paranormal and not so much the spiritual. She'd talk of women who had encounters with their husbands after they died as if they were unwanted ghosts infringing on their lives, and no matter how I tried to open her mind to see them as souls who had moved on, but simply wanted to help those they loved, it was difficult to do.

"Why did my grandfather want Grandma Anna Lee buried here in Hurtsboro?" I asked Uncle Henry, but Aunt Ida was the one to answer.

"He just didn't like the north. He said the folks

who moved away were losing their connection to their past and taking on a new one. This is how he explained it to me." Her expression turned faintly mocking. "Certain plants, certain people feel better and live better in the land where they come from. It can be deadly for most folks who move away from their homeland."

"Well, the way it is, if that's true most of the Africans shouldn't have survived being over here in America." Martha surmised.

"That's right," my mother said.

"But he didn't mean it like that," Uncle Henry explained. "He meant that people are more connected to this earth than most of us realize. Eli said, if people ate the vegetables from the ground where they lived, they would be healthier. Less folks would be sick."

For a moment I focused on the picture frame above Uncle Henry's head. When I was a child I saw the same artwork often enough. Like images of Jesus Christ, this image could be seen in most black homes. Martin Luther King, Jr., President John F. Kennedy and his brother, Robert; the three of them shown together in a flimsy, faux gold frame that showcased them separately.

"My brother said," Henry continued, "that's why folks who know about these kinds of things say the earth is our mother. And that people fare better when they remain in the land where their ancestors come from because they've already created that connection between the Earth and the cells of the people who live in that area. I'm telling you Eli was deep." Henry's lips pursed. "That's why I would sit and let him teach me because I understood how much he knew. His knowledge came from this world and the other." He emphasized his words with a nod. "My brother was deep."

Aunt Ida hunched her shoulders. "That's all a matter of opinion."

CHAPTER 7

The more Henry talked, the more I felt a kinship to my grandfather and wished I had been given a chance to know him.

"Do you have any pictures of Grandpa Eli, Uncle Henry?"

"The only picture I have of my brother is right behind you there, on that table."

I turned around.

"Go on. Take a good look." He encouraged. "Although it's mighty old and faded now. It was probably taken over fifty years ago."

I picked up the tin image and stared at my grandfather. He wore what looked like a black, felt cowboy hat, a short sleeved white shirt and dark pants. The photo stopped at the top of his thighs, but I assumed from the way his elbows stuck out that his hands were on his hips. Grandpa Eli's face was weathered and dark. His eyes penetrating.

"Let me see that, Rossi," my mother said.

"So, Grandpa Eli felt Grandma Anna Lee would rest better here in Hurtsboro." I said as I passed the photograph to my mother.

"Now that's a different story." For what little good it did, Uncle Henry cleared his throat. "You see, my brother had some strong feelings about that area of this country. He always said that area of Indiana next to Chicago, even up toward Michigan was special Indian land. Eli said Indiana in particular, had spiritual significance for Indians and all indigenous people here in America."

"Even though I said Indian, Henry, the right word to use these days is Native American." Daisy looked at me.

"I know that." Henry waved her off. "I'm not trying to be what they call politically correct right now, Daisy, I'm trying to make a point."

Daisy made a funny expression, turned around and went back into the kitchen.

"This is how it was, Rossi," he continued as my mother gave me the photo and I returned it to the table.

"Eli said all the medicine men knew about. It was a message to this country, that Indiana, which means 'land of the Indians' by the way, had a special-purpose for the red man in America. Especially that land right there at the tip of Lake Michigan." He swallowed. "Now that brings me to Gary, Indiana. And I remember it as if it was yesterday because Eli really didn't like it when Pearl moved there. He came over to my house that evening and said he couldn't stop Pearl from going because she was of age and her heart was so set on a new life up there and what she felt would be a better life. But Eli said he and Anna Lee were not going to follow her to Gary like so many people were following their children up North. He said that steel and metal wasn't good for the folks up there."

My mother moved closer to Henry. "That's right. Daddy wasn't happy with me but I had made up my mind. I know he didn't want me to go."

"Martha, can you come here for a minute?" Daisy called from the kitchen.

"Sure I can." Martha left the room.

"No, he didn't want you to go." Uncle Henry agreed. "So many folks were talking about all the jobs that were in Gary at that time because the steel mills were going strong. That mill in Gary was in its heyday back then. But Eli told me he had several spirits, Indian." He shook his head. "Native American, spirits come to him and tell him no good was going to come out of that city because its roots were built on the bones of Native Americans. He said there was death there. And that the Indian ancestors had been degraded on purpose." Uncle Henry crossed his arms. "And he said there was too much steel in that area. Too much fire. Eli said steel and fire have their own energy, like something live. And it was too much in that little town. He said in the end it was going to affect the people there in a bad way."

"Awww shoot." Aunt Ida sat down in a chair in the corner. "You're just like your brother talking nonsense. What bones?"

For me, what Uncle Henry said outweighed Aunt Ida's skeptical remarks. I thought of Pulaski and his photos of the steel mill.

"Hear me out, Ida." Henry remained calm. "Eli said that Gary's roots, the reason why Gary existed was because of the steel mill, and that some of that land under the mill was Indian burial grounds. That those folks had simply flattened that ground that the Red Man had honored for countless generations, disregarding the bones and everything, and built that big old steel monster right on top of it. He claimed any black folks with the least bit of Native American blood we're going to get caught up in that place."

"Now this is all news to me." My mother put her hands on her hips. "Caught how?"

"That they would be caught in a cycle of birth and death, birth and death—that they would continue to be born in that area, until the right thing was done."

"Henry, you're going to wear them out with that stuff." Daisy complained from the small kitchen. "Martha and I are getting the table ready and the corn bread is in the oven, so don't y'all let Henry make you too tired to eat."

"But what about people like me who simply moved there?" my mother asked.

"Eli said you were being drawn there because of your Native American blood."

"I can't believe all of the black folks in Gary have Native American blood. And it surely doesn't explain why we Black folks are up there killing each other. Because that's what's going on." My mother crossed her arms.

I glanced back at Grandpa Eli's photo and wondered what he would say if he were here.

"Is that right?" Aunt Ida shifted in her chair.

"It's horrible." My mother continued. "There have been some killings this year that make you wonder if Satan himself isn't in Gary. Two sisters." She looked at Uncle Henry before she cast her gaze over the rest of us. "Now you talk about Indians; their father was some kind of Indian and you can tell. They lived next door to Ben and me when we still lived with his parents, before we bought our house. They probably were about my age or little older with nobody else in the world but each other when it happened." She paused dramatically. "Those women were killed like something in a movie. One of their heads was cut off, and the other one was chopped up." She crossed her arms. "Then, who ever did it, burned the house to the ground. But even though their bodies were burned the police could still tell what had been done to them. And I knew these women," she looked at each one of us, "so how do you think that makes me feel?"

"I don't know if I could live in a place where people do those kinds of things," Martha, who had come from the kitchen said, truly horrified. "Did they ever catch the people?"

"No." My mother shook her head. "No. And those women were not into drugs or anything. I knew them because they used to live next door to me and they were from Alabama."

"My goodness," Daisy said.

Mother kept talking. "They were churchgoing women, but they never married and they stayed together just to make ends meet. Those young folks have gone crazy up there. Crazy, I tell you." She paused and the room remained silent because we were all sufficiently shocked. "Just the other day, just up the street from me and I don't live in a bad neighborhood, an elderly woman was found beaten to death in her home. And to make it even worse, they didn't find her body until a week later."

Aunt Ida's eyes widened. "Chile, no."

"Yes, just right up the street. They don't know if they were looking for money or what, but I even heard they raped her." My mother walked across the room as if the very words heated her up. "An eighty year old woman. Now why would somebody want to do that? I tell you those young folks have gone crazy. It's the drugs. They're always killing and shooting each other, but they should leave us old folks alone."

"Eli said no good was going to come out of that city." Uncle Henry snatched the opportunity to get back to his point. "And you have to admit a lot of the folks who moved from this part of the south, from around this area even, moved to Gary."

"Ye-es," my mother focused on Uncle Henry, "there are plenty of people that I know who moved there."

"So, just what are you trying to say, Henry?" Aunt Ida demanded.

"I'm trying to tell you what Eli said about it. You can accept it as truth or not."

"What did Grandpa Eli say?" I asked.

"Eli said there would be a lot of spiritual payback up there because the folks of mixed heritage, African and Indian, were a part of the ancestor's plan. A way to show America it was on a fiery path because of how it treated the people of color in this country."

Aunt Ida gave a loud sigh.

I rested against the back of the chair and caught a hint of dankness.

"Now this is how it went." He rushed on before anybody could interrupt. "He said the African had been taken from his soil in Africa and put to work on another man's land here in America, and because of that, that memory is in our cells,. Now, the Indian's land had been taken from them too. So when you mixed the two bloods together." He patted his unexpectedly strong sounding chest. "The offspring carried the purpose of both people within them. And now Pearl is talking about all the killing and stuff that is going on up there in Gary. That's going to bring the focus of this nation, this world, on that city, and to the plight of indigenous people in this country."

"Well we don't want to be known for that," my mother said.

Aunt Ida got up. "I hope the food is almost ready, Daisy, because Henry has gone too far, now."

"Everything sure does smell good." My mother took the opportunity and followed Aunt Ida into the kitchen.

My mind examined Uncle Henry's words. "Did you know Gary, Indiana is the murder capital of the United States?" I asked Uncle Henry who was moving to the edge of the couch.

He looked into my eyes. "No, I didn't."

"Yep, for the last nine years it has had that dubious mark of distinction." I told him.

"See there." He pushed himself up from the soft couch. "All I did was tell them what Eli said. Now I'm not saying it's all true, but he was right about so many things it's hard for me to believe he would be totally wrong about this."

I stood up too. "I can't say I believe every word of it, Uncle Henry, but something about it rings true for me."

He looked deep into my eyes. "You come with me. I want to show you something."

"Okay," I said.

I believe in karma, but to hear Gary with its murder capital crown was a part of a spiritual plan was tough to get my mind around. Again I thought of Pulaski who claimed a bizarre ritual had been performed on the spot where U. S Steel was built. It still sounded impossible, but I was certain there was a grain of truth somewhere in Eli's and Pulaski's beliefs.

I followed Uncle Henry as he slowly made his way to the backdoor through the kitchen.

"Where are you two going?" Daisy asked.

"I've got something I want to show Rossi out here," Henry said.

"Don't be lettin' Henry drag you out there." Ida twisted her mouth. "I'm sure she's had enough of you by now."

"No, I want to go," I quickly said.

"You do?" Ida looked skeptical.

"Let 'em go on," Daisy said, "but don't be out there too long, Henry, because the cornbread is almost done."

Uncle Henry didn't say a word. He simply opened the creaky screen door.

CHAPTER 8

I followed Uncle Henry to some white plastic chairs set beneath a fig tree. He sat in one of them and I sat in the other. In front of us, a chain link fence that leaned precariously on one end ran clear across the back of the yard. Two medium-size wooden boxes of flowering plants with a meager vegetable garden in the middle, grew against it. On the other side of the fence was a thick forest of pines, deciduous trees and under-brush. The air smelled of grass and a large, almost gone wild, rosebush burdened with pink blossoms.

"You see all that back there?" Uncle Henry pointed toward the forest.

"Yes," I said.

"All that used to be our people's property." In a stiff fashion, he swept his arm through the air. "All of it. And Eli and Anna Lee's place used to be back there. Now if you keep on down in front of our house, here and around," he swept his other arm in the opposite direction, "you would come to the main road and you wouldn't be far from the main part of town and the Hurt House. Our land used to butt up against the land owned by the Hurts, the man who this town was named for."

"It did?" Again Uncle Henry piqued my interest.

"Sure did. Our family had a place not too far

away from theirs', but we ended up losing our land. Truth be told we were cheated out of it. But we weren't the only ones." His chin jutted out. "That happened to a lot of black folks around here."

I leaned on the elbow nearest to Uncle Henry's chair. "What happened with our family?"

"Ohhh," he rubbed beneath his eye with the back of his thumb, "this white man who acted like he was our friend and was going to loan us some money against the property tricked my brother. Foley said Eli was signing a loan paper but actually it was a Bill of Sale and we ended up losing it."

"No way."

"Yep, he did. It didn't say Bill of Sale at the top or anything but it was down there in the writing. "Uncle Henry's eyes beamed. "Eli couldn't read or write or anything, and he trusted Foley. He had known him almost all his life." He nodded. "It was an ugly mess, and that's what really broke my brother's spirit. He ended up getting sick, and he died not long after that."

"How much land was it, Uncle Henry?"

"We had forty-five acres. But that deal involved forty of 'em. We sold four more some years back because we needed the money."

It surprised me to hear that my southern relatives owned that much property. "Where did you get all that land? Did the slave master give it to your parents or something?"

His forehead creased with incredulity. "No, the Indians gave it to us. There are stories of Indians giving quite a bit of land to black folks in Hurtsboro. They lived right along the Hurtsboro Creek back then." He pointed. "And part of the creek ran through our land."

"Native Americans gave land to black folks...I've never heard of such a thing," I said.

"Well, I know for a fact some of that went on," Uncle Henry said. "I don't know if all the stories are true, but I know they gave it to our family because, like I said, my father was part Indian. He was part Muskogee. Most people know them as Creeks, but my father said they were Muskogees. And back in the real early days when they were still trying to keep their land from the white man, they weren't into the slavery thing at all. Now I can't speak for any of the other tribes, but I know for a fact the Muskogee weren't into slavery. They married Coloreds and everything."

"Really?" I was surprised again. "Maybe that was true about the Muskogee, but I don't think that happened a lot," I said. "Recently, there have been lots of black people interested in finding out about their ancestors, and they've been taking these DNA tests. And what's come out of it is, there are less African-Americans with Native American blood than most people thought." From the look on Uncle Henry's face I wasn't sure if he understood what I was talking about, but he nodded anyway.

"Like I said, I don't know about the other tribes, but I know it is true about the Muskogee because our father was proud of his Muskogee roots. He even believed his father, which would be my grandfather, was a man called The Alabama Prophet. Now his daddy was Indian, full blooded, but my daddy said, because of the wars and politics that was going on back then, he didn't remember him much. He said he got to see him when he was real little, but after that he didn't get to see him anymore."

"So your grandfather was known as a prophet?"

"All I know is they called him The Alabama Prophet, and he was a famous Muskogee Indian." His countenance glowed with pride. "Eli said he was what they called a knower. He could see things in the future, and the folks in these parts depended on him for that."

This was a subject that was close to my heart, and to hear one of my relatives was known for it amazed me. "Wow."

"Eli took all that stuff very seriously."

"So do I."

Uncle Henry stared at me for a moment before he leaned toward me, his eyes intense. "My brother felt there was something special about our family because of our father, and because Mama's father was a bush doctor for his tribe in Africa." Uncle Henry continued to stare into my eyes. "Eli said the ancestors told him, the ones that had passed away, when you have two bloodlines like that come together; it is very powerful, and there's always a reason that they come together."

"Foods ready," my mother said as she held the screen door open.

"This is really something." I said as I watched her stand there.

"Yes, it is. There's a lot of history in this family." A crooked smile lifted Uncle Henry's expression as he stood, slowly, from his chair. "Lots of stuff flowing in these veins."

"There definitely is," I said, and I wondered if there truly was a reason behind it all.

CHAPTER 9

After eating I helped Daisy and the others with the dishes, but the entire time I was thinking of Aunt Tee. I had to talk to her. I thought of telling Uncle Henry about Pulaski, but I changed my mind because I wasn't sure what there was to tell. Yet deep inside I felt there was a connection. So the first chance I got I went outside, stood by the rental car and called Aunt Tee. I was about to hang up when she finally answered.

"Hello." She sounded out of breath.

"Hello, Aunt Tee."

"Rossi? Is everything okay?"

I could hear the wheels of her mind turning. "Everything is fine. Grandma Anna Lee's burial went fine.

"That's a relief to hear. I wondered how that was going to work out. So I'm glad to hear things went well."

"They did, and I just wanted you to know that."

"That's good." She paused. "I guess I wasn't expecting to hear from you so soon. What have you all been doing?"

"Well, we just finished dinner. My Great Aunt Ida, a cousin named Martha, Mama and I had dinner at Grandpa Eli's brother's house. His wife cooked."

"Well that's nice. That's real good."

I watched a crow stroke the wind high above me before he descended onto a magnolia tree branch. His blackness contrasted powerfully against a gentle, white blossom. "But I had to call you, Aunt Tee," and I guess my excitement reflected in my voice.

"I knew you were calling about something else. What's going on down there, Rossi?"

I thought about some of the things Uncle Henry said. "When I think about the synchronicity of it all, it's really bizarre, Aunt Tee."

"What's bizarre?"

"First of all, I asked Uncle Henry why Grandpa Eli wanted my grandmother buried here. You won't believe his answer made me think about Pulaski."

"Hush your mouth. What did he say?"

"Basically, he explained Grandpa Eli was a kind of medicine man, a spiritual man."

"I definitely have heard something like that before. I told you, I have relatives from Hurtsboro too. Elijah Jenkins had quite a reputation in those parts."

"Obviously, because from what I understand, Uncle Henry said Grandpa Eli communed with some spirits or something like that, and came to understand no good was going to come out of Gary because of how it started. That's why he didn't want Grandma Anna Lee to be buried in Gary. He didn't want her to get caught in the same cycle he said a lot of folks who are buried there are caught in. So, you know that made me think of Pulaski."

"Wait a minute. I don't understand," Aunt Tee said.

"You see." I had to make myself slow down. "Grandpa Eli believed the mill, U.S. Steel, was built on top of Native American burial grounds."

"Didn't Pulaski say the same thing?"

"That's what I want to ask you." I replied.

"I think he did." I could hear her mulling it over.

"Have you talked to Pulaski since he came to your house?"

"It's been a while since I've talked to him or seen him. I did call him the next day after he came to my house to make sure he made it home okay, and his son answered the phone." She paused slightly. "I don't have a good feeling about him."

"Why is that?"

"Well... after I asked to speak to Mr. Charles he asked who was calling. I told him who I was and he said real ugly like, 'Oh, you're that woman who my father went out in the middle of the night to see.'"

"No, he didn't."

"He did say that to me. But I tried to give him the benefit of the doubt, because I thought guess he was probably worried about Mr. Charles being out so late in that snow storm. Anyway, then in this authoritative voice he asked me why Mr. Charles had come over to my house so late at night as if me and Mr. Charles might have something going on. My God. The man is eighty-two years old and in bad health, and I'm damn near seventy. But I did get that distinct impression from the way he said it."

"I wonder why he would react like that?"

"I don't know, but I was offended. I started to tell him about the photos, but I remembered that Mr. Charles said something about how his son would probably think he was a crazy if he told him about them. Plus, I didn't want to tell him nothin' after how he questioned me. If he wants to believe that his sickly eighty-two year old father has gone out in the middle of the night for some hanky-panky then let him dream on. So I simply told him Mr. Charles brought back some things he had borrowed from me. He didn't sound like he believed me but I don't care."

"Have you met his son before?" An unfamiliar couple in a blue sedan slowly drove by. The man and the woman waved as they passed and I returned the courtesy.

"I met him at a Gary Historical Society Christmas party one year, but I don't remember his name."

"So did he let you speak to Pulaski?"

"Finally, he did. I asked Mr. Charles how he was doing, and he said he was doing okay, that he had made it home without any problems. Then he started whispering, and he asked me what I thought of the package. I didn't know what to say, Rossi, because you know, those photographs don't look like anything to me."

"They don't look like anything to me either," I said.

"So I said I thought they were interesting, and I asked him where did he get them. He said the wife of an old friend who died about a year ago was getting rid of some of his things." Aunt Tee coughed into the telephone. "Excuse me, Rossi." She stepped away to clear her throat. "He said the woman knew he collected things about Gary, so she called him and asked if he wanted a box that had a bunch of stuff about Gary in it. After he told me that I guess his son must have come in the room because he hurried off the telephone."

"I've gotta be honest with you Aunt Tee, I think your friend Pulaski has some problems. He sounds paranoid to me."

"I wouldn't say that, but I sure hope Mr. Charles isn't becoming senile. I surely do." She sighed. "But look here." Aunt Tee went on. "You know the young man I mentioned to you after the funeral. The one named Thomas."

"Thomas?"

"Yes. I told you about him when we were talking downstairs at the church, after the funeral. The intelligent young man that's a member of the Historical Society. I let him look at Mr. Charles' photos, remember?"

"Oh yes. I remember now. What did he have to say about them?"

"I told you, Rossi, we didn't have but a little bit of time so he just glanced over them." Then she hurried on. "But I know your mind was on other things, and that's okay. Anyway, I let him keep a couple of them to study."

"I'm sorry. I was having a hard time concentrating." I looked up at the house. My mother was standing in the window watching me.

"I told you, don't worry about that. But listen because there's something else that I want to tell you that he said."

"Tell me. Tell me." I felt instantly excited again because of the Grandpa Eli/Pulaski connection.

"Now once again, I want to remind you Thomas is a smart man."

"Believe me, you've made that very clear."

"I'm telling you that again because of what he said."

"Okay. Tell me, Aunt Tee." I began to lose my patience.

"Thomas said he wouldn't be surprised if there had been a ritual or something of that sort done there, because the men who were behind U.S. Steel, some of the really big names were into that kind of thing."

My eyebrows went up. "What kind of thing?"

"Ritual. Magic."

"What?"

"That's what he said, and he was serious. Thomas said they were associated with some kind of round-table or something."

"Come on now, Aunt Tee. A roundtable?" My eyes rolled upward. "We're not talking about King Arthur and Merlin, are we?"

"Now you're messin' with me. I told you Thomas was out there."

"He is really out there. I don't know who sounds the craziest him, or Pulaski. Where did this Thomas go to school? Or did he go to school at all?"

"See there, you're closing your mind to me, Rossi. Some of the greatest thinkers of our time didn't have a formal education. They may have read a lot, but they were not formally educated."

"So he doesn't have a degree."

"Yes he does. But what I'm trying to say is, you can go to a library and research all kinds of—"

"I know, Aunt Tee."

"Rossi, I need you to hear me. We've got to keep an open mind. We are not dealing with some ordinary subject matter. And I'ma tell you, through the years I've come to trust Thomas and his way of thinking. Not that I believe everything he say, because I don't. But Thomas is very knowledgeable when it comes to this kind of thing. That's why I showed the photos to him."

"Okay, I can accept that. But to say the founders of U.S. Steel were dealing in rituals, that's a mighty hard pill for me to swallow. And I am open-minded. I just can't imagine what academia would think of something like that."

"Thomas says academia is not interested in this subject. If you want to get him riled up start talking about what is acceptable to academia."

I no longer wanted to discuss this Thomas's merits and demerits. "Did he say anything else?"

"Yes he did, but I think you should talk to him about it face-to-face. You're coming back here to Gary, aren't you?"

"Yes, I'm coming back. I'm going to stick around for a week or so. Long enough to make sure Mama is doing okay."

"Good. So what I'm going to do is call Thomas and set up a meeting between the two of you."

I shrugged. "Sure, it couldn't hurt anything."

"It's as good as done then. It'll be better if you talk to Thomas directly because I can't explain everything the way he can."

"I said I'd talk to him."

"Good." She repeated.

There was silence on the line.

"Well," Aunt Tee said, "I'll see you when you get back then."

"All right," I said.

"Bye."

"Goodbye."

I listened as my aunt hung up the phone, and I couldn't help but wonder what I was getting myself into and if any of this was true. Was it possible such powerful men were into rituals and the occult? It wasn't that I was not aware of influential men and women who had turned to the occult for power. But there was something about the thought of these men, pillars of the financial and charitable institutions of America using such unorthodox means that made me feel very uncomfortable. I stood for a moment and thought about it. Then I found myself looking uneasily up the street before I started toward the house.

CHAPTER 10

Mother and I got up early the next morning and made the drive from the Columbus hotel to the Atlanta airport. Initially, she tried to convince me there was no need for me to stay in Gary, but with a little insistence on my part I was surprised when she gave in without much of a fight. In looking back, my mother's behavior over the next two days wasn't what I expected at all. She was gayer than usual, easier to talk to and our conversations, which rarely went well in the past, I would talk and she would talk over me, almost resembled authentic communication. I must say, I enjoyed those two days my mother and I spent alone.

On that third night before I went to bed, I lit a scented candle that I had thrown into my suitcase. It was a mixture of frankincense and lavender. I love the smell of frankincense. At home, scented candles were part of my nightly meditation. So that night I decided to contemplate Grandma Anna Lee's death, Grandpa Eli's truths and Pulaski's claims. When I awoke the next morning and went into the kitchen my mother was drinking coffee. I wasn't prepared for the drastic overnight change in her.

"Good morning, Mama."

She looked up over her coffee cup. Her body portrayed a resistance I had come to recognize over the years. "Good morning." She put her cup down. "What were you burning in your room last night?"

It was a definite accusation. "I didn't burn anything," I replied, defensively. "I lit a candle."

"I know I'm not crazy. I could smell something in there." She looked down at the table, and avoided my eyes.

"It was a scented candle." I straightened the napkins in the wooden napkin holder.

"It smelled strange to me. I'm not accustomed to all that."

"It was just a candle, Mama. You can buy them anywhere. In the grocery store, a department store...." I didn't understand why she was reacting the way she did.

"I don't like the smell and I'm not used to that strange stuff, Rossi. I'm too old for it."

Instantly, I thought of the frankincense they used in the church she attended; a much more potent frankincense than a candle could ever emit. I also thought of Grandpa Eli and the herbs he obviously used when she was a child. But I looked at her stiff, round shoulders and decided a scented candle wasn't worth the hassle.

"Okay, I won't light it anymore."

She talked as she got up from the table. "That smell will be all in my curtains and in my sheets." My mother walked over to the sink. "I'm not used to that stuff."

"I won't light any more candles, Mama," was all I could say. Actually I was a little stunned by the exchange." I'm going to take my shower now." I passed by her. "Aunt Tee wants me to meet this guy from the Gary Historical Society around lunchtime. Is there anything you want me to help you with this morning?"

"No." Her shoulders still twitched with resistance. "I'm going to be working out in the yard."

"Do you need some help?" I could tell she was trying to relax into my easy acceptance of her position, but the air still held a kind of electricity as if it was difficult for her to pull back.

Suddenly, her eyes bore into mine. "Help? I don't need any help. Every since your father died I've been doing this stuff by myself. Your grandmother surely couldn't help me. No, I don't need any help. You go on with Teresa," she blurted before she walked away with heavy steps.

"Fine," I said. I just didn't have it in me to take it any further. Perhaps she felt totally alone now that her mother and my father were gone, and felt I, who chose to move so far away at an early age, would not be there for her. It was truly a complicated situation; because deep within me I did not know if she really wanted my help. I recalled the countless times I had offered to fly in and help with my father when he was ill. Help with my grandmother and my mother herself when she was sick, but my offers were always vehemently turned down. I had spent many nights tossing and turning, trying to go to sleep as I replayed our conversations in my mind. I felt I could slip into slumber if I only understood why she constantly pushed me away.

So that morning I felt particularly hurt. Maybe I was hypersensitive because of my grandmother's death, but somehow I felt the whole candle thing symbolized how little my mother could take of me... that if my mother couldn't accept something as small as a lit candle, there was not much that I brought to the table that she was willing to accept.

By the time I showered and dressed, ate breakfast, and headed over to Aunt Tee's, the lingering hurt was almost imperceptible. An early riser like my mother, Aunt Tee had washed clothes and was in the middle of folding them when I arrived. We talked about the funeral, and Aunt Tee confidentially shared with me how many people were surprised that Grandma Anna Lee was being buried in Alabama.

"But knowing your mother," Aunt Tee's eyes twinkled, "no one plans to ask her why."

I didn't try to hide my smirk. "What did you tell them when they asked you?"

"I told them the truth." She nodded. "That Anna Lee's husband wanted her buried next to him. That's all they needed to know. I didn't go into any further details."

I feigned shock. "You didn't tell them my grandfather was a roots man and that he said anybody buried in Gary was doomed to be born here lifetime after lifetime?"

Aunt Tee stopped folding a towel. "Nope. I didn't tell anybody anything about what Eli was, and this is the first time I've heard this lifetime after lifetime claim."

I looked at the spiked clock on her wall. "Then I must fill you in when we have time. But shouldn't you be getting ready to meet the guy... Mr. Bates?"

"I'm not going." My aunt looked at the same clock. "And it's time for you to get out of here."

"I didn't realize you didn't plan to go with me."

"No, I didn't intend to," she replied. "Plus, I'm not feeling that well today, so it's all for the better. And I want you and Thomas to talk, alone. I don't want to be a distraction."

I narrowed my eyes. "I think you're trying to set up more than an informative meeting. You're not trying to hook me up with this Thomas Bates, are you?"

Aunt Tee crossed her heart. "Of course not."

"Okay now." I examined her face. She did look a little drawn. "That being the case, you know you won't be a distraction, Aunt Tee."

"I told you I'm not feeling well, and it is important that you and Thomas talk alone. I want you to see what you think about him and the things he has to say. And I think things would work better if I wasn't there."

I watched as she continued to fold clothes.

"If you say so." I glanced at the clock again. "But I thought you were going with me. I was going to tell you what Uncle Henry said about Grandpa Eli." I stood up. "We haven't had a chance to talk about that."

"And you know I want to hear it. But we've got plenty of time. Right now you need to go to the McDonalds that's near Fifth and Broadway. Thomas is going to meet you there on his lunch break."

I stretched. I realized I felt tired although the day had just begun. The encounter with my mother had drained me somehow. "What does he look like?"

"Tall. Medium brown skin, something like mine." She looked at her wrist. "He's got dreadlocks that come about to his shoulders, and most likely he'll be wearing a white shirt and tie."

"A somewhat militant dreadlocked brother in a white shirt and tie?"

"Thomas is a private attorney. He says he wears the white shirt and tie to throw people off." She smiled.

"His dreadlocks say one thing, and he keeps them blocked like Cochise or somebody. "Aunt Tee sliced the air right above her shoulder. "But then you take in the always impeccable, white shirt and tie and you just don't know what to think."

I kissed her on the cheek. "Seems like this Thomas of yours is a chameleon."

"Let me put it this way, Thomas is very unique. What can I say? He fascinates me." She smiled again. "His philosophy is, you have to give people something to think about, if you don't, they will fall into complacency and mental death.'"

"He said that?"

"I've heard it enough times that I'm quoting him," Aunt Tee said.

"Lord." I placed my hand on the door knob. "Who do you have me going to meet, woman?"

"Just go. And come back by here afterwards, if you have time." She waved me off.

Aunt Tee began to fold clothes again and I started for the door.

"How much longer are you going to be in Gary?"

"Maybe another week. I can tell Mama can't wait till I leave. Soooooo...."

"Well, I've scheduled a Mr. Patterson; I can't remember his first name, to speak about the Brownfields project at our next meeting."

"When is it?" I spotted a sparse trail of ants feasting on a bread crumb.

"Saturday after next."

"Most likely I'll be gone by then, Aunt Tee. But we'll see."

I left her folding clothes in the middle of her

living room filled with papers, magazines and articles about Gary and its past.

No sooner than I closed the door I was confronted with this throbbing bass music that vibrated all the old houses on Aunt Tee's street. I walked to my car, skirting the volcanic cracks in the sidewalk and before I climbed inside, I noticed an elderly man sitting on a shady porch watching the young men who provided the entertainment. I wondered what he thought about it.

CHAPTER 11

It took no more than five minutes to drive to the restaurant from my aunt's house. I couldn't imagine why a successful private attorney wanted to have lunch at the local McDonald's, but the truth was, there weren't many restaurants in the area. I stepped inside, looked around, and didn't see anyone who fit Thomas Bates' description. So I skimmed the menu board and decided the only thing that interested me besides the french fries was the fish sandwich.

"Are you Rossi Collins?" A man behind me asked.

I turned and looked up into Thomas Bates face. "Yes, I am."

In an exceedingly serious manner, he stretched out his hand and said, "Thomas Bates, here."

I almost said who else would you be, but opted for, "Hello," instead.

"Attorney Bates," a young man with a quarter pounder and fries on a tray called from across the room.

"What's goin' on, Franklin?" Thomas Bates said. "How's it goin'?"

"I'm doin' good, attorney." He flashed a smile revealing a couple of gold teeth.

"That's what I like to hear."

"I know it. I'm gonna do it this time," he said with conviction.

"That's the only way to make it work," Bates said.

"I'ma keep in touch with you," the young man said as he continued to his seat, "and let you know how I'm doin'".

Thomas Bates, looked at me again. "I guess we might as well order lunch and get right down to business." He shifted some papers under his arm.

"Sounds like a good idea," I replied.

I totally felt unimportant somehow as Thomas's gaze quickly left my face and began to scan the menu board, before he focused on the idle McDonald's worker behind the cash register. I took that as my signal to move up and order, which I did. He didn't offer any small talk, so neither did I. If Thomas Bates looked at me again I didn't see it, and I wasn't accustomed to being overlooked in such a way. Not that I'm the most attractive woman in the world, but I get my fair share of second glances, but not from Thomas Bates. We simply got our food, our condiments, and found a table in the corner of the fast food place.

The first thing he said when we sat down was, "I understand your grandmother's death brought you here. I'd like to offer my condolences."

I studied his face and found his expression to be sincere. "Thank you," I replied. It was at that moment that I sized Thomas Bates up in the way a woman sizes up a man. I thought he was rather cute, a little thin maybe, but attractive. But I also decided he was much too serious for my blood.

Again, in silence, we got down to the serious business of salting our french fries and squeezing out ketchup.

Thomas broke the silence and went straight to

the point. "I have studied the aerial photos your aunt gave me and I found something very interesting." He dusted off his hands, opened a folder and handed me a copy of one of the photographs with a circle drawn around a section of buildings. "I fully understand why Mr. Charles said they were important. You wouldn't be able to see this unless it was from the air. In one part of the site they have placed the buildings in such a way that the roads form, Moloch, the owl."

I stared at the picture but I didn't see a thing. "Moloch?"

He stopped just as he was about to take a bite of his Quarter Pounder. "Haven't you ever heard of the Bohemian Grove?"

"No." I did take a bite of my fish sandwich. I was not going to let his superior tone spoil my long over due McDonald's experience.

"It's a place in Silicon Valley where big shots, and I'm talking about leaders from this country and some from around the world, go to do rituals... and not pretty ones. Moloch is one of the main symbols they have there. It's a large great horned owl"

I wiped my mouth. I was surprised at how good my fish sandwich tasted. "So you're telling me Presidents and Vice Presidents would be seen at this Bohemian Grove?"

He looked directly into my eyes. "They have been."

I looked down at the photograph. I didn't believe him, and I still couldn't see Moloch. "Why? Why would men with that kind of power do something like that?"

"It's been going on for a long time," Thomas said. "The small group of people who run this globe believe in the power of the occult, and those that they have sanctioned have been taught some of their secrets."

Was this guy nuts? I focused on eating my french fries and how Aunt Tee put so much stock in him. "So this is a worldwide conspiracy."

"I'm sure they don't consider it to be a conspiracy. It's about them remaining in power, and never relinquishing it."

I looked into his eyes; I didn't know what to say. I was still trying to figure out if Thomas Bates was for real.

"Obviously, you've never heard of," he counted off on his fingers, "The Rhodes-Milner Roundtable." The Bilderberg Group. The Trilateral Commission. Skull and Bones. The Illuminati or Malthusian Eugenics."

From the way he rattled the names off he might as well have called me an idiot. "Not one," was my flippant response. Although I had heard of Skull and Bones.

For a moment he studied me as he ate his fries. "Well, if you aren't familiar with any of this, tell me, what is your interest in this subject, and how do you propose we go about discussing it?"

I stopped eating. Because I didn't know any of the things he deemed to be so important, it appeared he had determined our discussion had come to an end.

"My interest, if any, was piqued by pure chance," I replied. "I happen to be at my aunt's house the night Charles Pulaski dropped the package off."

He sat back. "My mistake." There was a moment of silence. "When Teresa suggested I meet with you after seeing the photographs, I assumed it was because you were well versed in this subject." He balled up his

McDonald's wrapper. "But it's obvious you don't know much about it and you don't believe it."

"Sorry you're disappointed, Mr. Bates," I said, icily. "But no, I don't particularly believe in a world conspiracy." There was much too much tartar sauce so I wiped my mouth again. "And no, I've never heard of any of the things you've mentioned, but I do have some knowledge of ritual and the occult." I filled my voice with as much authority as I could. "And what I know is this. The same power, the same energy can be used to do good or bad. It's all about intention."

Thomas cast a wary eye in my direction. "I can't argue with that. Sometimes it *is* a matter of perspective. Some people would say this world would be nothing without those secret societies that I just named. That without them material progress would have halted long time ago." He rubbed his chin. "What I am getting at is this, this is a profound, profound subject and there is so much water under this bridge, meaning within this subject, that it would take many days and nights sitting with you at this table, for me to even give you a surface understanding of how deep this is." He leaned forward. "But let me just say this. I am talking about rituals being performed by people who are determined to keep a society in power that is based on a master slave relationship."

Thomas continued to talk and I noticed a moth, one of those beige nondescript fellows, fluttering against the windowpane beside our table.

"And I'm not talking about slaves brought here from Africa. The masters I am referring to are the very elite, rich, old families on this planet, particularly, here in America and in Great Britain. The rest of us, be we blue, black or white, are the slaves. But of course, it goes without saying the people with the darkest skin would be at the bottom of that list." His face took on a cynical expression. "The truth is from where I sit the plan alone was so diabolical it didn't need hocus-pocus ritual to back it up." He shrugged. "But the ritual stuff isn't my forte. What I do know is," Thomas put his fist on the table, "these men were into power. And how did they figure they could gain power and hold on to it? By using control. They deeply believed they had to take and keep control of everyone. So they came up with a way to make use of the population *and* control it. We are being controlled, Ms. Collins, even if the majority of us don't know it."

CHAPTER 12

Thomas Bates's words sounded like a lofty philosophical discourse and to me, the moth's desperation was far more interesting. But I did think, perhaps... if what Thomas said was true, we pawns were like the moth, unable to grasp his situation. The insect could not comprehend the glass that kept him from the freedom he sought.

Thomas's chin tilted down. "The methodology they are using to control us is very old, and it started with a well, thought out plan. Within that plan, those races that they considered to be inferior, the darker skinned races were dispensable. Once those races were of no further use, they determined they would kill them off as a means of population control. I'm talking about indirect ways, like drugs and various means of genocide."

I crossed my arms over my chest. It was all so irrational. But I wondered why I felt a slight bit of fear. I wasn't afraid of Thomas Bates. Then I realized I was afraid of the possibility of it being true.

Thomas leaned forward. "A few minutes ago you asked, why? Why would anyone want to do this? Hey." He marked it off on the Formica tabletop. "Say they thought to themselves, we, the rich folks at the top, we're the minority. And we are bound to have some problems down the road with all of these people who outnumber us. So here's what we are going to do." His lips smiled, but his eyes didn't. "Let's create a working-class man and let's educate him. And although he will have some opportunities to share in the common wealth, in truth it will be a type of legal slavery, where this common man labors for those of us who are in power. The more he works, the more we make. And we will make laws and rules that serve us." Thomas's eyes brightened. "And the glitter of materialism will be so dazzling, this common man will be too busy trying to attain what we have to notice or even care. Now to top that off, we will make it a never ending process of control through loans and a financial system that binds him and his generations."

At that point I almost felt overloaded, but I managed to tap into my own belief system and I'm certain my eyes beamed doubt. I did not believe in a world wide conspiracy. I believe in the goodness of humanity and that we are all spiritual beings having a physical experience, that no particular person or group of people was innately evil. And although I must admit what Thomas was saying was very intriguing; I still felt it was too far fetched and I made a show of neatly folding my empty fish sandwich wrapper.

Thomas sat back and looked down. "I know this is a hard pill for most people to swallow."

"It most certainly is," I said.

"And that's a huge problem," he replied. "Because, I bet most of the people in this country who consider themselves highly educated, would scoff at what I just told you. It would be difficult for our great minds to accept this kind of thing goes on. So when you consider even lesser minds," I felt as if he was referring to me, "if they don't have the motivation to dig, to look into why people who are at the bottom don't seem to be able to pull themselves up, and how the people who are at the top got there." He shrugged his shoulders dramatically. "They end up living the lives of insignificant pawns to be disposed of or used by big interest. Slaves of our modern day aristocracy. But as I said before, even the greatest minds refuse to see what's happening. I call it the ostrich syndrome."

I couldn't believe how cynical this man was. I wondered how he could live with any kind of peace of mind believing the things he told me. "So where is God in all of this?" I found myself asking.

"Good question." He rubbed his eyes. "Probably the same place he was when that woman who put up a small shrine to him in front of U.S. Steel got arrested."

"Say what?"

"I'm just being facetious."

He was being facetious when I couldn't have been more serious. I looked at him and shook my head. I didn't know if I understood this man at all.

"I *was* being facetious," Thomas said. "But there was a woman who did get arrested a few days ago for setting up a kind of altar in front of the steel mill. It was in the Post Tribune."

"Really?" I thought it was a totally bizarre thing for someone to do, but the intuitive part of me could not ignore the timing. "Why did she say she was doing it?"

"She didn't. They said all she went to sing songs and she wouldn't speak at all. Wouldn't say her name... why she was doing it... anything. According to the article the authorities concluded she had some mental problems."

"They decided she was crazy, but they took her to jail anyway?"

"That happens all the time," Thomas said. "But they arrested her because she was trespassing. But since she wasn't harmful she's probably walking the streets again by now."

I rubbed my forehead. I didn't know what to do with the information Thomas had shared with me.

"There's a lot going on, isn't there?" He searched through his papers as he spoke. "If I was a superstitious man I'd say something is up. Old women praying in front of the steel mill, and old Mr. Charles giving Teresa aerial photographs that prove the men who planned the layout of U.S. Steel were part of a secret society. It's all rather intriguing." One eyebrow rose. "But I'm not a superstitious man. I need cold hard facts that prove these incidents are connected."

I shook my head again. "You claim the roads and buildings on the U.S. Steel site form a large owl planned by some powerful secret society, but you don't think there is a connection between that woman being out in front of U.S. Steel praying and singing and the photos?" I almost laughed. "I deal in more than cold hard facts and I am certain there is a connection."

"Perhaps." Thomas sucked deeply from his straw. "Either way, considering what you believe and what I've shared with you, neither would stand up in a court of law. But of course the laws were made by them." He thumbed through his material and gave me a manila folder.

I glanced inside. It was the aerial photographs Pulaski had given to my aunt and some other papers. "Investigating conspiracy theories, that's quite a hobby," I said.

"It's more than that," Thomas replied. "It's a passion of mine. Somebody's gotta keep their eye on the ball. I think—"

He stopped talking when a man approached the table.

"If it isn't the irrepressible Mr. Bates," the man in an expensive, pen-striped suit said.

The two men shook hands.

"Philip. What are you doing on this side of the border?" Thomas asked.

"I'm taking care of some business for Davies. You know they're building a new truck stop over there on 25th Ave."

"I've heard about it. I don't know if the folks who have houses around there and the people who go to St. Timothy's think it's such a good idea." Thomas Bates sat back. "But I've heard about it."

Phillip smiled. "He's part of that."

"Paul Davies has his hand in some of everything over here in this city, except for his personal life. Just like so many of the businessmen, who invest in Gary," Thomas made quotation marks in the air, "they keep their private lives separate from this city. You can believe that."

Philip turned up his palms and shrugged in a classy fashion. "What can I say? He's an astute businessman."

"Astute in a way that doesn't benefit Gary," Thomas said.

Philip stepped back. "You're not going to draw

me into this right now, Thomas. The man is my boss."
He looked at me. "How are you doing ma'am?"

I hate when people call me ma'am. It makes me
feel old, but I replied, "I'm fine."

"Good," he continued, "I've known Thomas all of
my life, and I saw how he was grilling you over here.
He's notorious for that, but I don't have time for him
to rake me over the coals today." He flashed a beautiful smile. "Thomas." They smacked hands and held. "I'll
check you later, man."

"All right," Thomas replied.

Things were quiet as Thomas watched Phillip
walk away. "Like I said," Thomas piped up, "somebody's gotta keep their eye on the ball. Money and
power makes too many turn a blind eye. It can be a
lonely game, and I'd rather it was a team sport, but,
hey, you do what you have to do." Thomas looked at
his watch. "I've got an appointment in about fifteen
minutes." He stood and picked up his tray. "The photos
are in there along with some papers about Gary's history that I have in my file. There's also papers about
some of the men who were behind the steel mill and the
secret societies they were associated with, just in case
you are interested."

I looked at the folder.

"Don't know if this meeting did any good but...."
He shifted the tray to one hand and offered me the
other.

"Never thought I'd be having this kind of conversation, especially not in Gary," I said. "The truth is I
never thought I'd have it at all."

Thomas smiled for the first time. "Then that's
another problem. People under estimate Gary, Indi-

ana. It was America's dream city at one time." Thomas glanced at his watch again. "If you want to talk some more, your aunt knows how to get in touch with me."

We said our goodbyes and I attempted to finish my fries, but they had turned cold and rubbery.

CHAPTER 13

I sat in the McDonalds' parking lot and looked over the papers Thomas had given me. At one point two teenage girls, one with hair styled and pressed into strips of blue and yellow ribbon, walked past. They made a display of laughter whenever a man drove by and craned his neck to look at them. They showed out even more if there were catcalls and whistles. I knew they liked the attention and had no way of knowing by some people's standards, right or wrong, they should have found the men's actions disrespectful.

I thought about how uneven life could be. If Thomas's beliefs were true, pawns like me, had no where to turn if they could not turn to their own family, their neighbors, the people we lived amongst every day. If the young girls that I watched disappear down the street, the future mothers of tomorrow had no one to teach them their value, what hope was there? I remember Sobonfu Some said, her people, the Dagara tribe of Africa, believed a village's health depended on the health of its women. If the women were not well, the entire community was ill. I thought of the women in my family and others in Gary. I knew, if Sobonfu's spiritual understanding was true, Gary was ill.

I didn't feel like going by Aunt Tee's house.

Thomas's words had created a weight on my shoulders. I didn't want to talk about the things he had said, at least not then. I had had enough, so I called Aunt Tee and told her I would talk to her tomorrow.

Part of the problem was, I'm a fixer by nature. If someone told me their problems, I would try to fix them. Of course, through the years I've learned sometimes it's better just to listen and not make the other person's problems your own. But the things Thomas espoused was not someone else's problem, they involved everyone, including me.

When I arrived at my mother's house I found her in Grandma Anna Lee's room. To my knowledge, the door to her room had remained closed since we returned from Alabama, and it was the first time my mother had entered it since my grandmother's death. As a child I wasn't allowed in Grandma Anna Lee's room and believe it or not, that afternoon I couldn't make myself cross the threshold. So, in an awkward kind of silence, I stood outside the doorway, in the hall.

"I guess there's no need for leaving her things in here like this," my mother said. "I've got to go through them at some time or another, might as well do it now."

I knew it was her way of making amends for what had happened earlier, and it was fine with me. I was open for putting an end to things, including my childhood rule that my grandmother's room was off-limits. Gingerly, I joined my mother and sat on the end of what had been my grandmother's bed. I've got to tell you, it was a strange feeling. I felt as if some boundaries had been crossed, some barriers broken. I realized the whole thing was like a sad, living metaphor. *Only after death am I allowed inside.* I didn't want it to be the same with my mother.

I looked into Grandma Anna Lee's open closet. It was extremely neat and orderly. Almost obsessively so. There was a small collection of dresses, three of them were black; the other two were white. All of the dresses were obviously fashioned maybe twenty-five, even thirty years ago. Three pairs of shoes, all-black of similar styles were on the floor beneath them, and three antique hat boxes were stacked on the shelf above.

"Grandma Anna Lee didn't have many things, did she?" I said.

"She didn't," my mother replied as she opened one of the drawers. "It was just her way. I tried to get her to go out and shop with me but she wasn't interested. But," she shrugged, "she said she didn't need them because she said she never went anywhere. And basically that was true." My mother looked through the drawers. "I remember when Mama first came to Gary she attended a church, but she stopped going there after awhile. After that she said she didn't need any more dress up clothes." She stood still for a moment and simply stared. "Yes, Mama said she was fine with what she had."

I watched my mother clear out Grandma Anna Lee's underwear drawer. There were only a few pieces and it hit me, every one of them was white. It wasn't that the articles were new, yet they were blindingly white from her panties to her bras, from her undershirts to her slips and thick white stockings. "Everything is so white," I said.

"Mama knew how to wash, now. She had her method," my mother replied. "She believed in using lots of bleach, and she always put it in with the detergent before she started the water. And she didn't like anything but white stockings. She said as she got older those darker colors made her legs itch. I believe she was onto something. I'm getting so where I can't wear any of those colors either." My mother placed the two stacks of clothes into a white trash bag before she moved on to a small jewelry box on top of Grandma Anna Lee's dresser. "Mama never was into jewelry." She placed a pair of pearl earrings on the dresser then picked up a silver necklace. "But she wore this all the time, for years and years. She said my father's mother gave it to her."

I remember seeing the chain around her neck, but I never saw the pendant. "May I see it?" I asked.

My question hung between us as she hesitated, then gave it to me. "You make sure you give it back, now. That's the only thing I have from my grandmother."

I took it but my eyes remained on my mothers face. "Why do to have to say that, Mama? Why wouldn't I give it back to you?"

"I'm just making sure that you do." She avoided my gaze.

It was difficult, but once again, something deeply ingrained in me made me decide to let it go. I studied the necklace I held in my hand. I had never seen anything like it. The pendant was shaped like a tree. "What was Grandma Eli's mother's name?" I couldn't ask 'what was my great grandmother name?' I couldn't ask because I didn't feel the connection.

"Mabel."

"Mabel? That sounds familiar. I guess you've told

me that before."

"Maybe." She knotted Grandma Anna Lee's stockings into one bunch.

"I wish I knew more about Grandma Anna Lee," I said. "Now that she's gone I realize how little I know. She didn't keep a diary or journal, did she?"

My mother gave me an irritated look. "So you could pry into her life?" Her face turned sour. "I've told you before that Mama couldn't write. She didn't go any further than the third grade."

"I don't remember you—"

"Rossi, there's too much around here that I've got to do for me to have to deal with you and these questions of yours. I'd be better off, if you're going to start asking questions, to do the stuff I've got to do alone. I told you, you could go back to Atlanta. That I was going to be okay." She closed the trash bag. "I'm use to having my own space."

On a dime, the sharing moment was gone and I was being put out... again. Instant rejection, that's what I felt; a feeling it seems I had been familiar with my entire life. I looked at her and I knew I couldn't take it anymore. "Mama," her name was a plea, "why do you treat me like this?"

"Like what?"

"Like an unwanted stepchild," I said.

"See there you go again talking all out of your head."

"I'm not talking out of my head. I'm telling you how I feel, and how I have felt all of my life."

Her shoulders twitched. "Well, I can't help how you feel."

That hurt me. "But you're my mother. You

<u>should</u> care," I said.

She opened another drawer of Grandma Anna Lee's while I waited in silence for her to say something, but she continued her task without a word.

I could feel the sting of tears. I closed my eyes to fight it. "This is how it always is between us. I reach out to you, and you don't answer."

"I don't know what you're talking about."

I opened my eyes. Could it be she really didn't understand? Was I being unreasonable? I didn't think so. "What about the eight-page letter I wrote to when I was thirty." I tried to make eye contact but she wouldn't look at me. "That was thirteen years ago. I poured my heart out to you, but you never answered it. You never even brought it up. It was like I had never written you at all."

Her mouth tightened, but she still didn't look at me.

An irritating tear escaped from my eye. I thought I had used up all my tears on this subject long ago. I felt angry at her for how she was treating me, and at myself for crying about it again after all those years. "What did I do, Mama, to make you be like this with me?" My heart beat faster. "Are you disappointed in me and what I've done with my life? I run a highly successful multi-level marketing business."

"You always had a knack for making things sound fancy," she replied. "You get that from your favorite aunt, Teresa. She loves being in the limelight. She can always make what she's doing or what she has, more than what it actually is. And you have the same ability. You sell vitamins, Rossi. And I'm not saying you aren't successful because you obviously make good money at it, but you could have been so much more. You were salutatorian of your class."

"So you are disappointed," I said, feeling the sting of how she had cut me down.

"I'm not disappointed. It's your life. You can do what you want over there in Salt Lake City."

Once again she forced distance between us and I wondered why, it seemed, she consistently wanted to hurt me. "You are holding something against me, Mama." Then the words just came out. I hadn't been thinking about it, but there they were. "Is it because I had that abortion when I was fifteen?"

We had never spoken of it since it happened. It was our secret that we had hidden even from ourselves. I was shocked that I had brought it up, and from the look on my mother's face when she looked at me, she was shocked too.

I rushed on. "That must've been mighty hard for you. God knows it was difficult for me. I couldn't look at movies with blood in them for years. It was all so crazy. The nurse that we met at the doctor's office who ended up performing the abortion came to our house about midnight and she was drunk and wearing an awful looking wig." I could see the woman in my mind's eye. "And she claimed she was her own twin sister. I couldn't tell you how scared I was. And when you left me at home alone until the baby passed, the entire time, I held on to Bowtie, that stuffed penguin you made me when I was a little girl." My tears came again. "I know you must have been mighty disappointed in me because I was so young. And believe it or not, I got pregnant the first time I had sex." I wiped my face with my hands. "And then that woman had the nerve to call a week or so later to try and blackmail you for more money." I shook my head. "It was an unreal situation." I paused. "I know you couldn't have forgotten it. But are you still holding that against me?"

She glanced at me, shook her head and said in a most sincere voice, "Of course not."

Instantly, a pain I didn't know I was holding drained away. I got up and hugged her. "I'm so glad you're not." Still, my mother never put her arms around me and within seconds her body was as stiff as a board. Finally, she pushed me away.

"Why won't you let me hug you?" I looked down into her face. "I wish I could be closer to you, Mama, but there has always been this distance between us."

"I just don't feel like being hugged right now," was all she could say.

"But you never do. At least not by me."

Silence filled the room. There were so many things I felt we needed to say to each other.

"You know," I continued, "you told me on more than one occasion that when you were a young woman and we were still living at Grandma Ruth's house, Aunt Naomi's first husband tried to rape you. That you had to chase him away with a big butcher knife."

"I did." She defended herself. "He tried to do it more than once, but this time I was serious because I was pregnant with you. I would've cut him if he had put his hands on me."

I saw fire in her eyes, and I didn't know if I really wanted to hear the answer to the question I was about to ask, but I had to know. "Is that man my father? Is that why you never wanted me around?"

"What?" She held Grandma Anna Lee's slip in her

fist as she placed it against her hip. "You can come up with some doozees, Rossi," she said. "Your father is your father. My goodness."

I was never so glad to see that irritated expression on her face in my life.

"I blame Teresa for your wild imagination. She was the one who was always encouraging you as a child when you were talking to folks nobody else could see. She encouraged that stuff. I didn't."

I breathed a sigh of relief. I even felt lighter. "You said I was born with a caul over my face, so what do you expect?"

"What did you call it?" Her interest was sincerely piqued.

"It's called a caul. It's actually a membrane that looks like skin."

"I've never heard of the word caul, but that's exactly what it looks like, a piece of skin. That's the truth. Dr. Murray sounded like he was shocked when he saw it." She closed the trash bag. "He told the nurse, and I could tell he was a little unnerved when he said it, 'She's got one of those things on her face.' And then he told her to hurry up and get it off."

"I looked it up on the Internet," I said, glad to have the issue of my paternity behind me. "He might have been surprised to see it because it doesn't happen that often. Many indigenous cultures believe if a baby is born with a caul on its face, it's deeply connected to the spirit world."

My mother nodded as I spoke although she replied, "I don't know about that, but you definitely had one."

After that I watched as my mother worked in

silence. I stayed with her until she finished going through, Grandma Anna Lee's drawers. Then she announced she was tired and she went to her room and I went to mine.

I had just begun to read when I heard it; the sound of my mother crying in her room. It pierced my heart, and I wondered if I was the cause of her tears. Or was life, in and of itself, the reason.

CHAPTER 14

After a while I couldn't read anymore. So I lie there listening to her soft sobs. It almost felt criminal to be privy to such deep emotion from my mother. I started to go to her room and offer some comfort, but I knew she couldn't accept that. So I continued to lie in my bed. In the end it proved to be too much for me. I wanted to drown out the sound and the strain it placed on my heart. The sound of her crying was evidence of how deeply my mother had chosen to hide her pain, her grief. Finally, out of need, I fished my cell phone out of my purse and called my friend, Stephanie. "Hey, Miss Jenkins. How are you?" I asked when she answered the telephone.

"I'm fine. The question is how are you doing?" She replied. "I started to call you a couple of days ago but I felt it would be better if I waited. I didn't know what you were dealing with up there. And I didn't want to intrude at the wrong moment, if you know what I mean."

"You know I understand. And, Stephanie, I've been dealing with all kinds of things. But I'm hanging in there."

"Are you really? From the way you sound you are hanging by your fingernails."

I sighed. "I think that's about right."

"What's going on? It's almost ten here, so it's got to be midnight in Gary, and I know how early you go to bed. Something must've really set you off today."

"There are so many things that have happened since I've been here, some of it ranging from interesting to downright strange. And you're right. I can't sleep."

"Things like what? What?"

I heard another gentle sob. "First, I've got to tell you this. You know how I've told you I've never seen or heard my mother cry?"

"Yes."

"She's in her room crying right now."

"Oh no." There was a pause on the line. "Maybe you should go in there."

"No way," I said. "She wouldn't appreciate that. She would definitely feel it was an invasion of her privacy."

"Is she loud?"

"No. Not at all, but still it breaks my heart."

"I'm sure it to does. Well…. It's only been a few days since she buried your grandmother."

"I know. But we had some words before we went to our rooms, and I'm feeling guilty about that."

"I see. Well, Rossi, death can bring out the best and the worst in all of us."

I focused on some ceramic pieces in the corner of the room. "Maybe that's what's happening, because my tolerance isn't what it used to be. Things I would have kept quiet about, let pass, I can't do it anymore. It's like coming back here at this time has opened something up inside of me, Stephanie. I don't know if my grandmother's death makes me think about my own death, and that we only have a short time on this planet so

Gwyn McGee

there is no time to mess around. I don't know what it is. But something is definitely going on with me."

"So you've just been cutting loose up there, huh?"

"Not really. I just—"

"You want me to pull your chart up on the computer?"

I truly hadn't thought about it, but instantly I knew I would be grateful for her astrological input. "Sure. If you feel up to it." I got off the bed and went over to the bookcase and I began to scan the titles. Some I had seen throughout my life; others were new to me

"I'd like to take a look at it," she said. "And you know me, I'm a night owl, so it's no big deal. I just need to walk in to the other room. The computer is already on. Because I'm definitely curious too. When was the last time we looked at your chart?"

"Probably," I thought about it, "three or four months ago. You said Jupiter was popping up everywhere, and you told me I would probably see growth in my business. And remember, right after that, I brought some real movers and shakers into my downline."

"I remember," she said.

As I waited for Stephanie to find my chart on the computer I realized my mother had stopped crying.

"Ooookay. Here we go," Stephanie said. "Let's see. You are coming up on your Chiron return. It's your wounded healer aspect."

I sat on the bed. "I've heard you mention Chiron before. But tell me, what does it mean?"

"Chiron is the energy that will make you go deep into the things that have hurt you and left a lasting impression. By acknowledging them, you will be able to heal them, and then help others with similar problems."

"Wow. I think I've already started. I told you my mother and I had some words. Well, I brought up something that we have never, ever talked about."

"Really."

I lay on my back and studied the ceiling; searching for something in the faint shadows above me like a reader divining tea leaves. "I told you about the abortion I had."

"Yep, you told me."

"Tonight I brought it up for the first time since it happened."

"Whoa. That was deep."

"I guess it was. It's not that we had a grand discussion or anything, but afterwards I could feel just saying it out loud, you know, acknowledging that it was something real that happened to me, purged something inside."

"I'm sure it did."

"And there have been other things." I turned on my side. "Things I found out about my Grandpa Eli, my mother's father, and Grandma Anna Lee. It's interesting because my Grandpa Eli was deeply involved in spiritual things. Actually people saw him as a kind of medicine man, a shaman. Even though some of my relatives in Alabama gave me the impression that some folks were afraid of him because of the things he knew and what he did." Suddenly, I wondered if my grandfather was lonely in ways only a person who walks that path can be. "And of course that scenario is as old as the hills; people being afraid of what they don't understand."

"Well, your telling me your grandfather was deep

into spiritual matters doesn't surprise me at all. Look at you."

"I know. But it's even deeper than that, Stephanie. Grandpa Eli's brother told me their father was a full-blooded Muskogee Indian known as The Alabama Prophet. He had a spiritual title, girl."

"Get out of here."

"I'm not kiddin' you. He was known to be what they called a knower. Somebody who knew the future." I paused as I thought of each one of my ancestors. "I've got to say Grandpa Eli's father is rather difficult for me to imagine, but not my grandfather. I really wish I had known Grandpa Eli."

"You've got some rich spiritual blood flowing in your veins, Rossi," Stephanie said.

"Grandpa Eli told Uncle Henry something very similar to that. Because according to him, their mother's father, my great great great grandfather, was some kind of shaman in Africa. I know it sounds like I'm making this stuff up." I picked at the sheet. "And who knows they may not know what they're talking about."

"Well, even if it's not all true normally, where there's smoke there's fire," Stephanie said. "They had to get the information from somewhere."

"But when I think about my mother, she's totally closed to this kind of thing. I can't share any of this with her. So if this was something that was passed down from generation to generation you would think I would at least be able to talk to her about it. So, so much for your heredity theory."

"Just because your mother won't talk to you about it doesn't mean she doesn't believe. She's got to believe something. It was a part of her up bringing."

"You're probably right." I paused. "She did do something that was absolutely shocking."

"What?"

"My mother had my grandmother's body shipped to Hurtsboro, Alabama. She was buried there."

"Wait a minute. So you didn't get to go to the burial?"

"I went. I made sure that I did and I got a ticket on the same flight as my mother."

"Rossi, I can't believe your mother didn't tell you she was burying your grandmother in another city."

"Not only didn't she tell me, I had to read about it in the funeral program."

"Oooo-we," Stephanie sounded. "Family can be something else."

"Tell me about it," I said.

"But why did she have her buried there?"

"It seems my grandmother promised my grandfather that she would be buried beside him in Alabama. We had lots of land down there, Stephanie, before it was stolen. It came from the Native Americans."

"Get out of here."

"Yep, and listen to this. My grandfather said some spiritual beings, some Native American spirits came to him and told him that no good would ever come out of the city of Gary because of U.S. Steel. You know, the steel mill?"

"Yes, I know what you're talking about."

"He said that mill is built on Native American burial land. He refused to even visit Gary and definitely didn't want to live here. My Grandpa Eli was Muskogee, African, and I don't know what else."

"Well, he knew something, because God knows

Gwyn McGee

Gary, Indiana has had more than its share of troubles."

CHAPTER 15

I heard the sound of running water in my mother's bathroom and the thought washed over me, when I returned to Utah my mother would be all alone. I didn't feel good about that. Without asking I knew my mother would never relocate, not of her own free will, and I could never return. "Every time I think about what goes on in this small city it blows my mind. I can't tell you how many times I have heard gunshots during the day, and it just doesn't seem right."

"Ummm, you know, but, that was kind of sweet."

"What's sweet about hearing gunshots?"

"Oh no. I'm talking about your grandfather wanting your grandmother to be buried beside him. It really is sweet."

"I guess it would be sweet if that was the only reason he wanted her buried there. But it wasn't."

"All shoot. What other reason was there?"

"Grandpa Eli believed anybody of African-Native American descent, who is buried in Gary gets caught up in a kind of karmic trap. That each time they reincarnate, they have to reincarnate in this area."

"Say what?"

"Amazing, isn't it? That's what I was told when I was in Hurtsboro. I guess they get caught in whatever energies have built up here in Gary, and they are born here, over and over again. It's like until the ancestors of the indigenous folks who have a connection to this area are honored, Gary will be forever plagued by problems."

"I have never heard anything like that in my life. No," Stephanie recanted. "That's not true. I remember several years ago during a big construction job in downtown Miami, they found this ancient circle. I believe it was made out of stones. Do you remember that?"

"Vaguely."

"Yeah. Well, I definitely do. And there was this Mayan shaman. It was a woman. After the circle was found, she went out there and sang songs and did ceremony at the place proclaiming it was a sacred site. It ended up being a big to-do," Stephanie cleared her throat. "I think they actually stopped the construction of whatever was being built, and I mean this was a big project. Millions and millions of dollars."

"Interesting." The woman Thomas mentioned, who had built an altar outside of U.S. Steel flashed through my mind. "Speaking of sacred sites, when I was in Gary the last time a guy named Pulaski gave my aunt some aerial photographs of U.S. Steel."

"That was a strange thing to do."

"Everything about this has been just that... strange." I saw Pulaski in my head. "Yeah, this old, from white guy came to my aunt's house in the middle of the night and gave her some pictures. Stephanie, it was storming outside and nobody should have been out there. But there he was talking about secret ceremonies and how he had to tell someone... it was bizarre."

"I can't imagine that."

"Well, it happened," I said. "Anyway, my Aunt Tee loaned some of the photographs to a guy named Thomas Bates because he knows about secret societies and all kinds of things that I can't begin to tell you."

"And this is a black guy?"

"Yes, he's black. And he seems to be an intelligent brotha with locs and all, but he is also a conspiracy theorist. And I mean he's deep into it."

"You have been going through it up there, haven't you?

"You just don't know. It's been wild. It's like so much spiritual stuff about Gary is coming at me. And things about the occult." I took a deep breath. "This man, Thomas, talked so much. Then, before he left, he gave me some papers that he felt substantiated the things he had talked about."

"Did they?"

"I mean... well." It was an important question that I had focused on for the first time. "Yes, I have to say there was information about the history of Gary and the people who built it, and how some of them were involved with the occult. When I think about it, based on what I read, some of the most powerful people behind U.S. Steel were very knowledgeable of occult practices, and they were the same people who built Gary, because Gary was actually built to house the people who worked at the steel mill. That was the purpose for this city. Where are all the folks who are going to man U.S. Steel going to live? Gary was their answer. And, Stephanie?"

"Wow. I'm listening."

"I know there is no coincidence that all of this information about Gary is coming to me at this time. I've been on the spiritual block long enough to know there's some reason, some message in all of this."

"Is there anything in the papers he gave you that say when Gary was incorporated?"

"There might be." I got up from the bed and picked up the folder. "I remember reading something about a meeting." I went through the papers. "Yes, there is something right here. Let's see. Gary was incorporated, July 17, 1906."

"Let me stick that into an astrology program, because it is possible to do an astrology chart for a city, a state or even a country. They have a kind of karma too."

"Really." Again I glanced through the paper's Thomas had given me. "I've never heard it said that way, but, I guess they would. Each city does have a different personality."

"I'm not talking about personality," Stephanie said. "Literally a vibration is anchored at the time of a city's incorporation. Just like when you were born there was a planetary influence, the same thing goes for the city of Gary. It's like its birthday. Okay, here we go. Give me a second. I'm going to put the phone down for a minute."

"All right." While I waited to hear what Stephanie had to say I took one of Pulaski's photos from the file and placed it beneath the yellowish lamplight to try, once again, to see Moloch. This time I did make out the form of what could have been an owl, but I wondered if I was just buying into what Thomas had said. I was about to put it down when I saw something else. I looked closer. There was a light impression of a list of words in one of the corners. It was as if someone had written on a piece of paper and their writing etched into the photograph. "What is that?" I looked even closer. It looks like Nepo ...Maescrap." I stared at the impressions. "Now that says Featherstone. I'm certain about that." I tried to figure out some of the other words. "Their written like a list of names but, most of them must be foreign because I don't recognize these at all." I went back to the top of the list. The letters there were the hardest to see. "That looks like the word Round...."

"This is amazing," Stephanie excited voice returned to the phone. "Gary's astrological chart looks so much like the chart for the United States."

I put the photo down. "What? Like the United States? Come on now."

"There's no doubt about it. I've studied America's chart. I know it when I see it, and there's quite a resemblance. But what I want to do, is compare your chart to Gary's chart. There."

The line went silent.

"Your ascendant, Saturn, is the same as Gary's sun sign. And Jupiter is definitely positioned where you will bring recognition to Gary. Oh. Now this is interesting. Your Chiron is at the exact same degree as Gary, Indiana's Chiron."

All the astrology talk was confusing me. I sat against the wall and pulled the covers up around me. "So my wounded healer is the same as Gary's? That doesn't make sense to me."

"It makes a lot of sense to me." The excitement was clear in her voice. "What this means is, you are very connected to your hometown. But for your Chiron's to be the same it means, if you do it consciously, when you heal your own wounds you can help heal the wounds of Gary."

I stared at the bookcase but I didn't really see it. "You're making my head hurt, Stephanie."

"I'm telling you. This is absolutely amazing. It's very clear to me that you can have a major impact on Gary, Indiana. This is such a cosmic set-up." She nearly laughed. "That's why you're hearing all these things. I think you're supposed to do this, Rossi."

"Do what?" I closed my eyes.

"I don't exactly know what you're supposed to do. But what is obvious to me is that there is a connection between you and your hometown, and if you consciously decide to heal your own wounds involving your family, it could make a difference for that city." She paused. "Mmmm, but you need to be careful. I don't know what other way to say it, but there could be some danger here."

I sighed long and hard. "I called you so I could feel better. Now you've laid some really heavy stuff on me and I don't think I'm ready to hear it."

"I'm just telling you what the charts say." She rushed on. "But you can handle it. You were born for this and I've had some practice runs, somehow. At least that's what it looks like me."

"Thanks a lot," I said dryly.

"You could look at it as an opportunity, Rossi."

"Stephanie, I'm too tired to look at anything as an opportunity. I'm simply trying to establish a decent relationship with my mother after forty-four years. And that feels like more than I can, right now. I surely don't know anything about healing a city."

"But that's it. Your intense need to make things

right with your mother, to talk about things that you haven't talked about that were significantly painful, is all a part of the process. I'm looking at it, Rossi, right here."

"Well you go ahead. I can't think about that right now. I'm going to sleep."

"Take your butt to sleep then. But tomorrow the same energy will be sitting right on top of you. You're not going to be able to avoid it. But call me back in a couple of days, if you feel like it."

"I'll think about it," was all I could say.

"How long are you going to be up there?"

"Who knows." I was angry at Stephanie for going off on some spiritual deep end when I needed some hardcore life understanding.

"All right. I'll talk to you."

"Bye." I hung up without waiting for her reply.

Instantly, I felt guilty again. That was kind of unusual because I'm not the kind of person who suffers pangs of guilt, but guilt had become a part of my life during those days in Gary. Then they guilt turned into anger, and I knew Stephanie was just a scapegoat for everything I had been feeling, but I didn't want to think about that. I didn't want to think about anything.

So I laid down and tried to get comfortable, but it was difficult because I couldn't stop thinking? Why couldn't all mothers and daughters love each other no matter what? See themselves in each others eyes. Why didn't my mother and I have a loving relationship instead of my being born with some weird connection to Gary? Why couldn't you answer that for me, Stephanie? Why couldn't you have seen that as my birthright written in the stars?

CHAPTER 16

When I awoke the next morning, I felt as if I had not slept at all. I was surprised to discover my mother, a notoriously early riser, was still in bed. That day and several others that followed, she wasn't quite herself. She blamed it on all the work she had to do to prepare for Grandma Anna Lee's funeral, and the thought of all the work that still lay ahead, but I suspected it was pure grief. Because of that and the sound of her crying that night, I tolerated my mother's gruffness with a new tenderness. Whatever the reason for the physical changes in her, I knew she was going through something profound when I offered to stay another week, and she quietly accepted.

With my mother not feeling well, I had a legitimate reason to remain at home. I didn't go inside when I dropped the photos and Thomas's papers off at Aunt Tee's house. I simply told her that I found Thomas's theory very interesting, but we would have to talk later because I didn't want to leave Mama alone for too long. Aunt Tee didn't seem to mind. She said she was still feeling a little under the weather herself, and that she was working on something. It was obvious whatever it was had her excited. But all Aunt Tee said was, she was deep into some research, and that she wanted to be prepared for the Gary Historical Society meeting with the representative from the Brownfields project. I didn't ask her when the meeting was going to be held. The truth is I didn't want to know. I was tired of the mind acrobatics and the emotional ones too. So I was relieved when Aunt Tee didn't insist that I come in and spend some time.

I didn't call Stephanie either, although the things she told me were never far from my thoughts. The fact is I wish I could have dismissed them altogether. But over the year's, by looking at my astrology chart, more than once, Stephanie had helped me make sense of my life and even accurately predicted my future. I couldn't throw that fact away no matter how it might simplify things. So I filled my days shoring up my downline, and by doing research on the Internet.

You would think with all the things that had unfolded to this point, when I discovered what I discovered, the shock value would have lessened. That was far from the truth. The more I read about people in the American government, men of power with connections to the Milner Rhodes Roundtable and its American counterpart which had indoctrinated thousands of Rhodes scholars into the kind of thinking Thomas had spoken of, and ended up in key positions in the American government, the more distressed I became. I believe what upset me most was, this was not a thing of the past, but according to the information that was available, it was alive and thriving today. Recent pictures of ex- Presidents at a place called the Bohemian Grove whose mascot was Moloch, a great owl, the same one Thomas claimed was symbolized in the lay out of the roads and buildings of U.S Steel, was among other photos of men of power and importance at The Grove.

There were things about rituals and more secrets than I could bear. Finally, I just stopped. The amount of information was exhausting, and to contemplate what it really meant, overwhelming. That particular morning I concluded what use was it to know all of this, if I didn't know what to do about it? If the people that compiled this massive stock of information had not found a way to make it count, how could I? I felt I couldn't.

That was my conclusion until Aunt Tee called that afternoon while my mother was napping and I was eating a piece of spongy angel food cake.

"How you doing, Rossi?"

"I'm doing okay, Aunt Tee. How are you?"

"Ohhh, I'm not a hundred percent, but the big Gary Historical Society meeting is being held this evening. I figured you'd want to be there."

Aunt Tee's timing couldn't have been worse. To be honest, at that moment, because of the things I'd found out I felt somewhat afraid. Maybe afraid isn't the right word. Perhaps it was a kind of hyper- apprehension. But I felt helpless for certain, and Lord knows I didn't feel up to going. But Aunt Tee had no way of knowing that.

"You know I've got to go, even though I really haven't been feeling that good. But I've been keeping busy. I've been going to the library whenever I could muster up the energy and I've been researching, Rossi. Researching this Brownfields thing. Knowledge is power, you know. And we need to get some answers from the man who's speaking tonight. If we can't, at least we've got to let the folks downtown know we deserve answers at some time or another. And I've got something for him. Eminent domain, my ass." She blurted a rare cuss word. "We can't just lay down and die and let the folks with money do whatever they want to us, can we?"

"I can't say it sounds like the right thing to do." I lamely replied.

"I know I can't. It's not what I'm made of. But I want you there with me, Rossi. I got the word out about the meeting as best I could. And even though the meeting is about the Brownfields project, they'll be folks there who are upset about the layoffs at Methodist Hospital, and the talk that they may close the Fifth Avenue location, leaving us without a big hospital. Isn't that crazy? That hospital has been there forever."

My heart sank. My father and Grandma Anna Lee had been treated at that hospital. I was born there. I couldn't imagine Gary Indiana without it. "That is absolutely crazy."

"Yes, it is. And there were also be folks there," Aunt Tee continued, "who are upset about the high property taxes, because people really haven't had a place to voice their feelings about these issues. And I'm sure there'll be some representatives from the other side of the fence there too just because I called in a few favors."

"I see," I said.

"So it should be quite a meeting, and what do you young folks say? I'm gonna need my posse with me." She chuckled. "I can come and pick you up about six thirty?"

I drew a deep breath. I really wasn't up for it, but I couldn't tell her no. "I'll pick you up, Aunt Tee."

"That's even better. That's even better," she repeated.

"Where is it being held?"

"At the main library on Fifth Avenue."

"Okay. I'll pick you up at six thirty."

I hung up the phone and looked at the clock. It was a quarter past two. I had about four and a half hours to get my feelings under control, and to put the information I had come to accept as true about secret, powerful forces operating in America in perspective. See, you have to understand that at that moment, I was functioning out of a feeling of powerlessness. But I knew no matter how much I felt that meetings like the one I planned to attend with Aunt Tee were insignificant, because the people in power had already stacked the cards in their favor, I couldn't let my elderly, favorite aunt go up against them alone. And there was no doubt in my mind that I saw the Brownfields projects as an extension of that power

Maybe it was the act of surrendering to the situation. But that did it. I don't know if you are familiar with, or even buy into the spiritual belief of empowerment through surrender. Aligning with that, that has created the bigger picture. But just as I was going to the door, on my way to pick up Aunt Tee, I thought of the photograph and the impression of names. I don't know how to explain it, but I felt if I looked at it again I would find something there. I would recognize something. So I returned to my room, took out the photograph and held it once again under the yellow lamplight. "It can't be," I said. "It just can't be." The top letters were still the most difficult to distinguish. "But that does say Round."

Hurriedly, I found the drugstore reading glasses

in my purse. And there it was. I couldn't believe it, even though I was seeing it as plain as day. The words that capped the list of names on the photograph were The Gary Roundtable."

Chill bumps covered my arms. "Roundtable. The Milner Rhodes Roundtable. This is crazy. These names can be connected."

"Rossi," my mother called from her bedroom, "I thought you said you were picking Teresa up at six thirty. It's almost six thirty now."

"I forgot something." I placed the photograph in my purse. "I'm leaving now."

As I left the house I wondered if the things I had come to believe over the last few days were impairing my judgment. It was because of that information that I even conceived the notion that the names imprinted on the photograph were somehow affiliated with the Milner Rhodes Roundtable.

There was a part of me that thought I didn't know enough about conspiracy theories to make a sound judgment. You know that old saying, 'a little bit of knowledge can be dangerous' or something like that. I feared I was wading in those waters. The only things I knew for certain were, the timing was uncanny, and that the words Gary Roundtable were present on the U.S. Steel photograph. I had no idea how they got there, or how Charles Pulaski got hold of the photograph. But I knew those two things for a fact. Everything else was pure speculation; the kind I didn't feel emotionally or mentally able to handle.

This was heavy on my mind when I picked up Aunt Tee at the appointed time. She asked about my mother, spoke of her own low grade, but lingering sickness, and asked about my meeting with Thomas.

"So what do you think about him? I noticed you didn't seem too eager to discuss what you two had talked about."

I glanced at her.

She tilted her head. "Yes, I noticed it. Now I know you said you were in a hurry because Pearl was sick, but I know you well enough, Rossi, to know when you're trying to avoid me. And I could tell that's what you were doing."

I kept my eyes on the road. "I know you know me, Aunt Tee."

"Yes, I do." She gave my thigh a pat. "I just wanted to make that clear. Because I spoke to Thomas briefly a day or so after you two talked, but he was on his way out of town and we didn't go into any details. So I am very curious about what went on between you two. He said he planned to be back for tonight's meeting. I hope he makes it. When you need a good mouthpiece Thomas is the man for the job."

Her question made me revisit what I felt about Thomas Bates. "He's a very interesting man. He talked about a lot of things I had never heard of before, and actually, it kind of surprised me."

"I know it did," she said. I think it was about four years ago when a few of us got together to have something to eat after a Gary Historical Society meeting. That's when I first heard Thomas spout off. He and another guy had gotten into a somewhat heated discussion, and Thomas was a faucet nobody could turn off. He started throwing these questions out about secret societies and organizations, and calling off names of important people in this country." She drew a deep breath. "Now I can't even tell you what all he said, but by the time he was done I think most of us thought he was a little crazy. I know I did, and I decided to avoid him at all costs." Aunt Tee hacked several weak coughs. "S'cuse me, Rossi. I don't know what's wrong with me. I don't have a cold and I don't cough all the time. Maybe it's allergies. Anyway…. Then months went by, and he consistently attended the meetings, and he spoke intelligently about so many other things that I thought I should reevaluate my conclusions about him. And that's what I did. He's really not a screwball. Not at all."

"Well, that's exactly what I thought after our meeting, that he was crazy, but I don't believe that now."

"But were you able to have a conversation about the photographs?"

I thought of telling Aunt Tee about the list but I didn't want to sound as crazy as Thomas Bates had initially sounded to me. Not only from Aunt Tee's perspective but from mine. "It wasn't much of a conversation, Aunt Tee, because he did the majority of the talking. As a matter of fact I felt like he was lecturing me."

"That's Thomas alright," she said.

"And I know you warned me, but I've got to say I really wasn't prepared for the things he said. I had never heard anything like it."

"I totally understand that."

"Thomas gave me some papers but I decided to do my own research and… have you ever come across something that just shifts your view of reality?"

She nodded deeply. "Yep. Yep."

"Well, when you called me this afternoon that's where I was."

"Oh my goodness." She focused on my profile.

"Oh my goodness is right," I said.

"So you really didn't want to be bothered with any of this stuff tonight, did you?"

I glanced at her then back at the road. "I could do without it, Aunt Tee."

She was silent for a moment. "Well, let me say this, Rossi. When I finally decided to accept that there was a lot of truth in the things Thomas talked about, I felt like someone had cut me off at the knees. I mean, to think that this whole thing may have been planned out on a level that the average person like me would never consider, it's mind blowing. But to make a long story short, once I got past feeling like a victim I got angry." She shifted toward me. "Now, I may not go around speaking as openly as Thomas about some of the things I have come to accept as true, but I haven't collected all that stuff in my house, stacks and stacks of it, for nothing." Aunt Tee threw up her hands. "My house is full of it. Do you remember my house being so messy when you were growing up?" she asked, as we waited at a red light.

I looked at her, but the woman in the car next to us caught my attention. She was about thirty years old and she had three children in the car. One of the boys, I'd say he was five or six, stuck both of his arms out of the window of the old, rusty Pontiac that burned oil.

"Get your arms back in this car," the woman snapped. "You gon' get it when we get home. I'm tired of you. You hear me?"

Immediately, the boy sat back and the car drove off.

"Well, was it?" Aunt Tee insisted on an answer.

I focused on Aunt Tee's question. "To tell the truth, I don't believe it was."

"It wasn't," she replied incredulously. "I was as neat as a pin. But I decided I wanted to do my part in this war, because that's what it is, a war. You see, I began to see Gary as a perfect product of the system Thomas talks about." She grabbed her little finger with her fist. "Gary was created to make money for the big steel tycoon's, but once they hit their high point and things started coming down the other side of the slope, the workers and their families who lived in Gary, had served their purpose. And it's been like this place has been thrown away ever since."

"I can't argue with that, Aunt Tee."

"I made another decision," she continued. "No matter how unimportant little Gary may seem to other people here in this city and outside of this city, that I was going to be a source for information about this town. You know why?"

"Why?"

"Because I want people to be able to look back and see the life of Gary, this city's life, its entire existence from being the apple of America's eye to one of the most ridiculed cities there is."

"That's a long fall." I sighed. "A very, very long fall."

"Yes it is. And I know that it's hard to believe, but it's true. No matter how much most folks want to distance themselves from this town, we are a perfect example of America's corporate might, be it for good or bad. In my opinion, right now this Brownfields Project idea, it's bad for common folks like me." Her mouth set stubbornly. "And if Gary is the perfect example of what corporate America can lead to," she closed her eyes and shook her head, "there's a fly in this milk somewhere."

"You've thought about this a lot haven't you?"

"Yes, I have, Rossi. And I thought about Mr. Charles an awful lot lately. And I figure somehow he came to know what I was doing. He never talked to me about it, but in recent years I can see how he supported me." She paused. "You know, I consider him my Gary Historical Society buddy. Nothing more."

I could feel Aunt Tee focusing on my profile.

"Now let me tell you the truth about Mr. Charles. Mr. Charles has got money, and he's got plenty of sense. Don't think he doesn't. He used to be an engineer before he retired." She gave me a look that only Aunt Tee could give. "And it makes me downright angry that that son of his treats him like some incapable child. That he's so out of his mind that he doesn't know who to talk to, or what to do. I feel bad," she said, "because I thought the same thing that night he brought those pictures over to my house. But you see, he caught me off guard, and I really feel bad about that, Rossi. Just because somebody gets old, doesn't mean they've lost all the sense they accumulated throughout their life. It burns me up, Rossi. It really does. Until somebody declares that I'm demented or that I have Alzheimer's, I want you to believe any and everything I say. Do you hear me?"

Aunt Tee had taken up the entire drive talking from her house to the main library. "I hear you, Aunt Tee. I hear you."

We pulled into the library parking lot and the timing wasn't right to bring up The Gary Roundtable. There was too much to discuss. So I held onto it, and because of her beliefs that Aunt Tee had shared about

Gary, Indiana, I had a gut feeling that the list was significant. But how? I could not have fathomed.

CHAPTER 17

We parked and went inside the building that looked practically new compared to the other libraries in Gary. Aunt Tee spoke to several people downstairs before I followed her into an elevator. We rode up to the second-floor and exited into a large foyer. The space was practically empty except for a group of women standing and talking outside of a meeting room.

"Teresa, how are you?" One of the women asked as we approached. The others nodded and looked on.

"I'm doing okay," she replied, looking inside the meeting room. "Can't seem to shake whatever has taken hold of me, but you know me." She smiled at the women. "I'm not going to let it stop me."

"I know you won't," the heavyset woman replied. "Teresa is the backbone of the Gary Historical Society." She explained to her companions.

"Is Mr. Patterson here?" Aunt Tee looked in the meeting room again.

"Who?"

"James Patterson, our guest speaker for tonight."

The woman looked through the open doors. "I don't know. I haven't been inside."

She barely finished her sentence before Aunt Tee was on her way into the meeting room. I acknowledged the women with a nod before I followed my aunt. There were twenty-five to thirty people seated on padded chairs inside and although he was seated Thomas Bates long frame stood out.

"At least there's one reporter here." Aunt Tee said to me, motioning with her head toward a man sitting alone with a steno pad.

In silence I followed as my aunt worked the room, speaking to one person after another before she took a seat next to Thomas. I noticed an instant air of camaraderie as I sat beside her.

"I'm so glad you made it." She patted his arm.

"Hey, Ms. Tee. I told you I would. I couldn't miss this one."

"I'm so glad," she repeated. "I might need you for back up tonight."

"I got your back now." Thomas looked over at me. "How you doin'?"

"Oh I'm sorry." Aunt Tee leaned back in her chair. "Forgive me you two. My mind is racing about this meeting."

"You're all right." I said before I gave Thomas a slight smile. This time I determined he actually was a good-looking man with a thinness that played up a masculine angularity. "I'm doing fine. How was your trip?"

He smiled back. "I can't complain. Life could be worse."

Peculiar as it sounds, I knew somehow he felt my newfound respect for him. "I had to take care of some things, so.... not as much fun as it could've been." Thomas looked at Aunt Tee who was shuffling through some papers in a folder. "You are chomping at the bit," he said. "You've found something, and I have too."

"Have you?" Aunt Tee looked over her glasses.

"I have, but this isn't the right time to bring it out to the public. I'll talk to you about it later. What about you?"

"I've definitely come across some interesting information, Thomas." Her lips thinned. "This thing could turn into a big mess if— There's Mr. Charles!" Aunt Tee looked over Thomas's shoulder.

I noticed Pulaski slowly walking beside a younger man. I also noticed the crowd had increased to about fifty people. I leaned toward Aunt Tee. "Is that his son?"

"Yes," she replied, as she watched them take a seat. "And here comes the other side of the fence, Philip Jones."

I turned and looked at the entrance. I recognized Jones from McDonalds.

"Paul Davies never shows up," Aunt Tee said. "He always lets somebody else do his dirty work. There goes Dr. Michael Sparks and our illustrious City Councilman Samuel Tillman. I wonder what they've got to say about this mess."

Just then, another man in a business suit entered the room. He took one glance around then strode confidently toward the podium.

"That must be James Patterson," Aunt Tee said, looking at her watch. "I need to go and introduce him."

Aunt Tee made her way to the front as I watched Patterson smile and speak to some of the people. When Aunt Tee reached him, they exchanged a few words before she turned on the mic.

"Good evening. I'm Teresa Collins, president of

the Gary Historical Society. This is an important meeting tonight and I don't want to waste any time. Our focus tonight is the Brownfields Project initiative in Gary, and our speaker is Mr. James Patterson. Hopefully, Mr. Patterson will be able to address any questions and concerns that we have concerning this issue. Mr. Patterson." She stepped aside and returned to her seat.

Mr. Patterson took his place behind the podium. With his hand in his gray suit pants pocket, he appeared to size up the audience before he tested the microphone and began to speak.

"Good evening everyone. As Ms. Collins said, my name is James Patterson, and I am your speaker this evening." He looked down then up again. "I was told the Gary Historical Society was a very small group. But from the number of people who have come to this meeting, there appears to be a greater interest in Brownfields projects than we anticipated at this early stage of the game. Actually, I'm serving in a temporary capacity, and I was very reluctant to come before you today because this is such a new area." He paused. "The person who will spearhead this effort was just hired. His name is Dexter Bonner. Mr. Bonner comes to us highly qualified, but he will not actually start work for another month. But the people behind the Brownfields project did not want to turn down your invitation, so until the time Mr. Bonner comes aboard, you are stuck with me." He flashed an even smile.

I remember thinking that I doubted if there was any response to his mild joke when I caught the faint scent of a piercingly sweet perfume. Another wave hit me as an elderly couple dressed as if they were going to a church meeting sat down at the end of our row. As outdated as their clothes were, particularly the woman's crushed straw hat with faded silk flowers, I have to admit they were absolutely styling, down to the gentleman's white patent leather shoes.

I focused on Patterson again.

"And of course with the limited information that is available, I'm sure you have surmised this project is just in the beginning stages," Patterson said. "But nevertheless, those of us associated with the local Brownfields Acquisition Task Force are very excited about what this will mean for Gary, its present and its future." He paused. "I'm going to attempt to sum this up rather quickly because I am certain you have questions that you want to ask, and we will shape our program around the things you want to know." Patterson looked around the room. "Basically, Brownfields involve the expansion, redevelopment, even the reuse of real property that may not otherwise be developed, or may be condemned because of complications that are the result of pollutants." He put his hands back into his pockets. "That's it in a nutshell."

I pressed my back against the chair, distancing myself from Patterson's light approach to the serious matter. The cushion was surprisingly stiff and I was certain the conference room chairs, and therefore the conference room, wasn't used very often.

"Environmentally speaking, reinvesting and redeveloping those kinds of properties is a great thing because taking that approach, we can leave the undeveloped lands alone; lands such as the dunes," he counted off on one hand, "the wetlands, and others of ecological importance in and around Gary. Let them be the precious lands that they are to this area, this nation and in some instances the world." Patterson nodded with reverence. "And of course, what this ultimately means is, we both improve and protect the environment through this process. Now, will that mean that some personal property might be compromised in the process, most likely. But that is not the intention of Brownfields projects. And I will guarantee you that we will do all that we can to save as many homes as we can, and that we will financially compensate the owners of those properties in a fashion that would allow them to settle elsewhere and continue their lives in a respectable manner." His expression softened.

"I must tell you, the people that you have elected, the public officials that you have chosen to bring new life to this city, like Councilman Tillman," he pointed, "are very proud that Gary is a member of one of the first Brownfields coalitions in the United States, the Northwest Indiana Brownfields Redevelopment project."

I watched Tillman smile and nod.

"We refer to this project as The Gary Brownfields Initiative," Patterson continued. "And you can rest assured we plan to raise civic awareness to the benefits of this effort, and will use the best people we can find, the best of the best, to make Gary Brownfields Initiative a grand success." He looked around the room again. "In brief, that is what this Brownfields project effort is about. And as I said earlier, I want to shape this program around your concerns, the things you want to know. So I open the floor to your questions at this time."

CHAPTER 18

Out of the corner of my eye, in the row behind me, an elderly woman with a substantial walking cane pushed her barely willing body out of a chair. She remained stooped even as she stood.

"What is your name again?" She leaned heavily on the walking device.

He smiled. "James Patterson."

She licked her lips. "Mr. Patterson, I don't know if you noticed, but it took a lot for me to even stand up out of this chair." She exhaled, forcefully. "I want you to know I was born here in Gary, eighty-five years ago, and I live in the same house that I was born in; the house that my parents scraped up the money to buy. Now according to," she reached behind her and picked up an article she had apparently cut out of the paper, "according to this article, if the entire southern part of Gary could be eaten up by this Brownfields thing, that means my house. And I don't care how much care you folks plan to take in paying and resettling people like me, it will never be worth it in my eyes. You saw how slowly I got up out of this chair, how am I supposed to move out of my house? Move some place I'm not accustomed to?" Her bluing eyes pinned him. "My body is too old and my spirit isn't willing, and there is nothing you can do to change that." Slowly, she descended into the chair.

Several people said, "I know that's right."

"Pay us what our houses are worth." A man loudly grumbled. "I'll believe it when I see it. We already having trouble paying these property taxes that are way too high. And now we got to deal with this."

Instantly the energy in the room shifted.

"Where we gon' go? Another female voice sounded. "Most of us who own property in this city are old? It ain't that easy to just pick up and go somewhere. This is the only life we know. Good, bad or ugly. And Councilman Tillman, I'd like to know if your house is a part of this Brownfields project? I bet it isn't."

"My private home is not," Tillman said. He stood up. ""But I do own a couple of properties that are in Brownfields property zones, and I believe once the projects are enacted it will clean up Gary, bring in new businesses and we will all benefit from it."

"But you just said it, Councilman. It's not your private home," she added a special air to her last words. "This is nothing but another business deal to you. Something that you are doing, not something that's been done to you. "

Patterson stood straighter beside the podium. "Once again," he spoke above a growing consistent undertone, "I want to remind all of you that this is in the preliminary stages. Reviews are being conducted and—"

"I don't know much, but from what I understand I don't like this eminent domain stuff." Someone proclaimed.

"On the surface, it can sound rather scary," Patterson said. "But let me explain, the law of eminent domain normally takes precedence when the property is found to be blighted."

"What's that mean?" The woman in front of me asked.

"That means that there is a presence or potential presence of hazardous substances, pollutants. So by redeveloping that land, cleaning up the environment, cleaning up pollution, utilizing the Brownfields project approach, it benefits the greater good, which means the entire city." Patterson smiled. "<u>And</u> it stimulates economic progress and new business, which results in new energy being pumped into areas that have been somewhat depressed."

"It must be someone else's greater good." A tall woman stood and placed her hand on her hip. "Because we've been living with this all our lives, and I don't see how taking our property is any good for us."

"There is another aspect of this that puzzles me," Aunt Tee said. She stood up. "Although all of this as you have said, is in the beginning stages, it is only the south side that is being targeted. And if the chosen area is based on pollution, all of Gary is polluted. U.S. Steel has seen to that. So why the south side of Gary when the entire Grand Calumet River area is a major concern for environmental groups?" She pulled a sheet of paper out of her folder. "I found a pollution check off list on the Internet, and the entire Grand Calumet River area is of environmental concern. Not just Gary. There were all kinds of pollutants and indicators of the presence of pollutants, and there was a check mark by everything. Some of the specifics, fish with tumors and birds and animals with deformities."

"Oh, my God," a woman moaned. "If it's doing that to the animals, what is it doing to us?"

"And even though this is not my area of expertise by a long shot," Aunt Tee continued. "There seemed to be every heavy metal known to man in the waste site runoff from the steel mill. It states the sediment in the ground water was contaminated. And this is most interesting. They call it, atmospheric deposition." She looked up from the paper. "In other words the very air we are breathing is contaminated, and I don't think there's a wall between our air and the air of the surrounding cities. How about Hammond? Lake Station? Chicago for that fact. But I do admit folks living in Gary are sitting in a pollution fishbowl. So does that mean you will eventually level the entire city? Because if pollutants are one requirement for determining the use of the Brownfields project approach, you better level everything."

Conversations erupted all around.

Patterson's face turned red . He shuffled uncomfortably. "Ma'am, we have no intention of leveling the entire city of Gary. I know it is an emotional issue for most of you—"

"You damn right," a man said. "You'd feel the same if we were talking about your house. I bet you don't even live in the city limits of Gary."

"Sir, taking homes is not the purpose of the Brownfields project," Patterson stressed.

Thomas stood up. "On the surface the idea of a redevelopment and environmental cleanup sounds very positive," he began. "And in the long run this area will probably benefit from the current plans that are on the table."

"It will, sir." Patterson said.

"I'm sure it will," Thomas repeated. "And there

will be many people who will benefit. People like your-self and others who have generationally benefited by this nation's financial machine. It's financial system."

A camera flashlight went off in Thomas's direc-tion. I turned and looked. It was the reporter. He had taken a seat near the front of the room.

"And I see a common link, here," Thomas de-clared. "I am sure no matter what city you go to, the areas that are most highly polluted are the inner cities, the places where the large industrial plants have op-erated for years and years, and folks of color, and the poor who can't afford to live anywhere else, live in its fallout. They get the short end of the stick once again. You might not see it this way, but it's an environmental civil rights issue. Another face on an age old problem."

Patterson cleared his throat in the microphone. "This is not what Brownfields projects are about. Be-lieve me."

I looked around at the faces of the people in the conference room. Most of all, what I thought I saw in their expressions was anger, and rightfully so. But I knew underneath what they were really feeling was fear, a fear born of powerlessness, from the thought that even here in the United States of America, the home that parents or grandparents had finally been able to claim as their own, could be taken away in the name of progress. It was mind-boggling. I thought about my father's father, and the migration he made from the south to work in the steel mills of Gary. His dream wasn't to work in and be scorched by the fiery heat of the blast furnaces where all the black people and the Mexicans were placed, an extremely dangerous occupation. His dream was to find work that would pay for a home for his family and the generations to come. I was certain many of the people who shared the room with me had similar beginnings in their family history. I thought of my mother and my father as I looked at Aunt Tee who sat beside me. The reality of what was unfolding struck, hard. This city that I had left as a teenager was the place of my roots. The people's hearts, their pain was my pain, and I could feel it. And no matter how unwelcome my mother had made me feel through the years, it was the place of my birth. I was a part of the karmic cycle Grandpa Eli had tried to warn us about. It was very clear to me. I could see it and I could feel it. "That's what the Native Americans were told," I said, as I stood. "Some of my ancestors, who were Native Americans were told 'believe me'. Trust us who know what's best when it comes to progress. And where are they now? Their land was taken. I don't know about anybody else, but for me this is total déjà vu, because in the end it means that people, who own land, lose it. And it is not the folks who are calling the shots who lose their land. Oh no." I shook my head. "This country keeps doing the same old thing. New methodology, but the same old thing. Will we ever change?"

Aunt Tee tore her gaze away from my profile. "Good question," she said, and
I could feel she was proud of me.

The room went almost silent

"At this point, I feel totally incapable of adequately answering your questions. It's not that I don't want to." Patterson stepped behind the podium again. "I simply don't have the answers. As I told you at the beginning of this meeting, I am operating in a temporary capacity. But I want you to know I take your concerns seriously, and will present them to the task force and to others who are in decision-making positions. I will let them know how emotional this entire venture can be."

"They have to be crazy or dead not to have anticipated this." A woman shouted.

CHAPTER 19

A thin, "I've got something to say," could be heard above the clamor, and I saw Pulaski with effort, push up from his chair. "You go back to the people who have the power to make decisions as you call them, and you ask them something for me."

The room died down as Patterson addressed Pulaski. "Yes sir?"

"Ask them where will all the people go? How will they begin their lives again when many of them are at the end their lives? And you ask them, how they justify in their hearts, taking the land from these Gary residents whose families have lived here for generations. See if any of them are willing or capable of answering those questions."

Patterson looked down.

"You see, there is a pattern here, Mr. Patterson; one that started so long ago that none of us in this room can remember how it got started. Our parents can't remember and neither can their parents. But make no mistake, none of this is happening by coincidence."

Patterson drew himself up. "Sir, I beg to differ with you but, industrial waste is one of the biggest mistakes man has made in our quest for progress."

"Industrial waste is not the issue." Pulaski's voice became remarkably strong. "Using the common man to line the pockets of the elite, no matter what it will mean in the long run, is the problem. And neglect, Mr. Patterson, deliberate neglect of people that some deem to be inferior is the problem. Let them eat, drink, and breathe chemicals that should never enter a human body until we find a way that we can line our pockets again. Calculated neglect."

I was stunned by what Pulaski said, and his words struck Thomas too. We locked gazes.

"The aftermath of Hurricane Katrina is a perfect example of that," Pulaski said.

Patterson looked uncomfortable again. "Well sir, I can't comment on that."

"Dad, I think you need to sit down." Pulaski's son advised.

"I will not sit down," Pulaski said. He looked around the room. "And I will not remain silent any longer. This stuff is happening in the open right underneath our noses, and I will not go to my grave knowing that it is true, but I didn't have the courage to speak out. There are people who know exactly what is happening because it was intended this way." His body began to tremble. "Papa told me something was set in motion when this city was built. That this is not just about Gary. He told me this with his dying breath." Tears ran down Pulaski's face.

A powerful hush moved through the room and I thought about The Gary Roundtable. We're the men listed there involved in some of the things Pulaski referred to?

"Please, Dad." His son tugged at his father's arm. "Sit down."

Patterson cleared his throat. "I'm going to call

this meeting to a close," he said, although Pulaski was still standing.

Disgruntled comments could be heard all around.

"I have one last thing to say." Patterson looked upset. "If Gary does not take advantage of The Brownfields approach, what will we do about the pollution problem in this city? How will we bring economic vibrancy back to this town?" He challenged. "I will pass your concerns on, as I promised. Thank you for inviting me."

Before James Patterson could take a step away from the podium, he was surrounded by people with more questions.

"I told you." Aunt Tee looked around the room. "I told you this could really be a mess. In a few years we could all be kicked out of our homes. But if we didn't do anything else this evening, the folks downtown who are planning to go down this Brownfields project road will know there are many of us in this city who won't take it lying down."

The woman who sat in front of Aunt Tee turned around. "You can say that again. They ain't just going to take my house."

"Like Rossi said, this stuff is as old as dirt and all we can do is shine some light on it," Thomas said. "It's a big job but somebody's gotta do it. So I want to talk to you two about what I found out, if you're interested."

The energy in the room mirrored the adrenaline pumping in my veins. I was definitely up for more. "I'm interested," I said.

"Count me in too," Aunt Tee looked at Thomas then at me. "But give me a minute, I've got to go over there and say hello to Mr. Charles, and speak to a couple of other folks before they leave."

I followed her gaze and saw Pulaski's son leading him to the aisle.

"I wouldn't mind speaking to him," I said. Pulaski had stood up in front of all those people and said things most people wouldn't believe. Or even if they believed them, they wouldn't dare say it. I, for one, was beginning to believe and I wondered what did Pulaski really know.

"I'll wait," Thomas said. "We can talk at my house. It's just a couple of blocks away." He looked at me. "You can follow me in your car. "

I nodded as I edged down the row behind my aunt. "Excuse me," I said as I bumped a chair in the row in front of me. An attractive woman in an auburn wig threw a slightly irritated glance over her shoulder.

Aunt Tee and I caught up with Pulaski and his son just before they reached the door.

"Mr. Charles," Aunt Tee said. "I had to say hello before you left."

Pulaski stopped. Very slowly, he turned and faced us.

"Hello, Mr. Pulaski," I said.

"It's so good to see you." Aunt Tee touched his hand. "How you doin'?"

Pulaski nodded at me and gave her arm a couple of heavy pats. "Not so good, Teresa. But I had to come tonight." So I convinced my son," he motioned with his head, "to bring me. You remember Nathan?"

Aunt Tee looked at him. "We met once at a Gary Historical Society Christmas party," she replied.

"Hello," Nathan said rather tersely.

Aunt Tee refocused on Pulaski. "Of course you had to be here. There wouldn't be a Gary Historical Society if it wasn't for the two of us. There were many meetings when you and I were the only ones."

"I know." Pulaski's breaths sounded labored. "This city has meant a lot to me. Maybe it's because my father helped to build it with his sweat and tears. You know this year, 2006, Gary is one hundred years old."

"It most certainly is and we're going to have to plan something," Aunt Tee replied. But we'll wait on you, Mr. Charles. We'll plan it when you are feeling better."

Pulaski turned a sad smile before he leaned toward Aunt Tee. " July 2006 to 2007 is a very important time, Teresa. And not just because it's the centennial year. At first I couldn't remember because when your body hurts like mine has been hurting, you can't think of anything else. But I've been getting some sleep lately, and it came to me just as I woke up the other day." He looked deep into her eyes. "There is a kind of window of opportunity, a window to change the direction things are going in. The folks who planned all this studied cycles from the cosmic on down. They knew things most people would say are absolute fantasy. But these things exist, Teresa. They do. You just have to know how and when to use them."

Nathan put his hand on his father's arm. "Dad, I think you have said enough. These people are just humoring you."

"I'm not humoring him" Aunt Tee flung Nathan an irritated glance. "I've always respected your father. I may not understand everything he's talking about, but I assure you, I am not humoring him."

Nathan's patient demeanor disappeared. "You only help to feed his wild ideas and his hysterics."

"He doesn't look hysterical to me," Aunt Tee retorted.

"You don't know what my father is dealing with." His eyes were harsh. "I know what's best for him."

"But that's just it, Nathan." A spark entered Pulaski's eyes. "You think you know so many things, but you haven't got a clue. And even before I got sick you refused to listen to me. You said I was talking against the Freemasons, and because you wanted to get ahead, and you wanted to use your Masonic connections to do it, you discounted everything I said." He took what appeared to be a couple of deep, uncomfortable breaths. "Now, I don't blame you for wanting to get ahead, son, but there was so much I could have shared with you, things your grandfather shared with me." Then the energy seem to drain out of him. "It's Masons like you, Nathan, who have no idea about the true knowledge." Pulaski looked at Aunt Tee. "Remember what I've said, Teresa." He cast an uneasy, but potent glance at me as Nathan began to lead him away.

The intensity of Pulaski eyes in such a weak body struck me. I knew there was something very powerful that could give such a weak man so much fire, and I felt urged to ask him about the Gary Roundtable, but I didn't know how. No. Actually, I didn't feel that I was the one to do it. So I took hold of Aunt Tee's wrist and almost pulled her after them. "Ask him if he has heard of The Gary Roundtable."

"What?" Aunt Tee said rather loudly.

Nathan Pulaski turned and looked at us as they continued to walk.

"The Gary Roundtable," I repeated. "Just ask him, Aunt Tee."

"Mr. Charles," she called. "Wait."

Pulaski and Nathan stopped and we caught up with them.

"Just one more thing," Aunt Tee said. "Have you ever heard of a Gary Roundtable. I mean, That Gary Roundtable."

Pulaski's eyes narrowed almost imperceptibly. He looked as if he was about to say something before he glanced at his son then hastily shook his head. "No. I've never heard of it."

A mild look of surprise came over Aunt Tee's face. "Oh, all right then.

"I've got to go now, Teresa," Pulaski said. This thing has worn me out."

"I understand. You go home and get some rest, Mr. Charles," Aunt Tee replied. Pulaski turned away and took hold of his son's arm for support.

Aunt Tees brow creased. "Humph. That's the first time that's ever happened," she said.

"What's that?" I asked.

"I could tell Mr. Charles was deliberately lying to me."

I thought of the imprinted list and Pulaski's response that had obviously caught Aunt Tee off guard.

"Are you certain?"

"I am." She glanced at the Pulaski's again. "So you've got to tell me about this. Gary Roundtable, but first," Aunt Tee said, "I want to catch that reporter before he leaves."

"Okay," I replied, as she headed back into the conference room. "I'll be out here in the lobby." I stood next to the door, thinking about Pulaski's answer. Aunt Tee was certain he had lied, and I wondered why.

CHAPTER 20

The reporter worked for the Gary Post Tribune and after the interview Aunt Tee quickly informed me, according to him, an article about the meeting would appear in the paper the next morning.

Minutes later I watched Aunt Tee thank Patterson for coming. She also solicited a promise from him that as soon as Dexter Bonner was available, he would address the Gary Historical Society. I watched all this physically and mentally from a distance, because in my mind I kept reviewing how Pulaski said, *"Remember, what I've said."* It was as if he wanted to let Aunt Tee in on something, but his son's, and perhaps my presence, kept him from doing it. Perhaps that was the reason he lied when she asked him about The Gary Roundtable.

Aunt Tee continued with her goodbyes, and Thomas, carrying a briefcase that looked as old as he was, joined me outside the door of the conference room.

"It got a little heated in there," Thomas said.

"Sure did." I looked at Councilman Tillman. "I think the councilman got more than he bargained for." He was surrounded by a small group of very vocal constituents.

"Hey, when you're voted into office it's your job to listen to the people. Where can we go if we can't take it to our politicians?" He kidded with a faux angelic face.

I smiled then turned serious. "I've got to tell you something. I've been looking into some of the things you talked about, and I can't say I believe all of it, but I do believe you're on to something, Thomas. I don't understand it, but I know there's some truth in there somewhere."

"I could tell something had changed. That was a pretty passionate speech you made." He smiled again. "I'm glad you decided to join the team."

"No, I've been drafted," I said as Dr. Sparks and Philip Jones exited the conference room together.

"I guess you've got plenty to report now don't you, Philip?" Thomas said when they were a couple of yards away.

"It was an interesting meeting," Philip said. "But I wish you'd use some of those smarts of yours to educate your fellow Gary citizens about business instead of some of these other things you're filling their heads with. They'd be much better off."

"I think they're getting a very good education observing how your boss brings businesses to Gary that don't benefit them. And some of his business is downright hazardous to their health."

Philips face turned stony. "It's not wise to make accusations like that, Thomas. Paul is a respected man."

"Don't waste your breath, Philip," Dr. Sparks said. Thomas has done it so long he can't help himself."

Thomas looked at the doctor. "Dr. Sparks, since you're the city coroner, I just thought I'd ask, is there anyway to check if someone has died from pollution?"

"The majority of the people I see have died from

much more obvious causes than that. Causes like bullet wounds. And when someone has bled to death from something like a big hole in their chest there's no need to check for anything else," Dr. Sparks said. "Pollution isn't killing the black folks around here, black folks are."

"But see, there's the rub," Thomas said. "Everything here isn't black-and-white. Pun definitely intended. You have to look beneath the surface of things in this city, Dr. Sparks."

Sparks looked irritated. "Don't think you are the only person who's concerned about what's really going on in Gary, Attorney Bates. Just because my approach may not be as radical as yours, doesn't mean I'm not concern."

Thomas nodded. "Concern is always needed, my good doctor, but sometimes action is appropriate."

Dr. Sparks gave him the eye. "Well, I've got to go," he said as he walked away.

"I'll see you around, Thomas," Phillip continued on with Sparks.

"Only if Davies sends you, or some of the other foot soldiers to this side of the border," Thomas said.

Philip didn't respond.

"You really like provoking them, don't you?" I said.

"Somebody's got to. Dr. Sparks has the ear of some influential people in this city, and I know he can have a great impact on some of their decisions. And as far as Philip is concerned, he is Paul Davies eyes and ears. Davies has got his own little empire going, and personally, I think the man does as much harm as he does good. He's got too much influence that Davies."

One of Thomas's eyebrows lifted. "Power always needs to be spread around."

"Is Davies a brotha'?" I asked.

I hate to admit it but, no matter how much I believe the soul is colorless, in matters of the physical world and especially in Gary, Indiana, skin color made a difference.

"For all intents and purposes, he's European," Thomas said. "But my grandmother told me that she knew Paul Davies folks. His grandmother was a friend of hers, lived all of her adult years right here in Gary, and was as black as you and me. But she had what my grandmother called a 'white child'. That was Paul Davies father. Then from there he married a white woman and so on so forth. And you can't tell by looking at Davies that he's got a drop of black blood in him." Thomas sat the briefcase near his feet. "Now, he doesn't go around telling anybody that, and neither do I. But since we're on the same team and I want to give you a little more insight into the dynamics of this game, I thought I'd tell you. Davies is one of the main people on the other side of the border—"

"What do you mean by 'other side of the border'?"

A nearly imperceptible smirk, touched his lips. "The other side of the border means all of those towns like Merrillville, Hobart, Portage, Crown Point. The towns that are near Gary's border, or actually border this city, and want to make sure that border," he brought his hand down in a karate chop, "is clear to the rest of the world and to them. They don't want to be associated with Gary in any shape or form."

I had one of Oprah's aha moments. "I get it."

He looked into my eyes. "Davies works real hard to keep that border as solid as possible, and I think that's rather ironic considering his background. But I also think Davies is doing some things here that he wants to keep his distance from."

Aunt Tee came out of the conference room, and Thomas picked up his briefcase.

"You ready to go Ms. Tee?"

"I'm ready," she said, and we walked out of the library together.

We trailed Thomas to his house. I was surprised to drive into a neighborhood of new townhouses. They seemed strange, almost out of place. That kind of development was unusual in Gary and it made me think about what the city might look like under the Brownfields influence. It didn't seem like Gary at all. You see, the older buildings, some of them even charred by crackhouse fires held a beauty of days gone by; a character, a steadfastness that would be lost under the bulldozer of progress.

Thomas invited us in and offered us a seat in his sparsely decorated, but adequately furnished front room. It was a man's space, colors and all.

"I'm convinced Pulaski knows something." Thomas said as we settled down on an overstuffed living room set. "He wouldn't speak out so openly, if he didn't. And *you*" Thomas looked at me "heard what he said."

"Yes, I heard him. And I looked at you because it reminded me of what you said during our first meeting at McDonald's."

"That's right." Thomas gathered his locs and tied them behind his head. "I'm sure he was eluding to some of the practices of the secret societies I mentioned."

"I think Mr. Charles knows something too, Aunt Tee said. "But what I'm not certain. And what was that Gary Roundtable stuff about, Rossi, that had my buddy lying?"

"A Gary Roundtable?" Thomas looked at me.

"I'm not sure what it's about, but I've been thinking." Suddenly I felt out of my comfort zone. "And I've got something for you two to consider."

"Okay. Shoot," Thomas said.

"What if there was a secret society named for this city."

Thomas and Aunt Tee looked at each other before, Thomas said, "I've never heard of it."

"Well, actually," I continued, "I think there was such a thing."

Thomas sat back eyeing me like an attorney would a client who might be a little shady. "And why do you think that?"

"This does." I removed the file containing the photographs and handed Thomas the photo with the imprinted list.

"I've seen this photograph before." He passed it to Aunt Tee. "It's one of the ones I gave back to you."

"Yes, it is. But when you look at it very closely in a particular light," I placed it underneath one of Thomas's table lamps, "there is a list of what I think are names imprinted near the left hand corner. Above those names, are the words The Gary Roundtable."

"Roundtable." Thomas squinted. "Swear."

"I'm not joking. You can see it right there." I pointed as Aunt Tee and Thomas crowded near me.

"I don't see anything," Aunt Tee said.

"Here," I handed her the photo and removed my reading glasses from my purse. "Use these."

"I see it," Thomas said. There was a hint of surprise in his voice. "It does say The Gary Roundtable. And what are these words beneath it?"

"I think they are names," I said. "Foreign names."

"I see Redman and Featherstone," Thomas said. "Those aren't foreign."

I looked at the list again. I didn't realize Redman was there. "I really haven't studied it," I said. "All this clicked for me, that Gary Roundtable was at the top, right before I left the house to pick up Aunt Tee. I discovered the imprint a few nights ago." I looked at Thomas. "But there was so much coming at me at the time. New theories. Conspiracies. Secret societies. I simply forgot about this until today."

"Let's write this down so we can really see what it is," Aunt Tee suggested, holding the photo inches away from my reading glasses.

"That's a good idea," I replied.

Thomas was already rambling in a slender drawer nestled in the side of his cocktail table. "Here's some paper and a ink pen."

I took them from him and wrote The Gary Roundtable.

"The entire thing is fascinating," Aunt Tee said, "but to think Mr. Charles lied about his knowledge of this Gary Roundtable makes it that much more interesting to me. He's got to be hiding something. Or this organization has something to hide."

Thomas placed the photo and the lamp on the cocktail table. "The first name looks like Nepo Redman to me." Thomas moved back so Aunt Tee to get a better look, before he continued. "You asked Mr. Charles if he had heard of a Gary Roundtable and he said he hadn't?"

"That's right." Aunt Tee tilted the photograph to make the imprint clearer. "Yes, that's the first one." She studied the next letters. "I don't know how you pronounce the next name, but it's spelled R-e-t-n-e. The last name is Featherstone."

"See. That's what I'm talking about," I said. "Nepo and Retne, I've never heard names like that, so they've got to be from another culture."

"I agree with you, Rossi," Aunt Tee said

"The third one is very difficult," Thomas said. "R-e-h-t-a-g M-a-e-s-c-r-a-p." He attempted to pronounce it. "You two may be right. The spelling for certain, and probably the pronunciation is very similar to the first two, first names."

"What's the last one?" I asked.

"D-e-m-r-o-f Logal," Aunt Tee said.

"L-o-g-a-l?" I spelled.

"That's it," Thomas said. "And the last name is listed as simply L-a-e-s."

"Only one name?" I said.

"Only one," Thomas said.

"They have to be foreign names," Aunt Tee said. "But I don't think any of these people or their descendents live in Gary."

"There might be some Redman and Featherstones," Thomas said, "but with white flight... I have to agree with you most of these people are probably long gone."

"That's true," Aunt Tee agreed. "But they could have lived here before. When Gary first got started there were a lot of foreigners living here. Maybe the first two people integrated into the society and married a Featherstone, a Redman."

"Maybe. But that would make them female," Thomas replied.

"Or they could have simply taken those names to fit in," I said.

Thomas shook his head. "I wonder how old this photograph is. But of course the age of the photograph wouldn't tell us when these imprints were made. They could've been made years later."

"I don't know how old it is," Aunt Tee said, "but when I spoke to Mr. Charles the day after he gave the package to me; he told me one of his friends had died, and this friend's wife knew that Mr. Charles was interested in historical things about Gary, so Mr. Charles guessed in cleaning out her husband's belongings she came across some Gary memorabilia and the photos among them." Aunt Tee scratched her arm. "Then I guess she called Mr. Charles and asked if he wanted them."

I looked at Thomas. "When I was researching the secret societies you spoke of, I came across the Milner Rhodes Roundtable. I believe you mentioned it to me."

Thomas rubbed his mustache. "I did."

"The only other Roundtable I have ever heard of besides this Milner Rhodes Roundtable is King Arthur's Roundtable." I felt like an idiot saying it. "And somehow for the life of me I don't see evidence of a group of old foreigners getting together and forming a Roundtable for the good of Gary. Maybe back during those days they did. Or maybe I'm just jaded after learning what I've learned about the Milner Rhodes Roundtable."

"So you think this Gary Roundtable would have principles similar to the Milner Rhodes Roundtable?"

I sighed. "I was thinking that but it seems so crazy now." I looked down. "I don't know what I think."

"Don't be so hard on yourself," Thomas replied. "You'll never see the big picture if you don't look and think outside the box."

"Yeah, right." I covered my eyes with embarrassment.. "I even had Aunt Tee hollering after Pulaski, asking him if he knew about the Gary Roundtable."

"And I believe he lied when he said no," Aunt Tee said. "Now I don't know what this Gary Roundtable is or was, but I do believe it was worth Mr. Charles lying about. And that's not like him, so there's something to this. Maybe it will come in handy while we are trying to rally the community together about the Brownfields properties, I don't know."

I heard what Thomas and Aunt Tee said, but I felt like Alice who had gone too far down the rabbit hole. I didn't know what The Gary Roundtable was but the things we were considering couldn't be true. My logical mind deemed them preposterous.

CHAPTER 21

"Like I said," Aunt Tee continued, "I do believe Mr. Charles lied about knowing about the Gary Round-table, but that's not what's bugging me. I don't get that son of his." Her forehead creased. "Unless he thinks his father is absolutely crazy, why is he ignoring what he's saying?" She crossed her arms. "And is it me, Rossi? Or did it seem like the first opportunity he got he lashed out at me as if I am the reason Mr. Charles is saying the things he's saying." She shook her head. "I just don't get it."

"Maybe he's jealous," I reply, as Thomas' telephone rang.

He got up to answer it.

"Jealous?" Aunt Tee repeated.

I heard Thomas repeat 'Hello' a couple of times. "Yes. I mean, if his father seems to be sharing a kind of closeness with you that they don't share, he could be a little jealous."

Thomas returned to his seat. "They wouldn't say anything," he said. "What's this about, Mr. Charles's son being jealous?"

"I don't buy it," Aunt Tee said. "Mr. Charles and I don't share a special relationship. We've become friends over the years because of the historical society, but other than that." Aunt Tee rolled her eyes. "And it's not my fault. Mr. Charles said he has tried to share things with him but he hasn't been interested. He said it right in front of us."

"And it really teed his son off," I said, "when Pulaski said he was like most Masons who think they have acquired some kind of deep knowledge, and they haven't. He didn't say anything but it was all in his eyes."

"Pulaski said that?" Thomas asked.

"He sure did," Aunt Tee replied. Her expression turned contemplative. "But sometimes Pulaski can say some off-the-wall stuff. I didn't get what he was saying about the 'window'. That this is Gary's 100th birthday and there's some kind of window."

"I think I understood," I said.

"You did?" Aunt Tee's eyebrows rose.

I nodded slowly as I tossed Pulaski's words and actions around in my head. "It's more an energetic thing than anything else. That whatever ceremonial, or ritual energies that were put into motion when Gary was first built, during this centennial birthday year there is a window, an opportunity to counter them. To change it."

"I never would have thought of that." Aunt Tee looked surprised. "So that really made sense to you."

"I've got to say it did." I nodded again. "And from what I understand, energetically speaking, it's true."

"They never should have sent that Patterson guy to the meeting," Thomas said, ignoring our spiritual conversation. "He gave us some basic information about the Brownfields strategy, but actually, what he said can be found on the Internet."

"I think the city wanted to make a point," Aunt

Tee said. "And that is, that they are open to talking to us regular Joe Schmoes and meeting with us. I've got to commend them for that."

"That's true. Oh." Thomas placed his palm on the coffee table. "Believe it or not, my mother did teach me some manners." He stood up. "Would you care for something to drink? I've got apple juice. Pink grapefruit juice. Water."

"I'll take some apple juice," Aunt Tee said.

"Water's fine for me," I replied.

Just then a rather polished looking woman with dark circles around her eyes walked into the living room.

"I didn't know you were here," Thomas said.

"Well, I am," she replied. "I didn't go to my meeting tonight."

Their eyes locked. I was slightly aware of how Thomas focused on the glass she held in her hand.

"Ms. Tee, this is my sister Marguerite. And this is Rossi, Ms. Tee's niece. My sister, Marguerite."

We exchanged hellos before Thomas disappeared into the kitchen then reappeared with three drinks. He placed them before us.

"You really stirred things up, Ms. Tee, when you started talking about the pollutants that are in the Grand Calumet River area as a whole."

"It stirred me up when I read it," Aunt Tee said. "It's a wonder we aren't all dying of some kind of rare cancer or some disease that they have to create a new name for. It's really awful."

"Now that surprised me," I said. "I didn't know it was that bad."

"It's worse than that," Aunt Tee said. "There was

so much in that report. They kept referring to these heavy metals that included mercury and lead, stuff like that. I remember those two in particular, but there were heavy metals in some of everything."

"That's not good. That's not good at all," I said.

"And that's exactly what I want to talk about," Thomas put his glass on the coffee table. "I found out that some scientists at Dartmouth College believe there is scientific proof linking pollution and violent crime."

"Don't you say it," Aunt Tee replied.

"Pollution and violent crime?" I couldn't believe what I was hearing.

"Yes. The information came from Dartmouth College. They did some research using controlled variables like income status and pollution density. Most experts believe crime is caused by social, economic and psychological factors. Well, guess what? This research indicated violent crime is associated with higher levels of environmental pollution. Specifically, heavy metals like lead and manganese."

Aunt Tee pointed. "Manganese. That was one of the heavy metals mentioned in the report that I have."

"I was going to ask you if it was," Thomas said.

"How is that?" I asked. "How are they relating violent crime and pollution?"

"Yes, how is that, Baby Brother?" Marguerite plopped down into a nearby chair.

Thomas glanced at her then focused on me. "The researchers say it's all in the way the toxic metals breakdown the inhibition mechanisms in our brains. And specifically the way the metals lead and manganese, breakdown. It causes what would be considered as natural violent urges to go out-of-control."

"Now I have heard everything," Marguerite said, twisting her mouth dramatically.

CHAPTER 22

Thomas sat back. "This is not something that I made up, Marguerite. This was a study done at Dartmouth College."

"So what are you saying?" She swung her crossed leg. "That all these black folks running around here killing each other are doing it because of pollution?"

"I am saying, look at the facts." Thomas sat forward again. "According to last year's police statistics, Gary leads the nation in per capita homicides for the ninth straight year. This little speck on the map. I believe this study and others like it gives us some insight into what is really happening in our city."

"Bullshit." Marguerite declared.

I looked at Aunt Tee.

"Pollution is not doing anything to these thugs." Marguerite continued rather loudly. "If the reason these folks act so crazy is pollution, it's the drugs they are polluting their own bodies with. That's their pollution."

"Those drug addicts could be self-medicating because of uncontrollable urges," Thomas replied. "But we are not discussing drugs. I am saying there was a scientific study conducted at a reputable college, and a hypothesis emerged as a result of that study." Thomas paced his words. "The hypothesis is that toxic metals like lead and manganese create an increase in aggressive behavior. They also cause learning disabilities and," he paused, "a loss of control over impulsive behavior. This is important information." He looked at each of us. "Maybe for once, there's something that scientifically proves that just because you've got a bunch of black folks together it doesn't mean there will be killing and utter destruction. Maybe there are real, tangible reasons that a city like Gary has turned into the hellhole that it is."

"You are notorious for looking for excuses for black folks," Marguerite replied.

"This isn't my excuse." It was obvious Thomas was getting irritated. His jaw muscle twitched repeatedly. "I just happen to read it."

"Is this information new?" Aunt Tee asked.

Thomas drew a deep breath. "I believe it first appeared in a magazine called New Scientist back in March or May, of 1997. I can't remember which one."

I followed Aunt Tee's lead in attempting to diffuse the situation. "I've never heard anything like this before. And if it's true the implication is tremendous."

"Tremendous." Thomas nodded. "They analyzed some statistics, including FBI crime figures and information on industrial discharge, similar to the discharge coming from U.S. Steel into the water and into the atmosphere in Gary, and they determined environmental pollution seems to have an independent effect on violent crimes. They specifically named things like aggravated assault, homicide, sexual assault and robbery."

When he said sexual assault it rang close to

home, and I felt like someone had punched me in the stomach. "You've got to be kidding."

"I'm not," Thomas said. "This research specifically focused on lead and manganese, and they said counties with the highest levels of those heavy metals typically had rates of crime three times the national average."

"Oh my goodness," Aunt Tee sounded. "And lead and manganese is in that report that I have."

I was as excited as Aunt Tee, but I was the closest to Marguerite who cussed and groaned under her breath.

"I don't doubt it." Thomas' excitement grew. "There's even a book that has this data in it. It's called Environmental Toxicology. These scientists are claiming pollution is as big a factor as poverty when it comes to crime, violent crime."

"Come on now," Marguerite said. "So now you're blaming everything crazy that happens in this city on pollution."

"I didn't say that," Thomas replied.

"That's what it sounds like to me." She crossed her arms.

"I think Thomas is telling us all of this," I attempted to intervene, "because we just came from a meeting addressing plans the city has that will probably take away people's houses to build new businesses. And what they plan to base their right to take away these private lands on is pollutants. You see, the way it goes is, if someone has the money, and can come in and do an environmental cleanup, even if it does displace folks who've been living in Gary for generations, then the city planners feel it is better for the city as a whole and there is nothing wrong with it. My aunt presented some information that proved Gary is inundated with pollutants." I looked into Marguerite's distrusting eyes. "That's how we got on this pollution kick. But when I think about it, "I looked at Thomas, "when you have a huge thing like a steel mill operating down the street, pollution has to be everywhere."

"I don't know anything about that." Marguerite gave me a deadpan look. "And if there is such information I want to read it for myself and draw my own conclusions."

I motioned to Aunt Tee. I was going to ask her to show Marguerite her report but Marguerite lashed into Thomas before I could.

"But I do know my brother. Any time he can jump on some conspiracy wagon to point the finger at someone else for our shortcomings, meaning black folks, he will. And no matter how much pollution is in this city, nobody has made these crazy folks smoke crack, shoot heroin, shoot up innocent folks sitting at stop lights and anybody else they can find. They've got to take responsibility for themselves."

"See there?" Thomas said. "Now it is *they* have got to take responsibility for themselves. What happened to the *we* part of this equation?"

Marguerite leaned forward. "Just because you have dreadlocks, dear brother of mine, doesn't make you more black than me. I don't see you living in the middle of the ghetto. You're out here where everything is brand new. You talk all that stuff but you don't live it. I was living it."

"This is not about who is living—"

"Yes it is." Marguerite cut him off. "I was in the

middle of it every day and I don't have no sympathy for them niggas standing on the corners waiting to commit a crime."

Thomas threw up his hands. "Okay."

"I know it's okay." Marguerite wouldn't stop. "That's why I'm here living with you today because one of them fools snatched my purse and forced me to give him all of my bank information so he could take my money. I'm lucky to have gotten away with my life." She shouted. "And it fuckin' pisses me off when you find excuses for them"

I looked from Marguerite to Thomas whose eyes remain downcast.

Finally, Thomas said. "If you want to see it that way, Marguerite."

"What do you mean, if I want to see it that way?"

Thomas sighed. "I think you should have gone to your meeting."

"I don't need those damn meetings."

He shrugged. "That's for you to determine, but one of the rules when you moved in here was, you have to go to your meetings. And I'm sticking to that."

The room went dead silent and it was obvious it took everything Marguerite had to hold her tongue. Finally, she stood up and said, "I'm sure you are," then she stormed out.

CHAPTER 23

"Well," Thomas cleared his throat, "a perfect example of impulsive behavior. Sorry." He tried to smile. "I didn't know there was going to be a side-show."

"No problem," Aunt Tee said softly. "As the old saying goes, you can choose your friends but you can't choose your family."

He rested against the couch. "Marguerite moved in a couple of weeks ago. She was having some problems."

"Hey, you're helping your sister out. I can understand that," I said.

"Well, I didn't feel I really had a choice."

"Don't be in there talking about me, Thomas." Marguerite called from another room.

"Believe me, I would prefer to be talking about something else." He called out, his gaze locked with mine.

"Let's get back to what we were discussing," Aunt Tee placed her empty glass on the cocktail table. "If there has been a scientific study about this, why isn't it all over the news? I mean, this is important information."

"It's out there. You just have to look in the right places," Thomas said. "There are many cities dealing with the same situation, but are they going to stop the steel mill production or any of the other corporate giants that are creating pollution? I don't think so." His eyes narrowed. "Then you are messing with this country's money, and they are not going to side with a bunch of folks who may or may not be having psychological reactions to pollution."

"So what good is the information?" I felt frustrated.

"Maybe in the long run if you can get enough people to care," Aunt Tee paused as she thought about it, "maybe some changes will be made."

"But in the meantime everything continues," I said. "This is so messed up."

"This system is like a steamroller," Thomas said. "It is in full motion and very difficult to stop, and if you are dealing with things that could be counter to the system, you could and probably will be crushed under the wheels." He leaned forward. "But we've got something working for us, solid information from reputable sources. This information about heavy metals can't be swept under the rug. It's bound to pop up again and again somewhere." Thomas glanced at the hall where Marguerite disappeared. "But some of the things I've shared with you, Rossi, and I have told you as well, Ms. Tee, have been ignored, especially when powerful people find them harmful to their causes." His features hardened. "There was a Georgetown professor, Carroll Quigley, who wrote a paper about the Rhodes-Milner Round Table, an organization many past and some present rich and powerful men belong to. This professor actually mentored President Clinton."

"Really?" Aunt Tee said.

"Yes, he did. And he exposed some of the strange

things I've told you about, because they are true."
Thomas stared at us. "And because he was a profes-
sor of a prestigious university people paid attention.
But in the end it nearly got him blackballed from the
speaking circuits. Quigley had gone back to the source.
He exposed Englishman, and deceased diamond king,
Cecil Rhodes', influence on our system here in America.
Some of the institutional foundations of this country...
the shadow government... were mandated in Rhodes's
seven wills."

I was awestruck by Thomas' newest revelation. I
wrapped my arms about me; a kind of verification that
I was actually sitting there. That all of this was real.

"You've heard of the Rhodes Scholars."

Aunt Tee and I both said, "Yes".

"They were named for Cecil Rhodes, and there
have been approximately thirty-two Rhodes Scholars
a year unleashed and promoted to powerful places in
this country since the early 1900s, to carry out Cecil
Rhodes desires." Thomas fiddled with his earlobe as he
looked at me then Aunt Tee. "And those desires weren't
pretty. Quigley wrote about Rhodes and other secret
societies. For a minute, articles popped up in esteemed
newspapers like the Chicago Tribune and in other pub-
lications, but after awhile things went quiet because
why? You do not cut off the hand that feeds you."

I closed my eyes. "This thing is so huge. Huge.
What can we do? What can we really do?"

"I don't exactly know," Thomas said, quietly,
"but I'm glad someone in Gary is finally listening
enough to ask."

The room went silent again.

It didn't seem real; this world of secret societies

and shadow governments. But I knew Thomas wasn't just spouting lies. I had read some of it with my own eyes. I scooted to the edge of my seat. "But... why?" I found myself asking.

"Cecil Rhodes deeply believed in creating a master/slave society," Thomas said. "Make them, those who you see as inferior work for you, and then once they have served their purpose, through whatever indirect means, be it pollution or drugs, dispose of them, kill them off. In the end you have fulfilled your philosophy of depopulation through the reduction of inferior races... human weeds."

"No. That's not what I mean." I looked deep into his eyes. "Not why did Cecil Rhodes put all of this into motion. Why was it allowed to happen? There's got to be a bigger picture."

"World domination was his ultimate goal," Thomas said.

I could tell he was reaching for an answer and it wasn't the one I needed. I shook my head, vigorously. "No, I'm talking about *the* big picture. I'm talking about God. Spirit. Why would a benevolent power allow this to happen?" I looked from Thomas to Aunt Tee. "And don't tell me there is no such thing as God because I know there is."

Aunt Tee shrugged, slowly.

Thomas offered his palms. "I'm going to be honest with you, I don't know anything about that. My religious experience, connection you might call it, is very limited." A look of impatience surfaced before he looked down. "I've never looked at this situation through a religious, or a spiritual filter."

But I didn't care what Thomas felt about my

question, if he perceived it as stupid or irrelevant. I didn't think so. "Well, I'm thinking about it right now," I said. "And I want to know why?"

"I'd like to know the answer to that as well," Aunt Tee eased the mounting tension. "But in the meantime we've got to use what we've got, and that is the information about the pollution in our air and in our water. It's not going to do any good for small numbers of people to know this."

I got up from my seat. I felt very uneasy. I couldn't let go of the subject the way Thomas had or push it aside like Aunt Tee did. I needed to feel there was a higher reason behind the events that had happened in Gary, and were allowed to continue. Thomas didn't believe there was anything higher, and I guess it simply wasn't important enough to Aunt Tee.

I walked over to a bookcase.

"What is it, Rossi?" Aunt Tee asked.

"I just can't sit down right now." I ran my hand down the side of an ornamental glass cylinder Thomas had displayed on one of the shelves. "This is pretty."

"It's a thermometer. One of Galileo's inventions," Thomas said.

"Does it really tell the temperature?" I studied the colorful glass objects that floated like Christmas tree ornaments inside a clear liquid.

"Within a few degrees," he replied.

"Interesting."

Thomas and Aunt Tee allowed me to meander in silence around the room.

Finally, I sat down and looked at Aunt Tee. "You're right. The information is too important."

She nodded. "We've got to get the information

out in this city and make people care." Aunt Tee moved to the edge of her seat. "And I haven't been a librarian all these years without acquiring a list of viable organizations in this city and other places. And I mean the people who head them up. The contacts that I've made through civic organizations, and my twenty plus years of being a part of the Gary Historical Society will come in handy too."

Aunt Tee looked into my eyes. I smiled, slightly. "I'm sure you do."

"Now, we've got a month before this Dexter Bonner is in place. And Rossi, I know you don't know how long you're going to be here." Aunt Tee continued to look at me. "I'm sure it won't be that long, but while you're here I want you to help me get the word out. Knowledge is power, and I think we can get a lot of people interested in this if they hear the hard cold facts, and that's what I told that reporter. I told him that we plan to make this a nationwide information campaign. We mean to inform the people here in Gary, and in places like Detroit, Michigan and Richmond, Virginia, which was also known as a murder capital at one point. And you know Richmond's got those huge cigarette plants there that use all kinds of chemicals. I bet that city is being eyed by people and businesses that are thinking about expanding their business interests through Brownfields projects too. And hopefully, when their plans start rolling, folks like us will gather in numbers to fight it every way we know how, because we will be informed." She focused her attention on Thomas. "I know you're an attorney, Thomas. And you've got contacts too. But I can't put any pressure on you to jump on this bandwagon because you're a busy man. You've got a reputation to protect."

"If I was worried about my reputation, Ms. Tee, my reputation wouldn't be what it is today." He smirked. "You can count me in. I think making some noise is exactly what we need to do."

We talked some more, and revved ourselves up for whatever was to come, but I could not, in my wildest dreams have imagined what that would be.

CHAPTER 24

When I arrived back at my mother's house, she was at the kitchen table signing thank you cards to send to the people who had attended Grandma Anna Lee's wait, and for the flowers she received. As I joined her at the table, I thought, life is such contrasts; something as direct as death and thank you cards to the complexities of Cecil Rhodes, secret societies and pollutants that alter the human personality.

I picked up one of the cards with an embossed image of praying hands just as the telephone rang. My mother answered it.

"Hello... hello-o." She listened for a brief moment, hung up and said, "I guess somebody's playing on the telephone." She sat down at the table again.

I replaced the card with the others. "You must be feeling better."

"Somewhat," she replied, with her head bowed. "But I've put this off long enough so I thought I'd get it out of the way tonight. How was the meeting?" She glanced up at me then continued to write. "If I had been feeling better, I would have gone."

"It turned out to be pretty interesting," I said then added, "Let me help you with this."

I was tired of profundities. I needed and wanted a break.

"Here's the address book from the funeral home." She positioned it between us. "The ones that I've done have a check mark beside them." Her puffy finger moved down the page.

"Okay. It seems like you've got this page under control," I said. "Why don't I take care of the opposite page and let you finish the one you started. And then we'll go from there."

A heavy, tired exhale eased its way out of her. "That sounds fine to me."

I chose one of several ink pens and began to address an envelope.

"Were there a lot of people there?"

"Probably about forty or fifty," I said. "But the guy who spoke didn't know much. They've got another man coming in a month to head up everything. But this Patterson guy who came tonight; he sure got an ear full."

"I'm sure he did," she replied.

"It's kind of funny though, I don't think he really expected that."

My mother looked at me. "I don't know how he didn't."

"That's what one woman yelled out." Her eyes looked tired and that bothered me.

"Mama," I hesitated before I asked, "are you taking your vitamins?"

She looked up again. "I'm taking everything the doctor told me to take."

"I wish you would try the vitamins that I sell. They are rated number one in all the nutritional magazines and—"

"The vitamins my doctor recommended will do

just fine," she quickly said.

I concentrated on the next name in the book. The writing was scratchy, and I could barely read it. Finally, I said, "I can't make this out. What do you think it is? Josie Simons?"

My mother studied the name. "Yes. That's Josie Simons."

We continued to work in silence.

"I don't know what I would do if they told me I had to move." My mother announced. "Maybe I'm just beginning to feel old and tired, but there is no reason in this world that our government should have the right to make us leave our homes if we don't want to."

"It doesn't seem right, does it?" I said. "It doesn't seem right because it's not."

She sat still and gazed off into space. "All these years, after downtown has been boarded up for I don't know how long; after all the white folks have moved out to Merrillville and Hobart, people like me have hung in with this city because no matter what, it is our home. None of them wanted any part of Gary during those years. Now they've found a way to come and take it back."

There was no anger in her voice. No fight at all; only a deep sadness that seem to come from a profound place. That saddened me. Throughout the evening I had felt a bit of anger, some disgust, had even experienced a kind of revelation when I compared what happened to the Native Americans to what could happen to the folks in Gary, but I had not felt sad. Tears welled up in my eyes as I attached another stamp. "Well, they haven't done it yet. So there's still hope." I was relieved I was able to control the flow. I made another check mark and went to the next line. "Now, what is this? It says, the Sisters of the Rose?"

"Let me see that," my mother said. She turned the book so she could get a good look at the writing. "Well I'll be. That's the church Mama used to go to."

I looked at the precise handwriting. "Grandma Anna Lee's church was called Sisters of the Rose?"

"No, that's what the women who attended the church called themselves. The church was called The Rose." She sighed. "I didn't think any of those women were still alive."

"The Rose. That's a different kind of name for a church. And they were all females?"

"Um-hmm. Nothing but women."

I was intrigued. I thought about the two white dresses that hung in Grandma Anna Lee's closet. "What kind of church was it?"

"They called it a spiritualist church." My mother made a face. "It was different from any church I'd ever been in. I went a couple of times with Mama, but it wasn't my cup of tea."

"Interesting. I've never heard of an all-female church."

My mother gave me one of her looks. "You probably would have found it interesting. They did things like call in angels. Go into trances. All kinds of stuff. My second visit to that place about scared me to death. That's why I didn't go back."

It amazed me that my mother knew about and had witnessed this kind of thing, and with all my attempts to launch a conversation about such matters, never once had she mentioned it. "How long did Grandma Anna Lee go to this church?"

"Probably a little over two years. And then she just stopped."

"Really? She never said why?"

"Never said anything to me about it. She didn't talk much anyway, so...."

Like mother liked daughter, and I wondered where I got my gift for gab.

"You know what?" My mother reached for the stack of cards that had been taken from the floral arrangements. "I believe they sent some flowers too. My mind wasn't working too well when I read it but I believe they sent a large vase of white roses."

"I put them in the sunroom," I said, looking in that direction. "I wondered who had sent them. They're gorgeous."

"So that's where they are, and I remember seeing them in there." She placed her hand on her forehead. "Lord, I must be loosing my mind."

"No, it's the grief, Mama." I looked at the top of her thinning, gray head. "It does funny things to you."

She sighed, nodded and chose another card.

"So when was the last time you saw some of the women who attended church with Grandma Anna Lee?"

"Oh, it's been years since I've seen them. Mama started attending that church maybe six months after she came to Gary, and that was..." she appeared to count the years off in her head. "That was about thirty something years ago. So I really haven't seen any of them since she stopped going there. I didn't have any kind of relationship with them outside of that church." She signed her name. "But the building was over on the east side. Down in the bottom, over there behind Diamond Street."

"Behind Diamond Street," I repeated. I vaguely remembered that area. "That's where Grandma Ruth and Grandpa David used to live before they moved."

"Yep, your father's folks started out over there."

Faint memories of playing at my grandparents house floated in. "Tomorrow, I wouldn't mind going to see if the church is still there."

"Chances are it's not," my mother said. "So many of those houses have been knocked down, and there have been fires on almost every street. Folks on dope have been using the abandoned houses as their hang outs. Sometimes they end up accidentally burning them down, or there's some kind of drug war and somebody caught up in that mess settles it with a fire. Either way the house gets burned to the ground. Hardly nothing over there looks the same."

"My goodness." It was distressing. "But I still would like to go," I said. "Want to come with me?"

She looked uncertain. "I've got to see the eye doctor at nine in the morning."

"We'll go after your appointment," I replied.

My mother shrugged. "I'll see how I'm feeling in the morning."

CHAPTER 25

That was good enough for me. Either way, I knew I was going. I didn't know what I would find but I felt it was important, if only to connect with a part of Grandma Anna Lee, I wanted to go.

"Dad had been working in the steel mill for quite a few years by the time Grandma Anna Lee came here, hadn't he?" I asked.

"He had." She nodded. "Probably thirteen, maybe fifteen years."

"That's a long time," I said. "You know, when I was little, I thought that he liked working at the steel mill. But after he retired I began to understand it was a tough experience for him. When I was growing up, because he was there all the time I assumed he liked it." I start writing. The truth, when it came to my father and the steel mill brought sadness again. "Boy, he worked there his entire life. I bet it consumed his life."

"It did," she said. "But what can you expect when you work in a place from the time you're nineteen years old until you're in your sixties. Especially a place like that."

My mother got quiet, but I felt she had more to say and she did.

"It consumed him all right. Now when I think about it, I don't know how he managed those first few years. It wasn't that your father was ever the most talk-ative man in the world, he was always rather reserved and had his own opinion about everything. That was one of the things that drew me to him. He was a strong man even when he was young. He wanted a home, and he believed he had to work hard to get it. So, he got a job at the steel mill." She smiled. "God, were we happy that day. It was like the heavens had opened up be-cause getting a job at the steel mill was a big deal back then, even if it meant you were going to be working in the blast furnaces." My mother shrugged a little. "And that's how he got started. In the blast furnace. And it was hard work. It was hard work." She looked down at the table and rubbed at a discoloration in the wood. "It never did get out to the public how many men actually died under those conditions. Your father surely didn't come home and tell me about it. But through the years he let me know how bad things actually were." She shook her head. "But he stayed anyway. He stayed be-cause he had a family. My-my-my." She closed her eyes. "And eventually all the stuff that was going on in that mill worked on him. And it changed him." My mother looked deep into my eyes. "It wasn't just the unbear-able heat from the blast furnace, because eventually he was moved out of there. It was the racism that changed him most, being treated like you didn't matter. Espe-cially in the very beginning when he had to swallow his tongue with the boss, just to keep his job. But then there were other things like when he had to get down deep and dirty with the men. There's no telling what kind of stuff was being said and done. And that's when your father found out in order to survive among all those different kinds of folks, you had to speak up for yourself in a way that would get them off of you. So you can imagine it would be mighty difficult to have to develop that kind of self-defense and then cut it off at the proper time, like with the boss men. And with a man like your father who had so much pride." She shook her head again. "So much pride."

We sat quietly.

"And all that stuff," she continued, "the total environment in that steel mill started an anger in him that lasted until the day he died."

As I listened to my mother I understood something for the first time. I understood that she developed her own anger to deal with my father's pain. Now, I don't remember any loud arguments when I was little, but they must have had them behind closed doors. I was certain as I listened to my mother talk, that her anger was the price she paid for how the mill shaped my father. "Wow." I took a deep breath. "That couldn't have been easy for you either, Mama."

"No, he wasn't the easiest man to live with." She rubbed her eyes. "And yes, that mill did change him from the young man I first married. But I changed over the years too." A directness beamed from her gaze. "And I know, perhaps the changes in me had a lot to do with what happened to him at the mill. But we made a good life together. A good life. And I guess in the end that's all that matters."

Was it really? I remember asking because I didn't agree with my mother. They made financial gains beyond what they believed was possible, but I felt there was something missing. My parents didn't have heart-to-heart communication with each other, nor with me, and I wondered if they knew how. I could tell my father longed for it as he grew closer to death. Yes, heart-felt communication, to me, that was essential for a good life.

But I kept my opinion to myself. How could I be in a position to judge when I didn't have a partner or children? But most of all I kept silent because it was the first time my mother had shared how she felt about my father so openly, and without anger, and for the time being, that was enough.

After that we finished the thank you cards. My mother went to her room and I went to mine. As I sat there I thought of Stephanie. I still wasn't comfortable with the things she said about my connection, and what felt like my responsibility to the city of Gary. But the truth was I missed talking to her. For ten years through boyfriends who came and went, Stephanie had been there. She was there when I needed to hammer out the heavy issues, and we had grown together on our spiritual paths. She was my best friend; no actually she was more than that. Stephanie was my family when I couldn't turn to my blood relatives.

CHAPTER 26

When I settled down in my room I called Stephanie. She answered the telephone right away. "Hello."

"Hey, it's me."

"Hey, Me. How you doin'?"

"Better than the last time we talked."

"Well that's good to hear. How's your mother?"

"I don't know. She seems more tired than usual to me. But I guess she's doing okay."

"That's good. So there's progress all around."

"I guess so. And I'm sorry I cut you off the last time we talked. It's not that I didn't hear what you were saying. It's just that when I called you things were already feeling pretty heavy. And then—"

Stephanie jumped in. "I understand. Forget about it."

"Yeah, right. You know I can't do that."

She chuckled. "I know you can't. So what's been going on?"

"I ended up at a meeting today with Aunt Tee and the guy I told you about, Thomas?"

"Oh yeah? And what brought the three of you together?"

"We as didn't get together," I said. "Well, actually we did, but it was after a Gary Historical Society meeting."

"I see," she replied.

"I know you don't listen to the news much but, there have been some stories in the media recently about eminent domain."

"You went to a political meeting?" Her disbelief was evident.

"It wasn't actually a political meeting. But I think things could get very political with time."

"So what is this eminent domain situation?"

"Basically, it boils down to quite a few people who live here could lose their houses under something called a Brownfields project."

"Lose their homes? What do you mean? Are they going to buy them out?"

"From the little I understand, they will get paid something. But the point is they won't have a choice in the matter."

"Really?" Stephanie sounded surprised. "Is it legal?"

"It's legal all right. Like I said, Aunt Tee and I got with Thomas after the meeting, and I found out the Supreme Court has already ruled on this thing. Some folks in, what was the name of the city? Oh, I remember. New London. Some people in New London, Connecticut, who were trying to fight the Brownfields project, which would take away their homes, lost their case."

"How can that be?" Stephanie sounded exasperated. "What are they basing this on?"

"Look, I'm just learning about this myself and I've got all kinds of thoughts going on in my head. But I think the guidelines say the property has to be blighted. I remember that word because I'd never heard of it before."

"Me either, so what does it mean?"

"It means contaminated with pollution, or abandoned. But up in Connecticut the US Supreme Court said the city *could* condemn private property even if it *wasn't* blighted if it was in the name of economic redevelopment. In other words, as long as it was in the interests of business, they could take the people's homes."

"This is insane. So what does that have to do with Gary?"

"Gary is one of the first areas in the nation that seems to be a perfect situation for a Brownfields project initiative, because we've got pollution coming out of our ears up here. And there are so many abandoned buildings."

I jerked the telephone away from my ear because of a loud clatter as Stephanie said. "Gary's situation doesn't sound good."

"No, it doesn't." I replied. "What was that noise?"

"Oh. I dropped a cookie sheet. I'm heating up some pizza."

"This late at night? Why don't you use the microwave?"

"Yes, this late at night because I'm hungry," Stephanie said. "And the oven makes it crispier. Plus I try to use those electromagnetic waves as less as possible."

I opened a bottle of lavender oil and placed a couple of drops in my hand. "We've got problems over here, Stephanie."

"If the folks in Connecticut lost under a Supreme Court ruling, Gary folks don't have a prayer."

"That's a wise choice of words." I shook my head.

"Because I wonder with every part of me why does God let things like this happen? You've got folks up here who have been beat down forever, and now they may lose whatever little raggedy houses they own? Now don't get me wrong. Every house in Gary is not some remodeling project waiting to happen. There are some good-looking houses up here." I exhaled something I didn't realize I was holding. "It's just not fair."

"Are your mother and your aunt's houses a part of this possible plan?"

"Yeah, they are." I sighed again.

"Maybe that's why your mother looks so tired. That's enough to send you to bed for a long time."

"I don't know. I think her problem is grief." I rubbed my bad knee. "She didn't go to the meeting because she said she wasn't up to it. So I decided to spare her the details. But the meeting was definitely on her mind and she asked me what went on. Afterwards she said she didn't know what she would do if they took her house." I paused. "It's funny, when I first heard about this whole Brownfields thing, Aunt Tee and I commented on how my mother would react if she thought someone was threatening to take this place, because over the years people have come to know, if my mother believes in something, she's going to fight for it. Yes sir-ree, Pearl Collins is known to be a fighter. And we predicted there would be hell to pay from my mother, if the situation ever arose. But Stephanie, when she talked about it there wasn't any fight in her. None. And it made me feel...," a lump formed in my throat, "we're being abandoned."

"Ohhh, Rossi. I know none of this seems to be fair on the surface. But it all has to do with karma. You know that. Spirit is always here. But we created our own karma. Don't put it on God."

"I knew you were going to say that." I felt a tinge of anger and I fought to smother it. "I believe in karma too, but I've got to say right now this karma business is getting on my last nerve."

"And that's allowed too," Stephanie said.

We held the line in silence.

Finally, I asked, "So this is a collective karma that the people in these cities are sharing?"

"Yep, that's how I believe it works," Stephanie said. "Some kind of way, what ever the circumstances are, they are perfect for the people who live in those cities to play out their karmic scenarios. Karma that probably deals with loss. That is if they end up losing their houses."

I took a deep whiff of the lavender. "I just thought about something."

"What?"

"That's what my Uncle Henry said my Grandpa Eli believed. I mean, it didn't have anything to do with pollution, but he basically said the people who were born and died in the city of Gary shared some kind of karma. I think Grandpa Eli was more focused on the dying part, though."

"It's all related. What your grandfather believed and what I believe are based on the same universal laws."

"I wonder if it's mutable." I mumbled.

"What?"

"If the karma is mutable," I repeated into the phone. "If it can be changed."

"Based on your connection with Gary, I'd say you

should be asking that question. There may be more than one person who should ask, but you are definitely one of them," Stephanie replied.

I nibbled my bottom lip. "I'm just asking, Stephanie, for the sake of asking."

"No, you're not. You're asking because something inside of you is making you ask. Think about it."

I did. "Well, it's not death," I said with a sigh. "Time of death is a karma that is very hard to change."

"But even death can be changed with grace," Stephanie said.

"Yes. That ah-all elusive grace," I closed my eyes. Then I softly, added. "But I believe in grace too. So I have to believe collective karma can be changed."

"And you just might be the key person who initiates that change in Gary, Rossi."

"See there. When you say stuff like that, things kind of go fuzzy for me. They turn into impossible concepts, impossible dreams. But when I take myself out of the equation, it makes sense again."

"That's because you're making yourself small, inconsequential to the big picture. There is no separation, remember? Separation is the big illusion."

"Oh yes." I made a face. "Two key spiritual words, *big illusion*. See that's another thing. The next time I'm on the other side, before I incarnate, I'm going to ask for a change in the rules over here. You know, make it a little simpler for us mere mortals on this side of the veil."

A familiar chuckle came through the telephone. "You might as well make light of it," Stephanie said. "Either way it's in your chart. And you know I've called some major life events for you before."

I recalled how Stephanie had prepared me for

my father's death and some medical problems I didn't know I had, suddenly I didn't feel like joking any more. "Yes, you have. More than once."

"It's up to you to make the conscious connection, Rossi. And to claim it. If you don't know how to do that, then ask Spirit how. Ask how you can make the connection. Because there's no doubt in my mind, that you're in Gary in the middle of everything that's happening, for a reason."

"A window of opportunity." I thought of Pulaski.

"Exactly."

I watched my feet while I patted them together like a little kid. "Tomorrow I plan to visit the church my Grandma Anna Lee used to go to. You know. Just to check it out. And get this. It was a spiritualist church, Stephanie, and all the members were women."

"Now that could be interesting," she replied.

"I think so," I said. "It's an old church and I don't know if it's still there, but I plan to find out and I've asked my mother to come. She didn't make any promises, but we'll see."

"Let me know what happens," Stephanie said.

"Stephanie?"

"Yes."

"Astrology can be a pretty exact science."

"You bet it can," she said.

"And people who are into astrology and who have a rich knowledge of the occult would probably put a lot of trust in it."

"I trust it implicitly. And you know me. Some of that occult stuff can really freak me out, but I definitely trust astrology. Now, I don't consider myself a master astrologist by any means, but I do stay on top of what's happening in my chart to help me make decisions. So I'm certain people who are deeply involved in the occult, and know astrology, would use all the tools at their disposal."

I thought about the things I had read on the Internet. I thought about Pulaski, the names that had rolled off of Thomas's tongue, the men of power who were involved in the occult, and I knew Stephanie was right. Those men would choose the perfect astrological time. A time that would support their victory. If Pulaski was correct about the window of opportunity during the centennial year 2007, those men were aware of it as well, and something inside me knew that did not bode well for Gary and its citizens. I absolutely knew it.

Intuition is a funny thing. It can be powerful, yet subtle. It is because of that subtlety that it can be easily missed or misunderstood, especially if the mind, the logical mind is preoccupied with other things. I told you I thought it did not bode well for Gary, I did not think events would take a much more personal turn.

CHAPTER 27

My mother and I arrived at The Bottom a little after noon. It was nothing like I remembered. My grandparent's home was gone and the only thing that remained of my childhood memories were the sunflowers. My Grandmother Ruth loved sunflowers. Now their offspring towered high above a variety of strong weeds and overgrowth.

"The church used to be on the corner of the street behind this one," my mother pointed, "and the house where those two ladies who were chopped up and killed lived on that street too."

I followed her directions only to be disappointed by the crumbled foundations of two buildings; one of a haggard red brick, and the other of a hay colored stone that resembled slate.

"Boy, this looks bad," my mother said. "I knew the clapboard buildings would all be gone." She rolled down the window. "But that brick building used to be a neighborhood store, and the other was the church."

"So the whole block is gone."

"Yep. Time takes its toll on everything, I guess."

I knew my mother was referring to more than the vacant lots and crumbled buildings. I looked to my right at an open field of weeds. Southward, I could see large patches of reeds sprinkled over the land. I remembered running in that field, chasing my cousin and playing hide and go seek. "Baron and I used to love playing out there," I said. "Especially near the water that came out of the big pipe. There were always huge dragonflies in that area and all kinds of frogs."

"And you used to scare me to death when you did," my mother replied. "That water was so unpredictable. Sometimes it would come rushing out of that pipe like nobody's business, and at other times it was calm enough. But you never knew how that water was going to act."

I looked at her aged but still attractive profile. "I remember I got one of the spankings of my life for playing down there. So now I get it. You whipped me because you were afraid that I'd get hurt."

She glanced at me before she looked out the window. "You could have drowned, Rossi. And I told Baron to stay from down there too. "

It was my mother's way of saying, yes.

"Well, believe me, I didn't go back after that. But Baron and some of the other boys from the neighborhood used to go down there all the time. Lots of fish came through that pipe, and they would catch them with their bare hands. I think they were carp."

"Most of them were carp." She agreed. "And of course there were fish out there because that's the Little Calumet River."

"It is?" I studied the landscape.

"You had to know that, Rossi."

"I think I've heard it before."

"You had to." She insisted. "Your father said the city put that pipe out there to redirect the river."

I thought about it. "So we were probably playing

in runoff water from the steel mill."

My mother thought for a moment. "I didn't see it that way back then but you're probably right. It did have a funny kind of smell. I remember that." Her forehead creased. "And there's still water out there." She pointed. "Look at those reeds. But there's not as many as it used to be, and it seems like they used to grow much taller. These reeds are kind of short and stubby." She placed her hand on the dashboard and looked around. "And there isn't a bird to be seen."

I felt something was missing, but I only realized what it was when my mother said it. "There's no telling what was in that water when we were playing in it," I said. "And what's out there now."

She pulled a tissue from her purse and blew her nose. "Well, it's no need of us sitting out here. It looks like that church has been long gone."

"Yeah, I guess you're right." I started up the car and turned around. When we were back on Diamond Street I wondered if any of the neighbors knew what had happened to The Rose, and the women who attended it.

I spotted an elderly woman sitting on a porch. "Maybe she knows something about the church."

"I guess it wouldn't hurt to ask," my mother said.

I slowed down as we drew nearer and rolled down my window. "Excuse me." I shouted across the street. "How are you doing today?"

"What?" She replied.

"How are you today?" I repeated.

Warily, the woman looked at me and the car. "I'm okay."

"My grandmother used to go to a church one

street over from here. It was called The Rose, and we were just wondering if any of the women who attended that church lived around here."

The woman shook her head, slowly. "I remember there was a church with a name like that, but you see, I moved in here with my sister about twenty years ago. She's been gone two years now. She was the one who knew everything about the neighborhood. But I don't know nearly as much as she did. I'm sorry," she apologized, "I can't help you."

"That's okay." I smiled. "Thank you anyway."

The woman looked up the street. "But there's another woman on this side of the street who might know. Her name is Frances. She's lived on this street as long as my sister had. Yes, Frances might know something. She lives in the white house on the corner with the white awnings trimmed in black."

I looked up the street. There were several houses, an empty lot and two structures that were burned and abandoned. I couldn't see Frances' house. I looked back at the woman. "Thank you," I said. "We might stop by and ask her about it."

"I'm sure she'd like the company." The woman smiled as she attempted to see who was sitting beside me.

"Thank you." I said again as I drove away.

"You're welcome. I don't think—"

I didn't hear what she said because a passing, noisy truck.

I drove toward Frances' house. "Do you want to stop by there?" I asked my mother.

She paused for a second. "No. I don't think it's a good idea. We don't know that woman and we just can't drop by her house. Besides, you never can tell with the people around here what you're going to meet up with. You've been away from Gary a long time." She held her purse close to her stomach. "You've got to be careful when you're dealing with these people in Gary."

I started to ask 'what could an old woman do?' But instead I said "Okay, we'll go back to the house."

But my mother found it necessary to continue her point. "She could have a crazy grandson, anything."

I continued to look straight ahead.

"I know what I'm talking about," she said. "Some of these old folks let there grandchildren move in and end up in some horrible situations. Especially the boys. Not too long ago there was a story in the paper where this elderly woman was shot while she was sitting in her Lazy Boy. Some young men who were after her grandson drove by and just shot up the house and her grandson wasn't even there."

I glanced at my mother. "Was she hurt bad?"

"They killed her!" Her lips meshed angrily.

"Nooo!"

"Yes, they did. The woman died." She tightened her hold on her purse and looked out the window.

"Oh no," I softly said.

While my mother continued to voice her fears, I acknowledged to myself that there were some horrible things going on in this town, , but I knew I would return to Diamond Street, regardless.

CHAPTER 28

Later that afternoon I went to Frances' house. As I walked up the walkway I realized it was extremely old. Almost as to confirm my observation the porch literally creaked as I crossed it. There were philodendrons and mother-in-law tongues that looked like they had been growing on the ledges forever; massive, jumbled plants that blocked large portions of the screens. The doorbell was a rusty antique so I decided to knock on the wood framed screen door. At first there was no answer and I knocked several more times. I was on the verge of leaving when the interior door opened, slightly.

"Yes." A female voice said.

Because of a combination of factors, the small opening, the shadowy porch and the screen that stood between us, I couldn't make out her face. "Hello," I replied. "My name is Rossi Collins and my grandmother used to attend the church," I pointed, "on the street behind us. A lady sitting on her porch said you might know something about it. It was called The Rose."

"What do you want to know?" She spoke through the crack.

"My grandmother used to go to there. She—"

"What's your grandmother's name?"

"Anna Lee Featherstone. We had her funeral a—"

"Lord, have mercy." The crack widened. "I believe I recognize you now from the funeral."

I strained to make out her features. "So you were
there?" I asked.

Her slender form came into full view. "I wouldn't
have missed it for the world. And we sent some white
roses to the wait."

A mixture of excitement and relief rushed
through me. " he roses are absolutely beautiful and we
really appreciate your sending them."

"I'm sorry. Come in." She unlocked and opened
the screened door. "Come in."

Of course, I accepted the invitation.

"My goodness," she continued, "I never would
have thought it after all these years, a part of Anna Lee
has come back to us. Yes, it has. Watch your step now."
She reached back in the semidarkness to guide me
through the room. "After we lost the church building,
we used to have meetings in this room, but we don't
anymore," she said. "Had you been out there knocking
for long?"

"Just for a little while," I replied.

"I don't hear so well. Not anymore. And because
we stay in the back part of the house it's really hard to
hear when somebody's knocking, which isn't that often
so...."

We emerged into a room full of light.

"Here we are. Now this is better, isn't it?"

I didn't think it would be polite to agree with her
so I looked around and said, "This is wonderful. You get
lots of sunshine back here."

"And we love sunshine. By the way, my name
is Frances Weaver." She offered her hand and I got a

good look at her face for the first time. She was a tiny woman, and I knew she was old because her hair was solid white yet her face was surprisingly wrinkle free.

"I'm Rossi Collins."

She gestured toward a chair and was about to sit down before she hesitated. "Would you care for something to drink?"

"No, ma'am," I said. "I'm not thirsty."

"All right," she sighed as she eased into the chair.

We looked at each other, and I decided she had a particularly pleasant face.

"Do you live here in Gary?"

"No, ma'am." I crossed my arms. "I live in Salt Lake City, Utah."

"I had a son who lived in Arizona. He's dead now. But I have two other children, another boy and a girl and they've got children." She smiled. "But none of them live here in Gary. Nobody wants to stay here anymore." Her eyes continued to shine. "Do you have any children?"

"No, ma'am, I'm not a mother." My response sounded charged even to my own ears. Motherhood was a sensitive issue for me. "No children," I said. "No husband. Nothing."

"Don't say it like that," she said. For a moment Frances studied my face. "Perhaps it's not for you to have children or a husband. Some people are here to accomplish other things. But I want you to remember something." She leaned toward me. "Because you haven't birthed a child doesn't mean you're not a mother. Oh no. A mother is someone who loves and cares when nobody else does." Frances dove into my eyes. "Everything in this world needs looking after.

Not only children. Everything needs love."

Suddenly, that part of my life didn't seem so bleak. I smiled. "I promise, I'll remember that.

She smiled too.

"You said, 'we'," I said. "Do you live here with your husband?"

"Oh no. My husband died a long time ago. I live here with— Here she is. I live here with Sally." She motioned toward the woman who entered the room. "We both attended The Rose. That's how we met." Frances smiled at Sally. "Back then I never would have believed we would be living and growing old together. But here we are."

"Hello, Miss Sally." I stood up and offered my hand.

Sally walked towards me. I could hear her humming, very softly.

"She doesn't talk that much anymore," Frances said. "She stopped about two years ago."

I thought there was something vaguely familiar about the woman whose eyes focused intently on my face. When she was within two feet of me, smelling of baby powder, she slowly said "Daughter of Mabel."

"Daughter of Mabel?" I looked at Frances who was obviously surprised.

"What did you say, Sally?" She came and stood beside her.

Frances was taller than Sally, but I, at five foot four, was taller than both of them.

Sally didn't reply. She continued to look at me.

"She said, 'Daughter of Mabel'", I said, and somehow the words were familiar.

"I can't believe she said anything," Frances

touched Sally's arm. "Why did you say that, Sally? It's been months since I heard you talk." She looked at me. "And even then it was one word here and there. Why, she hasn't said my name in years."

"Really?" I replied.

I knew I had heard Daughter of Mabel before, but I couldn't remember where.

"Daughter of Mabel." Frances repeated as she continued to look at Sally. "I can't believe she said that. Now singing." She went back to her chair. "That's another thing. Sally will break out in one of her childhood songs at the drop of a hat. I know—"

"I'm sorry, Ms. Frances," I interrupted her as I examined Sally's face, because it began to dawn on me the first time I met Sally her face was half bandaged, and she was somewhat heavier but I was certain it was her. "Was Sally in the hospital about three years ago?"

Frances appeared to think for a moment. "She sure was. She had had a bad spell and hurt her head. I couldn't go see her because I was down with my back. We were a pitiful pair at that time. But she was in the hospital."

"I saw Sally there." I couldn't believe it was true.

"Do tell." Frances crossed her arms.

"My father was in the hospital and I accidentally went into Sally's room."

Frances erupted into a smile. "Well, Spirit surely has something up for you two. Things just don't happen like that. That's the way Spirit works, you know. Just like a puzzle. A clue here. A clue there. Life is God's puzzle."

I was amazed at all, and I continued to stand there, staring at Sally.

Finally, Frances said, "If you're waiting for Sally to sit down first you might have a long wait, Rossi. So if I was you, I'd have a seat."

Grateful for the advice, I smiled and sat down. I also wondered about Sally.

"Sally and your grandmother, Anna Lee, were really good friends."

"They were?" I studied Sally whose long, wavy, gray hair was styled in three plaits, just like my mother styled my hair when I was a little girl.

"You best believe it. They clicked the first day your grandmother came to The Rose."

"So you actually remember my grandmother attending the church." I celebrated my good luck.

"I sure do. I was there from the very beginning because I am the one who started The Rose," Frances said. But I didn't consider it to be church. It was just a meeting place for women who had the same beliefs that I did. That's why I didn't name it so and so church." She folded her gnarled hands. "I named it The Rose. We had been open two years when Anna Lee came to us. I think it was about twelve of us coming to meetings at that time."

"Why did you name it The Rose?"

"Oh-h I've been asked that many times," Frances replied. She looked at her hands. "For me a rose represents the blood, the essence of human beings. That very thing that makes us human and allows us to connect to Spirit. So I called it The Rose.

"My mother told me it was a spiritualist church. I don't know if you remember my mother, Pearl. She said she came to a couple of the meetings."

"Did she now?" Frances looked puzzled. Then

suddenly she smacked her thigh. "She sure did. I remember now because I think we scared her away." Frances smothered her laugh with her hands. "Sally started off the meeting with some mighty messages from Spirit that Sunday, and then one after another it seemed all of us began to bring something through. I don't know if your grandmother did or not, but I think it was too much for your mama and she didn't come back after that."

I was stunned. "So my grandmother was a medium too?"

Frances placed the tip of her index finger in her mouth. "I remember Anna Lee did receive messages a few times. But she really was reluctant about that. And I think that's one reason why Spirit didn't come through her as much."

"I can understand that."

"Do you?" She studied my face.

"Yes." I looked into her eyes.

"I believe you do," Frances said. "Anyway, your grandmother was basically a quiet woman, and I think she attended our meetings because she knew what we did was real, and there weren't many other places that she could go. From what I recall, when she still lived down South, she was very close to her mother-in-law. Her mother-in-law was pure African, right?"

I thought of my Alabama visit. "Yes, she was."

Frances nodded. "That's right. You see, Sally shared a lot of things with me that your grandmother told her. Anna Lee loved her mother-in-law and she learned a lot from her."

"My Great Uncle Henry said the same thing," I said.

"While he was right," Frances continued. "I remember she told Anna Lee an African creation story that said the female spirit was first. And at The Rose we definitely believed that. As a matter of fact when you get to the root of most of the old ways of believing, they believed it all began with the feminine. That is where the creative power lies, you know. Think about it. It's the female who bears the children and who—."

Abruptly, Frances stopped speaking. Then she shook her finger. "Anna Lee's mother-in-law's name was Mabel. Your great-grandmother's name was Mabel. That's what Sally's talking about."

Maybe it was the excitement of everything I was being told but at that moment, I couldn't remember if Grandpa Eli's mother's name was Mabel or not.

"It's sure is," Frances said. "I remember Anna Lee told me herself how her mother-in-law never had any girls, and how she wished with all her heart that she had. So she told Anna Lee, from her way of seeing things, any of the girl children that came from her family line would be her daughters, and her mother-in-law drew joy from that."

Then it hit me. "Her name *was* Mabel," I said.

CHAPTER 29

"See there. Sally's something else." Frances looked at her friend. "Our best spiritual messages used to come through Sally. And she knew things." She squinted and nodded. "That's how Sally knew who you were. Now, don't get me wrong, you resemble Anna Lee a little bit too, but not enough for me to pick you out of a crowd and say you are related to her. Of course, I can see it now because I know you're related."

I simply nodded as Sally quietly slipped out of the room.

"So why did my grandmother stop going to The Rose?" I asked.

Frances looked in the direction where Sally had disappeared. "Like I told you, she and Sally were the closest of all. Now, it's obvious Sally's got some problems." She looked directly into my eyes. "But I believe before Sally came to The Rose she was already having trouble, if you know what I mean. With her mind."

I nodded again.

"You see, Sally is half Pottawatomie. Half Indian."

"So do the Native American... Indian things in here come from Sally's family?" I pointed out a very old turtle shell rattle with a bone handle. "There's quite a few of them in here."

"Oh no," Frances said. "Those are Sally's all right, but she brings those things in here when she goes on what she calls her journeys. We've got lots more of them down in the basement. They were taking over the house, so I finally made her understand she couldn't keep bringing them home because we didn't have room for them."

"Really?" I was amazed.

"I guess with Sally being part Pottawatomie and all it made that stuff attractive to her. They belonged to the Indians who owned this land before the white folks took over." Frances shifted in her chair. "Now, I don't know the whole story, but I believe Sally's mother decided to go on with her people when a group of them left this area. It seems you had to have some kind of proof that you were full-blooded Pot- tawatomie to receive some kind of benefits. I think with Sally being half black it was a problem for her mother, but what ever the reason was, she left Sally with her father. Then something happened and he died and Sally was basically on our own. And a young woman alone..." Frances gave me an insinuating look. "It can be horrible. And I tell you, when Sally was young, ooo-we, talk about a pretty woman. Sally was beautiful."

"I can believe that," I said, as Sally broke out in a rendition of Somewhere Over The Rainbow in another room.

"That Sally." Frances looked in the direction of the song. "I think some of the things that happened back then definitely messed with her mind. And with her being spiritually gifted too... it's been quite a chal- lenge for her."

"This is so unbelievable," I said.

"Life can be that," Frances replied. "When Sally used to talk more, she'd tell me when she was feeling the call as she referred to it. Feeling the call of the spirits of her ancestors." She closed her eyes and shook her head. "Now she just wanders off. That's how she ended up at the jailhouse about a month ago for setting up some kind of altar outside of U.S. Steel."

The light behind Frances that beamed through the thin, bric-a-brac trimmed curtains was so bright, I had to adjust my line of vision to see her face. "It was Sally, who did that?"

"Yes." Frances nodded. "For years she swore the land beneath U.S. Steel was sacred ground to her people. That's where she was getting all those things." Frances pointed toward a broken Native American necklace.

"My Grandpa Eli believed that too." My thoughts raced. "And I'm beginning to believe it's true."

"Sally, swore by it," Frances said. "And I knew about Anna Lee's husband. I believe that's one of the things that brought Sally and Anna Lee closer together. Anna Lee told Sally her husband believed the same thing she did about that land." Frances rushed on. "And Sally told me her mother, I'm talking about Sally's mother now, said when the last big group of Pottawatomie had to leave this area, from time to time small groups would come back and visit the burial grounds here in Gary. She named several places. One of the main areas was in East Gary, what is now Lake Station?"

I nodded and assured her I understood.

Then Frances lowered her voice as if she didn't

want Sally to hear. "She said they had ceremonies when they returned for those visits. Sally said she was a little girl when her mother told her these things, but she still remembered. Anyway, as I was saying." She leaned closer to me. "Your grandmother and Sally were very close when Sally's situation started to get worst. And the truth is, I believe Anna Lee stopped coming," she drew a deep breath, "because she was afraid of the same thing happening to her."

"What do you mean?" I asked.

"She thought Sally's problems were the result of her being so spiritually open. So Anna Lee was afraid if she continued to open to Spirit, and that was something all of us who attended The Rose claimed to be our right, that it might be too much for her too, and she would lose her grip on reality as well. I honestly believe that's why Anna Lee stopped coming."

I looked down at the yellowed linoleum floor. "I'm trying to picture that," I said before I looked up at Frances. "Grandma Anna Lee always seemed like such a grounded, serious person. Like you said she didn't talk a lot. Not at all. She ironed a lot." I forced a laugh.

"That was just her nerves, baby." Frances said. "Ironing was a habit she picked up in prison. It was part of the work they assigned to her, but it ended up helping her get through that experience."

I felt my breath leave my body. "Prison?"

Frances looked surprised. "You didn't know your Grandma Anna Lee served time for killing a man?"

"No-o." I sat back in the chair.

"Oh no." It was obvious Frances wished she could take it back. "Well, the cats out the bag now." She shook her head. "She did. She served time in Alabama. What happened was, Anna Lee was married and a man raped her and she killed him. But by the time she got out of prison her husband had died."

My hand covered my heart.

"Yes, it must have been mighty sad," Frances said. "Life sent your grandmother through quite a bit, but she held on to her sanity. I guess she couldn't see herself losing it, after all that, for any reason."

I tell you, to hear my grandmother had killed a man and had served time in prison shocked me to the point where I couldn't move.

Frances touched my hand. "So your family never told you?"

I shook my head.

She sighed. "I can surely see why. It's a hard thing to tell. And had I known you didn't know, I may not have told you either. But you asked why Anna Lee left The Rose, and I believe that's why she left."

I sat there not knowing what to say, and, Sally returned to the room as naturally as she left. She leaned against the wall. I looked at the two women who had known my Grandma Anna Lee in a way perhaps no one else had known her, but I didn't have another word to say.

"Would something to drink help?" Frances asked, her face marred by concern.

I shook my head again, and once again the room fell into silence until Sally started to chant a Native American song.

"Well, perhaps you'd like to go home and think about the things we've talked about." Frances rose from her chair. "It's not that I'm putting you out, but I can tell you need some time to think about this without two strangers looking on." She touched my arm. "I'm sorry I told you. I didn't know. I hope it doesn't cause you too much heartache."

I managed to say, "How could you know?" as I stood up.

Sally and I followed Frances through the dark front room and out onto the porch.

"I want you to know you are welcome here at any time," Frances said.

"Thank you," I replied as the setting sun bathed the last meeting room of The Rose in soft orange hues, highlighting images of female spiritual figures on the walls.

"Goodbye," I said.

"Goodbye," Frances replied. Sally just looked. I started to walk away but I found I couldn't. Instead, I came back and hugged Frances and then Sally. To my surprise, Sally whispered in my ear, "You'll make a difference. So don't be scared. She'll be okay."

I wanted to ask Sally what she meant. But there was so much on my mind. So much. And Sally had no intention of answering any questions. The moment she left my arms, she opened the screen door and went back inside, singing.

CHAPTER 29

I don't quite remember driving to my mother's house. I do recall sitting in her driveway experiencing wave after wave of various thoughts and emotions. Those waves were dominated by an intense feeling of not belonging. I felt, if I was truly looked upon as a member of my family, they could not keep something as profound as Grandma Anna Lee killing a man from me. I didn't feel it was possible, and all of my old wounds about family that I believed were finally beginning to heal were laid open again.

Finally I got out of the rental car and went inside. The house felt extremely quiet, still. Empty. But I didn't look for my mother because I was certain the emptiness had more to do with us than the house, itself. Instead I went and sat in the living room and stared out the large picture window.

Somewhere in the distant reaches of my mind I heard the telephone ring.

"Rossi," my mother called, but I didn't answer. I didn't answer because I wanted to shut her out as I believed she desired to shut me out of her life, out of the family. "If that's you, Rossi, answer that."

I still didn't move. I heard her finally answer the phone and hang up moments later. "I am sick of whoever is playing on the telephone," she said as she came nearer. "Didn't you hear me, Rossi?" She asked from somewhere across the room. "I called your name a couple of times to make sure it was you, and I asked you to answer the telephone. I didn't know who was in here. Somebody could have broken in, or something. Didn't you hear me talking to you?"

The next thing I knew she was standing near me. I didn't hear her approach. Perhaps the thick carpet masked her steps, or perhaps I was too far inside myself.

"What are you doing sitting here staring out the window?"

I looked down.

"What is it?" She asked.

I turned and looked at her face. She looked like a stranger as I thought about all the secrets in our family.

My mother put her hand on her hip. "What's wrong with you, Rossi?"

Then I told her. "No one in this family ever told me Grandma Anna Lee went to prison for killing a man."

She looked shocked.

"No one. Why is that, Mama?" I asked, softly. "Why did I have to find that out from a stranger?"

She recaptured her composure. "Who told you that?"

I couldn't take my eyes from her face. I felt if I stared at her long enough I could figure out if I really knew my mother at all. "That's not important," I said. "What's important to me is—"

"It is important if people are out there gossiping about your grandmother." She interrupted me. "I want to know who told you that?"

My voice sounded strangely detached. "One of

the ladies who went to The Rose told me. And she wasn't gossiping. She assumed I knew because Grandma Anna Lee is my grandmother."

"So you went back over there." The tone was accusatory.

"Yes, I did."

"You should have left well enough alone. I told you, you didn't know what you would find talking to does people over there."

For some reason, I don't know why, but some kind of internal light switched on. I was extremely present; aware of the colors in the room, the ornamental designs on the lamp posts, the guilt masked with a veneer of irritation in my mother's eyes, and it was clear what my mother was attempting to do. "I am not going to allow you to turn this into a conversation about how I found out, Mama." I stood up. "I want to know why, being a member of this family, I was never told that my grandmother spent part of her life in prison because she murdered a man. Tell me how that is possible, Mama."

Her lips set in a stiff line. "Maybe she didn't feel it was any of your business. Obviously, if she had wanted you to know she would have told you."

Her words cut. "None of my business." I squinted. "How did you find out? Did she tell you?"

My mother looked away. "She didn't have to tell me. Everybody knew about it."

"But you feel it was Grandma's place to tell me."

"I sure do."

I shook my head. "But you knew she wouldn't. You know how Grandma was. She had all but closed herself off from all of us, so you couldn't have expected her to tell me." I took a step toward her. "Grandma Anna

205

Lee didn't even allow me in her bedroom. That's how close she was to me. And that's where she stayed the majority of the time. She stayed in her room ironing. A duty they had given her in prison. "

My mother continued to look away. "Well. If she had wanted you to know, like I said, she would have told you."

By the stubborn look on her face I could see I wasn't going to win. And it wasn't that I wanted to win. "Why didn't you tell me, Mama?"

"It wasn't my place." Her body language noted the change in me.

"You're my mother. If you knew Grandma hadn't told me it was your place to tell me. Being your daughter I had a right to know. What if I had heard something like that out on the streets when I was a little kid?"

"Well, you didn't." She squeezed her hands. "So it was right that I kept quiet. This worked out perfectly. You're grown now. You can handle it."

"But that's so wrong, Mama. That's so wrong. All this keeping quiet has divided us into little pieces. Little tiny pieces." I created a mimicking voice. "Tell cousin so-and-so, but don't tell Rossi." I changed it again. "I'm telling you this, Rossi, but don't you tell your grandmother. All that keeping quiet has been nothing but poison because there were times when I should have spoken up, but I had learned all too well how to keep quiet."

"Now here you go blaming me again for your shortcomings," my mother said. "I'm sick and tired of being blamed for other people's shortcomings." She folded her arms tightly against her breasts.

Quickly, hot tears fell from my eyes. "I never

blamed you, Mama, for anything. Why would you say that? Why?" I literally reached out to her. "I've never blamed you. I'm just telling you the truth about what has happened in this family."

"One man's truth is another man's lie." She held on.

"That may be." I caught a salty tear with my tongue. "But I know somehow I learned to shut my mouth when I should've done otherwise, and I learned it here, in this family."

She placed her hands on her hips again. "So what is it, Rossi? You're dying to tell me something. That's what this is all about, isn't it?"

I shook my head.

"Then why is it, two weeks after I have buried my mother you dare to talk to me this way." Her voice trembled. "You better tell me something."

CHAPTER 30

At first I didn't know what to say. I could tell she was hurting and I didn't want that. But all the pain and the silence of my life would no longer be suppressed and the words just poured out of me. "I want to tell you, it hurts me to know the first time somebody attempted to rape me in Tolleston Park when I was thirteen years old, instead of coming home and telling my mother that I was okay, that I was able to fight the boy off." My voice broke. "But in the process he tore my favorite blouse that she had just bought me. Ripped it." I swallowed hard. "But instead of telling my mother I came home quietly, took the blouse off and threw it away."

She looked angry. "Well, that's not my fault. Why didn't you say something? Why didn't you?"

I didn't answer her question. "It hurts that I never told you," I clenched my fist, "two years later when a grown man with a gun, and I was so scared when he showed me the gun, Mama."

Shock filled her eyes.

"A member of the P-Stone nation attempted to force me into the *same* park because he had just gotten out of jail and he wanted a woman." I wiped my nose on the back of my hand. "So what did I try to do? I tried to use psychology on him. There I was fifteen, trying to use psychology on a man with a gun." I could barely speak. "I asked him why he would want to do something like that. And I told him, it wasn't the right thing to do, but he had me by the arm in such a way that people passing by thought he knew me. An even though cars passed us on the street, because of the gun I was too afraid to do anything."

My mother's face melted and my voice lowered to a whisper.

"Do you know how I got away from that man?"

She shook her head and looked down.

"We were on the sidewalk on 15th Avenue, opposite the park. And I knew if he got me into the park it would be too late. So he walked me across the street and when my foot stepped on the curb, I snatched away and I said, 'At least let me go get something to eat.'"

My mother's confused eyes looked into mine.

"That's what I said." I shrugged, slowly. "I did. Now when I look back on it, it was such a stupid thing to say. Such a young, stupid thing to say. But it worked," I paused. "And then I heard this click in my head, a literal click, and the next thing I knew I was in the middle of the street, trying to stop the cars that were coming toward me."

My mother placed her hand at her throat. "Did somebody stop?"

I stared into space. "No. They went around me. Nobody would stop. I guess they were afraid, so they went around me."

"Rossi."

She took a step toward me, but I couldn't stop telling the story that I had never told her before. "After that, I ran. Boy did I run. But mentally I was so out of it that I ran past a police car that was sitting on one of the side streets, and I ran to Aunt Velma's house."

My mother's face filled with pain. "And you didn't tell her what happened?"

I shook my head. My gaze followed the tangled path of a monstrous Devil's Ivy my mother had been growing for years. "She was in the backyard watering the grass. It was such a normal thing," I said softly. "So I waved and went inside, and I pulled myself together. Then I came home."

"I didn't teach you to be that way, Rossi," my mother argued with her finger. "I taught you to speak up."

"Did you?" I looked deep into her eyes. "So why can't I talk to you at the most important times of my life?"

"I don't know why," she said, and hurried on, "because I know I taught you to speak what was on your mind." Then, her expression turned uncertain. "At least, that's what I intended to do."

"Maybe it was what you intended, Mama," I said, softly. "And maybe I would have really understood it if you had only shown me."

Seconds later, I watched her mouth tremble before her eyes overflowed with tears. "I didn't know that's how you saw it. I didn't know, Rossi." She swallowed. "All I can say is, I did the best I could under the circumstances. I did what I knew to do."

"Don't cry, Mama," I said. "I couldn't stand to see her cry. After all those years of complaining that I had never experienced my mother's tears, I realized it was something I could live without. I put my arms around her and held on for the two of us. Finally, when my heartbeats slowed, I said, "I believe you."

"If I had known how to do things differently, I would have," my mother said. "If I could have made our relationship closer, I would have. But it just wasn't in me. And I can't change the things I did back then." She continued to let me hug her.

"No, we can't change the past," I said breathing in her smell, "but we can acknowledge our mistakes, can't we?"

She nodded, and deliberately, firmly wrapped me in her arms. They were heaven.

That moment, in my mother's arms, I felt as if there was nothing I couldn't face. "I know I've made mistakes too. And probably one of the main ones was not coming to you when I was hurting. I should have known to come to you no matter what, because you are my mother and in my heart I have always known that you love me."

"I do love you, Rossi." She up looked into my eyes. "I want you to know that. I guess your grandmother wasn't very good in showing me she loved me, so I didn't know how to show you that I loved you. But you have always been in here." My mother pressed her fist against her heart. "No matter where you were, you've always been in here. And, Rossi?"

"Yes."

"I didn't tell you about Mama because I didn't want you to think bad of her. I didn't want you to think bad of the family... of yourself."

"Wow." I shook my head. "Being family can be so difficult."

"Yes, it can," she replied.

"How did it happen?" I asked. "How did she kill him?"

My mother went and stood in front of the large picture window, and the soft blue sheers framed her like a painting. "I guess the man had been hiding behind the shed. Daddy was in town and Mama needed some chopped wood. It was outside." She exhaled. "The man jumped her, wrestled her to the ground and raped her. But somehow afterwards, she got hold of one of those pieces of the wood and hit him with it. She hit him several times. I heard he died right there in the yard." My mother looked at me. "When Daddy came home with another man, Mama was still sitting on the woodpile with the man lying right there."

I don't know how but I could feel my Grandma Anna Lee's state of mind. "She didn't know what to do," I said.

"Even though it came out in the court that he had raped her, they said she killed him after the fact. They still gave her ten years in prison." My mother added softly.

"Poor Grandma Anna Lee. That had to be so horrible. I can imagine she didn't want to talk about those things with any body. But it had to have had a huge impact on her life." I went and stood by my mother. "If I had had something to hit that boy with the first time he attempted to rape me, I probably would have killed him too because I felt my life was in danger. It wouldn't have been what I wanted to do, but in the heat of that moment I believe I could have. So believe me, I understand how Grandma Anna Lee felt."

"So do I," my mother said. "Remember I chased your uncle away with an axe."

"You did." I nodded my head. "So there is a kind of strength that runs in the veins of the women of this family." I took her hand in mine. "We have the strength to fight back, to survive. But we've got to make sure we use that strength in the proper way."

My mother looked at me with a new light in her eyes. "You're right. We are strong."

That's when the telephone rang. My mother wiped her eyes as she walked over to answer it.

"Hello. Yes, this is the Collins residence. No, my husband isn't here." My mother leaned against the table. "What is this about? Yes. Teresa Collins is my sister-in-law."

I went and stood beside her. "What is it?" I mouthed.

Oh, I see." My mother looked at me. "I see." She repeated. "Thank you for letting us know. Goodbye."

"What has happened to Aunt Tee?" I asked as she replaced the receiver.

"She was attacked in the library parking lot." Her eyes were wide. "She's in the hospital."

CHAPTER 31

Instantly, my insides turned to jelly. "Oh no. No. We've got to go see about her."

My mother began to shake your head. She looked down. "I don't know if I'm up to it, right now."

"We've got to go." I began to pace. "She doesn't have anybody else."

"You know how things are between your Aunt Teresa and me."

I stopped in front of her. "What happened between the two of you?"

My mother looked away.

"This is one of those secrets that's not doing anybody any good," I said. "Aunt Tee has been attacked and you don't even want to go see about her."

She pinned me with a look I knew very well. "As a person, particularly as your mother, I have a right to my secrets."

"I don't deny that." I backed down a bit. "Everybody has a right to their personal privacy."

"All right." My mother shook her index finger. "I need to establish that."

"And I agree with you," I said. "But Aunt Tee is in the hospital. She needs her family. She needs us. So what's keeping you from doing that?"

My mother took a deep breath. "Months after

your father and I first got married he started acting real funny. I knew something was wrong. It was right after he began to work at the steel mill." She paused. "And somebody told me Teresa had told him that I had been with another man."

"Did you ever ask her about it?" I asked.

My mother's face hardened. "No. There was no need to ask her. The woman who told me had no reason to lie."

My thoughts were filled with fear because of what had happened to Aunt Tee but I had to see this through with my mother. "Did you confront Dad?"

Her eyebrow rose. "I sure did."

"Well, what did he say?"

"He claimed Teresa never said it. But Teresa was your father's favorite sister and—"

I looked into my mother's eyes. "But you never asked Aunt Tee, Mama. You never gave her a chance to redeem herself. Maybe it was a lie. Maybe that woman had her reasons for saying the things she said. Reasons you knew nothing about. And after all these years you have held this against Aunt Tee, when she never deserved it."

My mother continued to look into my eyes.

I touched her arm. "A little while ago we said we were going to admit our past mistakes. Now, whatever happened between you and Aunt Tee was a long time ago, and Aunt Tee is Daddy's only surviving sister. She's a good human being, Mama. I love her. And this is one way, if we are going to start anew, we can start off together by going to see after her."

I waited for her answer. I knew it would prove if my mother and I were actually starting a new phase of our lives.

Finally, she dropped her head. "All right. Let me get ready."

I breathed a sigh of relief as the telephone rang again. My mother picked up the receiver. "Hello. Yes, you may," she said looking puzzled. She handed the telephone me.

"Hello," I said as my mother stood by.

"Rossi, it's me, Thomas."

"Thomas." This was the first time he'd ever called. "You must know about Aunt Tee. That she was attacked."

"Yes, I know."

"We are about to go to the hospital." I could hear people talking in the background. "How did you find out?"

"I'm standing in the library parking lot where it happened," Thomas said. "I just talked to the police."

I didn't understand. "You were there when she was attacked?"

"I may have been," he replied. "You see, Ms. Tee and I were supposed to meet here, at the library. We were excited about the article that was in the news-paper this morning, and—"

"What article?"

"There was an article about the Gary Historical Society meeting, but they didn't use a picture of Mr. Patterson in the paper. There was a picture of Ms. Tee, and it focused on how she said she was going to spear-head a grass roots campaign informing people about what can happen if their land is targeted as part of a Brownfields project."

My mother whispered that she was going to get ready. I nodded and she left the room.

"I haven't seen it," I said. "I've been in and out all day today. I didn't think about getting a newspaper."

"So you didn't talk to Ms. Tee. She said she was going to call you."

"No, I never talked to her." I had difficulty focusing. I started to pace again. "You say you're still there in the parking lot?"

"Yes."

"Well, what happened?"

"Like I said, we were both excited about the article," Thomas began. "We felt it was a good way to jumpstart the project. Because of the article people would have an idea of what we were trying to do when we contacted them. So Ms. Tee and I planned to meet and organize our contacts. We didn't want to call on the same people and duplicate our efforts."

"Which library?"

"The one on Fifth Avenue," he replied. "But when I drove into the parking lot, as soon as I got out of my car, a woman shouted that a woman had been attacked and she needed help. So I called 911 right away. When I got over there, I saw it was Ms. Tee"

"Thomas." I swallowed. "Was she hurt bad?" I had know.

"She was unconscious, Rossi. And she was still unconscious when they put her in the ambulance. They're on their way to Methodist Hospital right now."

"Oh no." I sat down at the dinette table. "How bad was she hurt, Thomas? I mean, was there a lot of blood?"

And few seconds passed before Thomas replied,

"There was blood in her hair." He rushed on. "But that was all that I saw."

I closed my eyes. When I opened them my mother was standing in the kitchen wearing her hat and sweater.

"Well." I tried to think positive. "I'm sure she'll be alright. She's got to be alright." My words turned into a prayer. "My mother's ready so we're on our way to the hospital."

"I'll meet you there," Thomas said.

"Thanks." I hung up the telephone.

"Who was that?"

I removed my purse from the counter. "That was Thomas. He's a friend of Aunt Tee's. He was supposed to meet her at the library when this happened."

The telephone rang again, and my heart pounded as my mother picked it up.

"Hello. Hello." She listened briefly then hung up. "Nobody said anything. They didn't say anything. That's been happening a lot lately."

I heard what my mother said to my mind was on Aunt Tee as we went outside.

"See there," she said. "It's just not safe to go out after dark anymore."

We climbed into the vehicle at the same time.

"You won't catch me out after dark, not unless I have to be." My mother straightened her hat. "What library was it?"

"The main library." I started up the car and backed out of the driveway.

"They attacked her in *that* parking lot." She was genuinely surprised. "It's so well lit. It's not dark at all. I thought it may have been one of the smaller libraries."

"No, it was the main library." I tried not to think about what Thomas had said about the blood.

My mother shook her head again. "What is the world coming to? Teresa has been a librarian for at least forty years, and now somebody ends up attacking her in a library parking lot. It's sad. Really sad."

"I just hope she's okay," I prayed. "Thomas said when they put her in the ambulance she was unconscious."

"It's really sad." My mother repeated as she stared through the front window. "Teresa's got to be about seventy years old."

"Aunt Tee is sixty-seven years old. She'll be sixty-eight next month," I said softly.

It took us no more than ten minutes to get to the hospital. We entered the building through the emergency room door. Lucky, I thought for us, there was no one at the emergency room counter. But that didn't seem to matter, it still took awhile before a nurse asked, "May I help you?"

"An ambulance just brought my aunt here. Her name is Teresa Collins."

"Just a minute." The nurse thumbed through some papers on a clipboard before she keyed something into a computer. "Yes, Teresa Collins is here. You say she's your aunt?"

"Yes." I watched a doctor disappear through some double doors. "May we go back and see her?"

"It says here she just arrived," the nurse said. "Give the emergency crew a few minutes to see what they can do."

"Was she conscious?"

"Ma'am, I told you all I can at the moment." She

stood up. "Please have a seat and we will call you as soon as we have some more information."

"But you don't have my name," I said.

She looked at me with a hint of impatience. "We'll call out the patient's name, ma'am."

"Thank you," I said, wishing she'd shown a little more compassion.

My mother and I looked for seats in the near capacity waiting room. We found some chairs against a far wall. Thomas arrived as we were sitting down. He spotted us right away.

CHAPTER 32

"How's it going?" He asked as he walked up.

I shrugged and looked at my mother.

Thomas looked at her too as he knelt beside me. "How are you, ma'am?"

"I'm fine," she said.

I drew a deep breath. "Thomas, this is my mother, Pearl."

They shook hands.

"We don't know how it's going," I said. "A nurse told us to have a seat because Aunt Tee hasn't been back there long enough for them to have any information."

Thomas looked down. "I'm sure they'll know something soon."

"Waiting is horrible," was all I could say.

"I had an opportunity to talk to the woman who found her," Thomas said. "She actually saw the men who did it. She saw them as they were running away."

"She did?" I said. "There was more than one?" I asked horrified.

"She said there were two of them."

"I bet they were some of these drug addicts trying to get money for more drugs," my mother said.

"I don't think so," Thomas replied. "Ms. Tee's purse was still on her arm when I saw her."

"Really?" I said.

"It was." He seemed bewildered.

"Maybe they saw the other woman," my mother said. "And they didn't get to take Teresa's purse."

"The lady who found her said something very interesting," Thomas replied. "She heard one of the men say, 'Did we get the right one?'"

My mother and I looked at each other.

"Did we get the right one?" I repeated the question.

Thomas nodded. "She said she heard it as clear as day."

"So they might have meant to attack somebody else and accidentally attacked Teresa," my mother offered.

"Maybe," Thomas said. "We were standing by the woman's car, talking. And I noticed she had the same kind of car as Ms. Tee. So I asked her did she think they had planned to attack her. I could tell the question really caught her off guard. She said she didn't know any reason somebody would want to specifically go after her. And I believe her."

"So you think they meant to attack Aunt Tee," I said.

"They meant to attack one of them," Thomas said. "But I'm sure if you asked Ms. Tee if she knew of a reason someone would attack her, she would have said the same thing that lady said."

"What did the men look like?" My mother asked.

"They were young and black," Thomas said. "But she said they looked different from most of the young men around here."

"Different, how?" I asked.

"She said she couldn't quite put her finger on

it. It was something about the way they dressed that seemed different to her. I think she said one of them had on khaki pants and a button-down shirt that looked like it had just been pulled out of the pants."

Instantly, I was angry. Angry at Gary with its pollution, drugs and young black men who attacked old, black ladies.

My mother rolled her eyes. "Now she saw too much for me. How does she figure that?"

"That's what I asked her," Thomas replied, "and she said his shirt was so wrinkled that she noticed it."

"A button-down shirt." My mother hugged her purse. "I can't tell you the last time I saw some of these young men around here wearing a button-down shirt. And none of them wear their shirts tucked into their pants. They wear their pants sagging off of their butts. And I don't remember seeing any khaki pants." She made a face. "It sounds strange to me."

Thomas squinted. "It does. It really does. And on my way over here what came up for me was that article that was in the paper.

"What article?" My mother asked.

"Thomas said there was an article in the Gary Post Tribune this morning about last night's meeting. They had a picture of Ms. Tee along with it." I noticed Thomas was looking around the emergency room.

"I bet she liked that." My mother said under her breath, but I heard her just the same.

"What is it, Thomas?" I asked.

"I thought, maybe—there's a paper over there." He retrieved a mangled newspaper that was stuffed between a built in table and the tiled wall. "I don't know if this is all of it. It seems rather thin." He looked through the stack. "Here it is. This is the article."

It was a good photo of Aunt Tee. She was talking with her folder in her hand and the headline read 'Librarian Plans Campaign Against Brownfields Project.

My mother leaned over and got a closer look. "And that's a big picture too."

It was a large photograph. I glanced over the short article. "So you think this had something to do with Aunt Tee's attack?"

"I don't know, Rossi. But I'm an attorney, remember? So I think like one. And I've got to say I agree with your mother that something about this is strange."

My mother sat up straighter. "It is strange. Anybody can see that."

I looked at the nurse behind the counter. She was busy talking to a man with a woman leaning heavily against him. I felt for the couple, but I wondered what they were doing to Aunt Tee in the back. "Why would someone attack Aunt Tee because of this?" I asked, although some opinions were already forming in my mind.

"They may not have. That's a valid possibility too," Thomas said. "But think about it. Gathering opposition against Brownfields projects is going up against the big boys."

"People do information campaigns every day," I replied. "But I can't believe they are attacked for it."

"Maybe there's something in this that we're not aware of. Maybe it's the idea of a nationwide campaign that is threatening, because if it works it would affect some deep pockets. And when you start messing with people's money, and I'm talking serious cash." Thomas shrugged. "I'm just saying, think about it."

"It's still hard for me to believe that...." My words trailed away.

"What was Teresa planning to do?" My mother took hold of the paper.

"Teresa Collins. The family of Teresa Collins." The nurse announced from the counter.

My mother and I got up with Thomas close behind.

"Yes," I said, holding onto the counter top. I didn't notice the doctor until he walked over and joined us.

"Teresa Collins is your aunt?" He asked.

"Yes. She's my father's sister."

He looked at my mother. "And you're Ms. Collins sister?"

"Teresa is my sister-in-law," my mother explained.

"Okay. I understand." He pulled at his stethoscope. "Now, we had hoped Ms. Collins would regain consciousness while she was in the emergency room, but she hasn't."

My hand covered my mouth. "What's wrong with her?"

"She's got a concussion and her right arm is broken. We think she broke her arm when she fell."

The image of Aunt Tee lying in the library parking lot bleeding from her head with a broken arm sent a visible chill threw me. My mother grabbed my wrist.

The doctor continued. "Sometimes it takes longer for some patients than others to regain consciousness. It's based on the individual. So what we are going to do at this point is put a cast on Ms. Collins' arm, then move her into ICU. After that we will conduct some tests to find out if there are any other complications that may be prolonging her unconsciousness."

I closed my eyes. I tried not to think this but the thought crossed my mind that I might never speak to Aunt Tee again.

"You're taking her to ICU right now?" My mother asked.

"We are going to take her up there after the cast is applied." He shifted his weight. "It's late. ICU visiting hours are over. But we will allow you to go back and see her before we put the cast on and take her to ICU. Of course, she won't know that you're there."

"Do you want to do that?" I asked my mother.

"If you want to," she replied.

I nodded. "We'll go back and see her."

The doctor looked at Thomas. "Are you a member of the family also?"

"No, I'm not."

"We are only allowing members of the family to go back," he said.

"I understand," Thomas replied.

The doctor walked off.

Thomas looked down at me. "I got to go out of town again. I'll be back in two days. The timing couldn't be worse, but.... "

I didn't want Thomas to leave. I didn't know him that well but I felt as if he, Aunt Tee and I were in this thing together. It was also drained. What had happened to Aunt Tee had literally taken my strength. I searched his eyes. "After what you're considering about Aunt Tee and that newspaper article, I do wish you were going to be here," I said.

"If I could I would stay but believe me, Rossi, I

can't back out of this."

I noticed he didn't say it was a business trip. I looked down. I had no right to depend on Thomas Bates. He didn't owe me or my family anything. "It's okay," I said, "Thank you. Thank you for coming."

"There's no need to thank me, Rossi." He pressed my hand. "You know me and Ms. Tee are like this." He crossed two fingers. "I'm the one who's sorry that I've got to leave, but I'm sure she's going to pull through this. Ms. Tee is an exceptional lady."

"You need to go back, if you're going." The nurse said without looking at us. "We need to clear that station out as soon as we can. As you can see there are a lot of people in this emergency room that could use it."

"I'll call you sometime tomorrow and find out how Ms. Tee is doing." Thomas said as he walked away.

I nodded at hand before we went through the double doors.

CHAPTER 33

Another article appeared in the Gary Post Tribune the next morning, Librarian Attacked In Library
Parking Lot. There was no picture.

I went to see Aunt Tee everyday; morning and
evening. The first day my mother went with me, but
by the third day when Aunt Tee was still unconscious
she decided to stay at home. In the evenings when I returned, my mother and I talked for hours late into the
night, and on a couple of occasions she complained that
someone had made a habit of playing games on the telephone. She said the phone would ring when she entered
the house. She would answer it, but the line remained
silent.

They ran a battery of tests on Aunt Tee, but the
only thing they determined was her immune system
was extremely weak. During that time, I prayed for my
aunt. They were child-like prayers where I promised
to do this or that if my Aunt Tee recovered. In other
words I tried to bargain with God. I wanted it to be that
simple. Yet, deep inside I believed Aunt Tee's recovery
had more to do with her karmic path. If she had accom-
plished all that was intended for her to accomplish during this lifetime, her physical life could be over, but if
not, I believed I would walk and talk with my Aunt Tee
again.

Thomas and I spoke briefly while he was out of town. I felt strengthened by our short conversation. There was one thing about Thomas that was reassuring. He did not falter in his belief that Aunt Tee would recover, although Thomas didn't consider himself a man of faith.

One afternoon after visiting Aunt Tee I drove to a mall in Hobart. I went there because Aunt Tee and I had gone there during my last visit to Gary. We did some window shopping, and a particular pair of shoes had caught her eye. I tried to convince Aunt Tee to buy them but she refused, saying they were too expensive. So after everything that had happened I decided to buy them for her. I wanted her to have them. I wanted to see Aunt Tee stepping high in those camel colored high heels, and I decided they would be waiting for Aunt Tee when she woke up.

I bought the shoes and left the mall. After driving a few minutes, I slowed down as I approached a line of vehicles waiting at a red light. Out of habit, I looked in my rearview mirror. There was a man wearing a hat and sunglasses coming up behind me at an alarming speed. "He's not going to be able to stop," I said, as I braced myself with my steering wheel, and just as I feared he rear ended my car. My body lurched forward on impact, and my car hit the SUV in front of me.

For a moment, I just sat there. "He hit me! I knew he was going to hit me." It couldn't have been more than thirty seconds that I sat looking in my rearview mirror, when I became aware of what I felt was an absolutely inappropriate nonchalant expression on the guilty driver's face. I mean, he could've been sitting on a park bench instead of being the person who had just hit my car! Armed with all the stress I felt I got out of my car and approached him. When I arrived at his vehicle his window was up, and he didn't let it down, even as I stood beside it. That's when I became steaming mad and I tapped on the glass. Finally, the window came down.

"What is wrong with you?" I asked. "You drove up behind me as if you weren't aware there was a line of cars waiting at a red light. Now you've hit me and made me hit them." I pointed at the SUV.

The man kept his profile to me. All I could see was, t he was a middle-aged white man with somewhat heavy jowls. The hat and the sunglasses, kept me from seeing his hair or his eyes.

"Did you hear what I said?" I demanded.

He never looked at me. Instead, he rolled up the window.

I didn't know what to make of him. "Of all the rude things," I said, and I stepped back from his car just as a police car approached. At that point I assumed the driver of the SUV had called the police or that the policeman had witnessed the accident. So I began to walk back to my car. The police car pulled up beside me.

"Get back in your vehicle, ma'am," the uniformed officer said. "Pull over into that parking lot," he pointed, "and stay in your car."

So as I was doing what I was told, in my rearview mirror I saw the police car pull up beside the SUV. I assumed he gave them the same instructions that he gave me because they pulled into the same parking lot and stopped, as did the vehicle that hit me.

Moments later, the policeman got out of his car, spoke to the driver behind me, bypassed my car as he walked toward the SUV and spoke to the driver within that vehicle. I didn't understand why I was being singled out for last, and my perplexity increased when both cars pulled away as the policeman, finally, walked over to my vehicle.

"Officer," I said as he rested his elbow on the rim of my window. "I don't know what you've been told but the man behind me is responsible for what happened here. He hit my car, knocked—"

"You've been receiving a lot of wrong phone calls lately?" He said in a mechanically flat fashion. "They're watching you and yours, Rossi Collins. You're meddling in something you have no idea the magnitude."

Mental earthquake. Twilight zone. Call it what you may. That's what I felt as I stared into his sunglasses. Then he pointed his finger close to my face.

"The people I work for don't play around. Ask yourself, who can you really trust, Rossi Collins? Just as those cars have disappeared after involving you an accident," he paused meaningfully, "the people you care for could be set up and disappear just as easily."

That was it. As he was turning to walk away I found the presence of mind to look for a name tag. There was none.

Terrified, I sat and watched him drive away. I didn't realize I was holding my breath until I exhaled, "Oh my God, what is going on?" My life felt like fiction. My thoughts were garbled, and I had difficulty processing what I had experienced.

I began to play the whole thing over in my mind. I thought about the man who had hit my car... how quickly the police had arrived on the scene...the times I had been over Aunt Tee's and at my mother's house when the telephone rang with no one saying a word. "Someone is watching me. Watching us," I whispered to no one.

Frightened, I looked in my rearview mirror. "It sounds crazy but it must be true. Someone is watching us, and that police officer..." I shook my head. "He may not have been a police officer." I looked in my rearview mirror and around the car. "He was probably posing as a policeman. And those people in the other cars were all a part of it." My breathing increased. "They were all a part of it."

I tried to figure out what to do and logic tried to surface through the unimaginable situation. "I've got to call the police."

I took out my cell phone and started to dial 911, but I stopped. "The man who threatened me was in a police car. He said I had no idea of the magnitude of what I was meddling in. Maybe he was a real police-man? How else could he get his hands on a police car?" I closed my phone, and it was at that moment that I real-ized, of the people who were involved in the incident, there was no one but me who would say what had just occurred, had actually happened. And even though it had happened to me, there was a part of me that ques-tioned the reality of it all.

Grasping for proof, I thought of my car. I got out and ran to the rear of my vehicle. I searched for any evi-dence that it had been hit, there was none.

When I climbed back into my car, I thought of my mother who was home alone, and I thought of Aunt Tee who had already suffered a criminal act. Those were the only two people I truly cared about, and who ever had staged the accident threatened me with their disappearance. Not much more could be done to Aunt Tee but my mother was another situation.

I drove back to the house as quickly as I could, but after an experience like that the slightest incident provokes a sense of paranoia. I watched the cars behind me as I drove; the people who crossed the street in front of me at a red light, and those who drove beside me on the road. But the relief I felt when I saw my mother watering her flowers in the backyard as I turned the corner is indescribable. I got off the car and joined her.

" How's Teresa doing?" She asked as she watered her hostas. "Any change?"

"No," I said, looking across the street. "She's still the same."

"Lord knows, we need some help in this city." She pulled the water hose. "There's something wrong when older residents like me and Teresa have to be scared when we walk the streets." My mother shook her head. "And it's at times like this that you can't not have faith. Because it's my faith that's getting me through right now. It really is."

During my drive to my mother's house I questioned what I would tell her. Now I knew the answer. Nothing. So I sat and watched each car and the individuals inside of them that went by as my mother continued to water her flowers. I wondered what Aunt Tee and I had done to make someone want to harm us. Pollution problems had plagued Gary for a long time. It was a known fact, and although Aunt Tee knew people with muscle in high places, who could cause problems for big interests, I didn't know anyone. I didn't get it, and I needed to understand.

I thought of calling Stephanie, but there are

times when the future might hold something so fearful, so frightening, you don't want know. This was one of those times, not only for me but for Aunt Tee. I didn't want to hear Stephanie say she saw a door, like the one she had seen for my father, for my favorite aunt. I couldn't bear it.

"Look, Rossi," my mother called.

I took off my shoes and walked across the wet grass. Somehow feeling the raw earth beneath my feet helped to ground me and stabilize my emotions.

"I plant sweet potato plant about a month ago, and look how it's growing. It's just the right thing for this hanging basket."

"It's beautiful," I replied. I noticed the hanging basket was attached to some wire wrapped several times around a chain. "What's that for?" I asked.

"Oh, someone stole my other hanging basket. So I thought I'd make it a little harder for them this time."

Beautiful flowers in hanging baskets locked down by chains... something's got to change I thought as I scrutinized the car that passed.

CHAPTER 34

A day later, Thomas returned to town. We agreed to meet at Methodist Hospital to have lunch after my morning visit with Aunt Tee. I had decided to tell Thomas about the accident. I needed to share the weight of it with someone and I felt Thomas was that person.

"I'm glad you called me last night," I said, when I saw him. "It's hard to wrap my mind around some of the stuff that's been going on." I wanted to launch into what happened in Merrillville right away, but we were standing in the front foyer of the hospital so I held back. "Actually, I was laying in bed thinking about Aunt Tee. It's really tough seeing her unconscious, and I hoped it would be different today. But no such luck."

"I was hoping you'd have some good news." Thomas looked down at me. "I called you right after I got in the house. For me it's kind of a blessing and a curse that Ms. Tee is in ICU and I can't see her. But I thought we could get together, have lunch, talk."

"Yeah." I exhaled. "I can use the company."

We looked at each other without saying anything and I felt something. What? I wasn't certain, but something. I'm sure he did too.

I broke eye contact. "So how was your trip?" I tried to keep the moment light. "Last time you said

Gwyn McGee

things weren't as pleasant as they could be. Any better this time?"

"Well..." Thomas hesitated. "There's a lot going on with me, Rossi, and I feel like I need to tell you something."

I didn't know what Thomas was about to say and I wondered if he had experienced something similar to what had happened to me. "What is it?"

He looked directly into my eyes. "You and I have developed a special connection." He swallowed. "I know you feel it because I feel it."

"I feel something. Yes." I shrugged slightly. It was an old protective mechanism. "But we've been in some unique situations, and under some strain. It's easy to feel closer to people when you need to," I said.

Thomas looked away, then back at me. "That's true, but I still need to acknowledge what I 'm feeling, and to let you know the reason I went out of town is because I have a daughter," he paused, "and a wife."

My surprise must've been obvious. I didn't know what to say.

Thomas continued, quickly. "We're not together, of course, but we never divorced, and there was an emergency with my daughter, at least that's what my wife said."

The words 'my wife' flowed from his mouth easily. "I see."

"The problem is, her emergencies are not always real," he said. "She can and does make a mountain out of a mole hill sometimes, but there's no way for me to judge until I go down there. My daughter's still too young to really let me know what's going on."

I looked in his eyes and glanced away. It was a

236

Universal set-up. Here I was about to reveal everything to Thomas, what happened in Merrillville with the fake police, and even how I felt about him, and the Universe, God, whatever you want to call it, sets up a situation where I just couldn't do it. I knew about relationships with men who were already committed, pseudo committed, or didn't know they were committed. I had been well trained, and now, like Pavlov's dog my immediate reaction was to back off. I asked about his daughter. "How old is she?"

"Five." An awkward moment followed before Thomas continued. "I just thought I'd let you know what my situation is."

I said what I thought was the proper thing to say. "You didn't have to. You don't owe me or my family anything." Yet I was confused because I felt a little hurt.

"I know that, Rossi. Still I wanted you to know what's happening with me. That's the kind of man that I am."

"I can appreciate that," I said, hoping my tone was light enough.

Thomas and I walked outside, and I found myself feeling that when he left to see about another human being while Aunt Tee was still in the emergency room, that Thomas had betrayed Aunt Tee and me. Silly, I know, but for that moment I felt it deeply.

We walked several feet from the building before a taxi pulled up. An elderly man, struggling with a bouquet of flowers, slowly climbed out of the back seat.

"That's Pulaski," I said.

"It sure is," Thomas replied.

We waited for him to pay.

"Mr. Pulaski," I said as he nearly walked past us.

He turned and focused his watery blue eyes. The bright sunshine was of little assistance. "You're Teresa's niece, Rossi."

"Yes, sir, I am."

He looked at Thomas. "And Thomas. How are you doing, young man?" Pulaski started to extend his hand, but it trembled something fierce and he nearly dropped the bouquet.

"I'm fine, Mr. Charles." Thomas lightly patted his arm. "How are you?"

"Good enough to come see Teresa," he said. "I came as soon as I could."

"You came here from Porter County in a cab?" It was quite a distance.

"I wasn't about to ask my son to bring me." He gave a sad smile. "And although I am feeling better, I don't feel well enough to drive. So I called a taxi."

A group of people approached the door, and our best solution to the traffic jam was to move back inside.

"I'm sure Aunt Tee would appreciate your coming to see her, Mr. Pulaski, but she's in ICU."

He looked surprised.

"The only people who are allowed to see her are family members. I'm sorry," I said.

"I didn't know Teresa was in intensive care." Pulaski scratched his head. "I called the hospital before I came and all they told me was she was still a patient here, so I hung up and called a cab. I had the driver stop by a florist shop on the way." He looked at the bouquet. "Would you give these to Teresa, and tell her that I came to see her?"

I accepted the flowers. "Thank you, Mr. Pulaski.

I'll take them to her room." It was obvious he didn't know Aunt Tee was unconscious and I didn't want to tell him.

Pulaski looked across the street. "I guess I'll just get another taxi and go back home." He sighed. "But as long as you tell Teresa I came to see her and you give her the flowers, I'll be okay."

It moved me that Pulaski would go through so much for my aunt. "Do you have to go back right away? Thomas and I were about to have lunch. You're invited if you want to join us." I glanced at Thomas.

"We'd be glad to have you," Thomas said.

Pulaski looked uncertain. "I could eat a little something," he said. "I'm on some medication right now that requires I eat every two hours."

"Well, you should join us," I insisted.

Again, Pulaski looked across the street.

"Rossi and I were going to a restaurant around the corner," Thomas said. "But since we're back in the hospital, how about eating in the hospital cafeteria?"

"That will work fine for me," Pulaski said. "They've got lots of vegetables here. When you get to be my age you need to watch what you eat."

"I think that's a good idea at any age," I said as we headed toward the elevator. "I tell you what. Why don't you two go to the cafeteria. I'll drop the flowers off in Aunt Tee's room and then I'll join you."

They agreed. With a nurse's help I set the bouquet up in Aunt Tee's room and minutes later I entered the busy cafeteria. There were clusters of nurses, doctors and people visiting patients throughout the well worn space. I noticed Thomas and Pulaski were at the cash register so I picked up a tray and got in line. There was a choice of your basic cafeteria food which included the vegetables Pulaski sought. I decided on a turkey sandwich with potato chips. After I paid the cashier; I joined Thomas and Pulaski at a table in the corner of the room.

"Did Teresa like the flowers?" Pulaski asked as I sat down.

I opened my chips. "Mr. Pulaski, I didn't feel like telling you this when we were standing outside the hospital, but... Aunt Tee is unconscious. She has been unconscious since the attack."

Both of his hands began to shake. When Pulaski looked at me again it was through a veil of sadness. "My God, I had no idea."

"I know," I said.

"Do they know what's wrong?"

"She's got a concussion," I replied. "They still aren't sure what else is wrong with her, if anything."

Pulaski looked down at a bowl of green beans.

"How did you know Aunt Tee was in the hospital, Mr. Pulaski?"

"I read it in the paper yesterday morning. It said she had been attacked."

"That was in the paper three days ago," Thomas corrected him.

"I know." Pulaski nodded. "You see, some of my days are better than others." He ate a few green beans. "I felt pretty good the morning the big article came out in the paper; the one that had Teresa's picture in it. But by that afternoon I wasn't doing well at all. I was so tired. And when I get tired like that I can sleep a good day and a half before I feel better again. And that's basically what I did. So yesterday I was catching up on my reading when I read Teresa had been attacked."

"What do you think about all of this, Mr. Charles?" Thomas asked.

Pulaski looked up from beneath his thin, but long eyebrows. "It's according to what you mean by all."

"I mean the timing of Ms. Tee's attack."

Pulaski's shoulders rose slowly.

"Personally," Thomas said, "the more I think about it; the more I'm convinced it isn't a coincidence that Ms. Tee was attacked after that article appeared in the newspaper."

Pulaski went stock still. "Why do you say that?"

"There was a woman who saw the men who attacked Ms. Tee." Thomas leaned on the table. "She said, and I'm paraphrasing here, that at least one of the men didn't look like he belonged here in Gary. But on top of that she overheard one of them say 'Did we get the right one?'"

Pulaski's thin, pale skin turned ashen. "She did?"

Thomas nodded.

Pulaski put his fork down. "So you think it was a planned attack?"

"They didn't take Ms. Tee's purse." Thomas spoke with his hands. "If it was a purse snatching or a robbery they would have taken her money. All they did was hit her in the head. So yes, I think someone was out to hurt her."

Pulaski stared at the bowls of vegetables spread out in front of him. Several tears drifted down his cheeks. "Now that I'm old, I cry so easily," he said, embarrassed. Time either softens an old heart or it toughens it. Thank God, it has softened mine." He looked at

241

me and sighed. "I didn't think it would turn out like this."

CHAPTER 35

"What do you mean?" His words caught me off guard.

"When I gave Teresa the photographs and told her those things, I wanted to show her she was on the right track. I didn't think she would come to any harm. I simply wanted to pass the information on to someone. My son wasn't open to what I had to say and I have always admired your aunt's spirit." He looked down. "Her integrity." Pulaski looked up again. "And like my father, I didn't want to take what I knew with me."

I glanced at Thomas. "Wait a minute, Mr. Pulaski. You think all of this is tied together?"

He thought for a moment. "If what Thomas suspects is true, it is."

I sat back in my chair. Once again, I felt angry. "Mr. Pulaski, I don't mean any disrespect, but you have been dropping hints ever since you brought those aerial photographs to my aunt's house that night. Now, I think you owe us," I moved closer to the table. "You owe Aunt Tee some answers. What is this really about? What do you know?" I demanded.

Pulaski exhaled, and his shoulders shook, slightly. "You're right. You deserve to know and I'm old enough to let go of my fear of telling you." He looked into my eyes. "But even my hesitation is proof of the kind of hold this thing can have on a person." Pulaski looked around the room as if someone might be watching us. "But I'm willing to let go of my fear now."

I drew a deep breath. "Alright. If you've got the time, I've got the time." I looked at Thomas.

He slouched down in his seat. "I'm not going anywhere. I think I've waited a long time to hear this."

Pulaski picked up his fork again. "All I can do is tell you what I know. Some of it I got from my father, and the other information I got from studying and digging for myself. It was like putting a jigsaw puzzle together."

"That's a valid methodology," Thomas said. "A little here, a little there."

Pulaski looked at Thomas. "I think so." His eyes narrowed. "You see, I believe the people who built U.S. Steel knew they were building on Native American land. They probably suspected it when they bought it, but they had to know it when they started digging because evidence of it would have been everywhere. The Pottawatomie were living all along the Grand Calumet River." He wiped his hands on a napkin. "Once word of that got back to some folks in high places, folks who were into ritual—"

"Wait a minute," Thomas said. "How did the word get back to them?"

"I don't know that," Pulaski said. "I just know my father was there when a ritual took place. What he called a bizarre ritual." He looked at his food. "And from what he shared with me I'd have to agree with him." Pulaski looked up quickly. "And he said the men who performed it were no underlings."

"But how did he know that?" Thomas asked.

"It could've been some men with new money in their pockets simply out to have some fun."

"How did that woman who saw the men who attacked Teresa know that they seemed out of place? You just know sometimes." Pulaski said, agitated. "My father may not have been educated but he was no fool. He said they were dressed like they were going to an important meeting, suits and all, and they arrived in an expensive new car. Brand new money from the steel mill back in those days couldn't have bought all of that. Plus the ritual they performed would not be considered as fun by any stretch of the imagination."

I touched Thomas' arm. "Thomas, we know you're an attorney, but Mr. Pulaski is trying to tell us what he knows the best way he can. Come on now, give him a chance."

Thomas sat back. "Alright." He folded his arms. "No more question. Go ahead."

I focused on Pulaski. "Mr. Pulaski, you say there was a bizarre ritual?"

"There's no other word for it." He almost looked sick. "My father said they had a skull. And it was real."

"How do you know—" Thomas interrupted him.

I touched his arm. "Thomas, please."

He looked down. "Go ahead, Mr. Charles."

Pulaski continued. "He said they had things that probably came from Indians. You know, Native Americans. Back then that's what they were called, Indians."

"What kind of things?" I asked.

"There were some rattles, some kind of head-piece, and there was a long pipe with objects hanging from it. My father said they were caked with dirt. And he said," Pulaski hesitated.

Thomas and I waited, silently.

"He said there was something that looked like an Indian's hair that was still attached to the scalp and it had some kind of hair ornament in it." Pulaski sat back. "My father said the first thing they did was take a stick and draw a circle on the ground. Then they sat inside the circle."

"How many men were there?" Thomas asked not able to stop himself.

"Three. There were three of them, and my father said one of them had a brown paper bag. He couldn't tell if it had something in it because he was too far away."

"How could he see at all?" Thomas sat up. "Was there a full moon?"

"He said there was a moon, but it wasn't full. But one of the men had a flashlight," Pulaski said. "And my father said because the light was localized it was difficult for him to see everything at once. But he did see one of them pick up a stone and hit something with it. Then he heard a cracking sound. The next thing he knew he saw the man with the paper bag empty the contents from the bag into the skull. That's what they had broken with the stone, the top of the skull."

I felt myself cringe. I picked up my turkey sandwich but I couldn't take a bite. I put it down again.

Thomas looked at me then Pulaski. "What did they do next?"

Pulaski wet his lips. "They began to eat whatever was in the brown bag out of the skull. And then my father said two of them took a rattle and started shaking it. The other one put the Indian scalp on top of his head and picked up the pipe. That's when they started saying some words that my father said was not English. He was sure it wasn't. He didn't know what the language was, but he was sure it wasn't English because he didn't understand a word of it."

"This *is* crazy," I said.

Thomas shifted in his chair. "You should hear some of the things that come across my desk."

I rolled my eyes.

"Were they done?" Thomas asked.

"No." Pulaski shook his near bald head. "Once they finished chanting, they got up and started imitating Indians. My father said they were whooping and hollering inside that circle, and dancing around with the skull in the middle until they finally stopped and pissed on the skull."

"What did you say?" I said.

Pulaski looked me straight in the eye and said, "They urinated on the skull."

"Now I've got to say that's some crazy shit," Thomas said. "I was expecting you to say something off the wall, but I wasn't expecting that." He leaned on the table. "Some men in fancy suits arrive in a fancy car. They eat out of a skull then piss on it?" He shook his head and looked at me. "As a lawyer I do encounter all kinds of things, but in the end it usually makes some kind of sense." Thomas looked back at Pulaski. "This doesn't."

"Well... that's the ritual my father saw." Pulaski held firm. "He told me this on his death bed. And he said while they were peeing they were using some of the worst language you can use. My father said he recognized those English words because in the part of the steel mill where he worked, cussing was the norm."

"So they were cussing out the skull." Thomas said almost laughing.

"They were degrading the Indians," Pulaski replied with all seriousness. "First they consumed their power by eating out of the skull and using their power instruments. But after they consumed their power, they expressed how they really felt about the people. They urinated on the Native Americans after they got what they wanted. They were of no more use."

"When I think about it, it kind of makes sense." Thomas sat straight up. "It's tied to Malthusian eugenics."

"You've heard about that?" Pulaski looked surprised.

" Yes, I've conducted some research on the subject," Thomas said.

"So that's what they were out to prove by doing the ritual?" I asked. "It was an act of racism?" My ceramic plate clattered against the cafeteria table when I accidentally struck it.

Pulaski leaned in. His neck was pencil thin inside his heavy jacket that was out of season. "The ritual was about consuming the power of the people who owned the land before U.S. Steel owned it; consuming the spiritual power that they had been generating for hundreds of years. Letting the ancestors of those people know that they knew there was real power there, and now it would be used for their benefit." Pulaski's hand began to shake. "But that's not all. That's not the worst of it."

My stomach clenched from the look in Pulaski's eyes. "It's not?"

He shook his head and looked at Thomas. "Earlier you asked how did I know the skull was real."

"I did," Thomas said.

Pulaski drew a deep breath. "After the ritual was over, my father said one of the men went to what must have been a designated spot and got a shovel. He picked the skull up with it, then all three of them went over to a patch of bushes near this area that had been cleared," he swallowed "and they dumped the skull on the ground. After that, each man dug a few shovelfuls of dirt, and when the last man was done digging," Pulaski swallowed again, "my father could see there were more bones there." He looked at me, then Thomas. "He said because of the flashlight he could see that there were quite a few of them... and another skull."

"Another skull?" I said.

He nodded. "One of the men used the shovel to pick up the skull that had been in the ritual, and he dropped it on top of the pile." Pulaski shook his head. "Then they covered all the bones up with dirt."

Thomas leaned on the table. "So you're saying there were bodies buried there. Two bodies to be exact. Quite possibly Native American."

"I'm saying there were other human bones there, including a skull." Pulaski's faded blue eyes bore into me before he asked, "How did you find out about The Gary Roundtable?"

I was so stunned by what Pulaski had just revealed; there was no pretense in my answer. "There was a list of names imprinted into one of the aerial photographs that you gave to Aunt Tee. Above that was the title, The Gary Roundtable."

Surprise and apprehension mingled on Pulaski's pale features. "I wonder who they are and how did Pembroke know about them. Pembroke is the man whose wife gave me the aerial photographs." Pulaski's breaths quickened. "You see, I believe the men who performed that ritual started The Gary Roundtable."

"Why?" I asked.

"When my father drove those men back to the city, he said he heard those words: Gary Roundtable, over and over again. One man would say it and then another would say something else as if they were choosing a name. And they would always come back to Gary Roundtable."

I thought about the stage accident. "And those men murdered someone," I said.

"I doubt if they actually did it, but I believe they were behind the murder. Murders." Pulaski added softly. "And I believe The Gary Roundtable was formed as a pact of secrecy between them."

"They were murderers were serious about occult rituals," Thomas said. "That would be an interesting court case."

"They were," Pulaski said. "And so are their descendents. Spiritual power is very important to these people, at least those who understand it. They believe that energy is the foundation of everything."

"So there is a present day Gary Roundtable," Thomas said.

"I think so," Pulaski replied. "I'm sure they would have passed the knowledge down to their sons, if they were willing to listen." He looked down.

I'm certain he was thinking of Nathan.

"So who were these people? What were they? I mean, are they warlocks? Into Black Magic? What the —"

"What I know is," Pulaski replied, "they formed

The Gary Roundtable because of what they did, and I am almost certain they were also Freemasons."

CHAPTER 36

"Freemasons," I repeated. "Ever since The Da Vinci Code people blame everything on the Freemasons." I lowered my voice. "But I know a few, like my good friend Stephanie's grandfather; he's a mason. And I don't believe he would do anything like that. What he does do, on a regular basis, is go to his Freemason meetings in his funny hat and they do good things in the community."

"That's what most Masons do," Pulaski said. "It is as simple as that. They become masons for the brotherhood, for the fraternity, and most of them have no idea where the rituals they perform as Masons come from. It's just something that you do as a Freemason." He squeezed his wrinkled hands together. "And the background information is not readily available to them. That knowledge is available to the core group. If someone, who is not among the chosen group, really wants to find out the deepest truths, they have to dig for it. They really need to want to know. The majority of the time there is nothing that pushes Masons like your friend's grandfather to do that. They can see the positive effect Freemasonry has on the community and that is good enough for them. I know what I'm talking about." Pulaski looked at me then at Thomas. "I was one of them. But after my father told me what he witnessed. I needed to know what I had gotten myself into. What were the roots of Freemasonry."

"What are they?" I asked, incredulous.

Pulaski exhaled. "What I know about Free-masonry is long and complicated. And I know I don't know everything."

He ate some what had to be by now, cold mashed potatoes, and I took a bite of turkey sandwich. I felt a little queasy, and I didn't know if it was my blood sugar or the things Pulaski was saying. If it was my blood sugar I figured the turkey sandwich would help. Thomas had finished his meal.

"There's got to be something you can tell us," I urged between chewing. "A general summary or some-thing."

Pulaski wiped his mouth. "Alright. In a nutshell, this is what I understand. Their recent beginnings, simply put, the Knights Templar resurfaced as the Free-masons. But the ancient history is a different story. Freemasonry came out of the young civilizations of Sumer and Egypt. And those cultures believed in the power of the planet Venus which they saw as the God-dess."

"You've got to be kidding." I said as I thought of Grandma Anna Lee, Frances, Sally and The Rose.

"No, I'm not." Pulaski's brow folded into perfect lines. "The oldest information I was able to dig up showed Freemasonry was based upon a belief system in the Goddess, even though most Masons don't know that. But in the beginning it was very clear they be-lieved true power came from the Goddess, the female aspect of God, if you will."

"But what about Moloch?" Thomas said. "What

does Moloch have to do with the Goddess? Because I saw the form of Moloch in those aerial photographs you gave Ms. Tee."

"Moloch is there," Pulaski said.

I shook my head. "I never saw it. Even after Thomas circled it, I felt I was forcing myself to see a large, great horned owl."

Pulaski's eyes shone. "I believe Moloch's form is there in the road formation of U.S. Steel. You see, in the beginning Moloch was a God of Child Sacrifice."

"Moloch is also associated with the Bohemian Grove." Thomas jumped in. "That's the place, Rossi, where I told you a lot of big shots go in Silicon Valley. But their ceremony is called the Cremation of Care. There's a similarity here. God of Child Sacrifice. Cremation of Care."

I looked at both of them as if they had lost their minds. "How morbid," I said. "Both of those things are absolutely morbid."

"I'd say so." Pulaski nodded. "But based on the ritual those men did on the U.S. Steel site, I believe Moloch represented the Child of Sacrifice to them. Because at the end of the ritual they acknowledged Native American land and their spiritual energy had been sacrificed for the steel mill's cause. For its success."

I poured my potato chips onto my plate as I mulled over what was being said. I'd loved Jay's Potato Chips ever since I was a little girl. They were one of my simple pleasures. I needed a little bit of Jay's right then.

Pulaski looked at Thomas. "You asked what does Moloch have to do with the Goddess. It's all about the horns, Thomas."

He traced what I guess were a set of horns on the

time stained table top. It looked more like a U to me.

"You see Venus's movement around the sun gives a horned effect, and you can trace the history of the Goddess by studying the Egyptian Goddess Hathor's evolution through the centuries. Now, in this day and time, the horns are represented by an owl, the Great Horned Owl. Moloch, the huge owl that is the mascot of the Bohemian Grove." Pulaski showed a thin smile. "As I said, Freemasonry has a long and complicated history."

"I hear you," Thomas said. "And I connect with a lot of this but see, all that energy stuff seems like smoke and mirrors to me." He paused. "I think it's all about money and power."

"But money and power are energy," I said. "They are energy in a different form."

This time when Pulaski looked at me it was with a steely clarity. "You are absolutely right, Rossi." Finally, he focused on Thomas. "For those Masons with high degrees of knowledge, meaning the inner circle and those they have empowered, those Masons truly understand it has always been about power. They believe in using spiritual energy as a generator to get what they want," Pulaski continued. "Those men understand spiritual energy can be stored and harvested like anything else."

"Excuse me." Thomas apologized for kicking me as he crossed his leg.

"It's okay," I said and refocused on Pulaski.

"So those people have sought places where that spiritual energy *has* been, and still is being stored." Pulaski moved one of his bowls aside before he leaned on the table. "And who are the people across this planet who have generated the most spiritual energy through their ancestral rituals? The indigenous people, be they in South America, Africa, India or be they the Native Americans right here in the United States." Pulaski paused for emphasis.

I looked at Thomas. He didn't look like he was buying it, but I was.

"Now more recently, for some of the Masons it has been about money and material gain." Pulaski continued to hammer away at the subject. "Join the fraternity, the brotherhood and benefit from the networking. And networking is an accepted way of getting ahead in business all over this country if you are a Mason or not. You don't need any ancient spiritual knowledge for that."

He grinned, showing slightly yellow teeth for the first time.

"Connected businessmen have put into place a system that makes sure the wheels that grease their money machines are always in motion."

Thomas pointed. "Now that I believe. I've researched this myself and from some of the names of the early Freemasons, to members of groups like the Council on Foreign Rights and the Trilateral Commission, I believe it was always about the money and power. I think the secret societies were formed," he made two fists," as organizations to ensure certain men remained in power. The rituals and all of that stuff are just what I said, smoke and mirrors. Almost like a game. Those are the things that the men with real power get behind closed doors and laugh about because, once again, they have been able to use the average man. They have enticed him into the system to work for them, always making sure their coffers are full."

I finished off my turkey sandwich as Thomas and Pulaski traded knowledge. Their words were white noise, a background for my personal thoughts which were back on Aunt Tee.

"And because Average Joe wants to be like them so much," Thomas continued, "have what they have, he performs these rituals that he has no idea what they are about. Puts on the outfits. Does the bizarre stuff; things no one else could ever talk him into doing. And for the men with real power, Moloch, the torch, the all-seeing-eye; those things are just a kind of stamp that says, this is our work. We claim this. We know what is really going on here."

Pulaski tilted his head and shrugged. "There are many ways of looking at this and that's one of them."

"It certainly is." Thomas ran his hands over his locs. "Some people will do anything to get ahead and to protect what they have, and I think that was the reason Ms. Tee was attacked. Somebody looked into her background, not only as a librarian, but as a woman who over the years has sparked movements in this city and other places. They looked at that and decided Ms. Tee could stir things up enough to cause some real problems. You know what I'm saying?"

Pulaski nodded his head, slowly. "I'm afraid I do. It was because of those same qualities that I shared the information with Teresa. Those qualities, and others." He glanced at me, before looking down.

Thomas rubbed his chin. "Do you think there is a network of businessmen collaborating across this country, planning to take advantage of the Brownfields project initiative?" He asked Pulaski.

257

"I don't know, Thomas." Pulaski sighed and shook his head. "And I don't think I have the strength or the time to find out. Meaning I'm too old to dig any further. I'll leave that up to a young man like you."

His eyes closed.

"You look tired, Mr. Pulaski," I said.

"I am tired. This conversation has taken a lot out of me. But I'm glad we had it. He sighed. "And if you don't mind, Rossi, I'd like to ask a favor."

"What is it?" I couldn't imagine what he wanted after all of this.

"Would you give me a ride home?" Pulaski looked at Thomas. "I'm assuming you have to get back to work."

Thomas looked at his watch. "Yes, I've stayed away long enough. I do need to get back."

Pulaski looked at me again. "So can you take me?"

"Of course I'll take you home. No problem at all," I replied.

"Good." He pushed back from the table. "Now, if you'll excuse me, I need to find the men's room." Pulaski got up slowly and walked across the cafeteria.

For a moment Thomas and I sat there looking at each other.

Finally, I said, "Never in a million years would I have dreamed of having a conversation like that."

"I'd hoped for it," Thomas said. "But not under these circumstances, considering Ms. Tee and all. Mr. Charles simply confirmed what I already knew. I don't get the energy thing." He said point blank. "But being an attorney I can't help but look at the evidence. Maybe the inner circle as Mr. Charles called it, really knows something. Something I don't understand, but the truth be told, I don't believe I want to."

I thought of Aunt Tee lying unconscious in her hospital room. "Right now contemplating what is behind all this is not going to change anything. Understanding the pie in the sky doesn't allow you to enjoy the taste, if you know what I mean." Thomas shook his head. "No, I don't get that."

"I mean, we live in a physical world so we need physical solutions no matter what we might know otherwise."

"That's true," Thomas said. "And I'm more convinced than ever that somebody deliberately attacked your aunt because she planned to shine a continuous light, in a real way, on the pollution problems in cities like Gary."

I nodded. "Not only can pollutants cause you to lose your home, but they can cause you physical, emotional and mental problems. I think most people are aware of the physical threats pollution poses, but they don't know about the others. It's the kind of subject that weaves its way through the news every once in awhile just enough to lull us into apathy. We hear it. We know it's a problem. It's out there somewhere but what can we do?"

"Yeah, well." Thomas's mouth set in a hard-line. "I plan to see if I can find out who attacked Ms. Tee." His anger rose. "These people can't be allowed to get away with this."

"No, we can't let them get away with it, Thomas, but finding those two young men is a microscopic part of this."

"That may be." His pointed chin tilted up and there was revenge in his gaze. "But at least we'd be doing something."

I looked into his eyes. "What we are dealing with, Thomas, is profound. It's enormous. And we have to treat it as such. Now you know I want to find the men who hurt Aunt Tee. They need to be punished for that, but we can't stop there."

"Oh no. Don't get me wrong," he said. "But I've got private investigators that I deal with every day, and I'm going to call in some personal favors." Thomas' jaw was rock hard. "And I know it's not just about that, and I don't intend to stop there. But we have to be careful, Rossi. I really think we do. That original Gary Round-table bunch murdered somebody."

I sat back. "You think the people operating as The Gary Roundtable are responsible for what happened to Aunt Tee?" And to me? I thought but did not say.

"Actually I hadn't considered that." Thomas leaned toward me. "The truth is we don't know who did it. I'm saying when money and power are the stakes people will do anything; like that crazy ritual that was performed on the U.S. Steel building site."

"Yeah, you're right," I said as Pulaski walked toward us.

You must be wondering why I didn't tell Thomas and Pulaski about the staged accident. Later, I wondered about that too. Perhaps old habits die hard and I had closed down as I had done as a teenager after being attacked. Or perhaps, the policeman's question of who can you really trust was a deterrent. Either way, at the time, I didn't feel it was the right thing to do.

But there is something else. I was in a kind of denial. Although the events were unfolding as they were, this aspect of it was especially difficult to accept because, if I accepted The Gary Roundtable had been responsible for someone's death in the past, what did that mean for my life I wasn't willing or able to look in that. Now, in hindsight, I know Divine Timing is everything. We characters, still had our parts to play.

CHAPTER 37

"So are we ready?" A stiff Pulaski asked when he reached the table.

Thomas looked at me. "I'd say we are."

We took the elevator to the main floor and exited the building. Thomas and I had parked in the same parking lot. We said our goodbyes and Pulaski and I went on our way.

At first we rode in silence. I had a lot to think about and I thought Pulaski's silence was evidence he did too. I was right, but not in the way I thought.

"Rossi, I had a reason for asking you to drive me home."

"Other than your needing a ride." I said.

"Yes," he replied. "I didn't want to talk about this in front of Thomas because I don't believe he understands. Or perhaps he just doesn't believe in it."

"Believe in what?" I kept my eye on the old Barritz that wove slightly in front of me.

"He called it smoke and mirrors, the spiritual aspect of this whole thing. But it's not."

Out of my peripheral vision I could see Pulaski squeeze his wrist as if it pained him.

"The original Freemasons were occultists and they knew their stuff. Spiritual energy is very real, and from the things you said in the cafeteria I believe you know that."

"Yes, I know it's real. But it's the kind of thing you have to experience for yourself in order to really understand it."

Pulaski looked straight ahead. "So you're saying you have had personal experiences."

"What I'm saying is," I formed my words carefully. "I am consciously pursuing my spiritual path. And I say consciously because I believe everyone is on a spiritual path no matter what they might think. But as a result of my *seeking* out spiritual truths, I've come to experience the truth of spiritual energy."

"Does Teresa think like you?" His voice softened.

"Aunt Tee?" I glanced at him. "Not really. We've talked. She knows I have an interest in it and she's never shot me down because of it. But let's say it's not something that she feels drawn to."

Pulaski laid his head back against the car seat. "I know she goes to church every once in awhile, but going to church doesn't necessarily mean you believe the things we're talking about. And sometimes, if you're curious about them, you're not supposed to investigate it, or it's seen as evil."

"That's true," I said, "but not all churches take that position."

Pulaski sat quietly before he spoke again. "I told you and Thomas I shared this information with Teresa because of her integrity, and her ability to get things done, but if you recall I said there were other reasons too."

"I heard you," I replied. "And I noticed you never shared them."

"I know I didn't." He shook his head. "That night

before I drove out to Teresa's in that snowstorm, I had a fainting spell. I remember I came to and looked around, and things looked so strange to me, then I fainted again. I'd already been dealing with one physical problem after another, so I didn't know if the fainting was part of my dying process."

"So you thought you were dying," I said.

"Yes." Pulaski closed his eyes and massaged them with one hand. "Yes, I truly did and I was scared." He drew a deep breath. "We are still so racially polarized in this area of the country. And I'm not proud to say this but, back in the days when I met Teresa I'd say I was a ring leader of that mindset. You see, Teresa was the first black woman I really got to know. I mean, I've been around a few black women in various settings but that was as far as it went. But through the Gary Historical Society I really got to know your aunt, and it amazed me how full of life she was although her husband had only been dead for about a year. And I knew it wasn't because it was a bad marriage because in the beginning Teresa talked about him quite a bit. Finally I realized she was just a positive human being who believed if there was a problem, it was just a matter of finding a solution. She believed there was always an answer. And when...." Pulaski got quiet for a moment before he continued. "And when Bonnie, my wife, was sick and dying with cancer, seeing Teresa at those meetings was the one thing that seemed to give me some escape from all I was experiencing at home. I felt good around her. I'd put on one of my favorite shirts and my brown penny loafers because I liked them the best and I'd go. Teresa would bring sweets that she'd baked and, she always wore the same perfume, Estee Lauder's Youth Dew. I know the name of the perfume because I asked her one day." His voice was full of the past.

"You remember an awful lot about my aunt, Mr. Pulaski," I said.

"I do." He glanced at me before he focused out the front window again. "I know I do. She was quite attractive when she was young, and maybe because of where I was in life I couldn't help but see it. And that was something I never thought I'd do is find a black woman attractive." Pulaski looked down. "I remember Bonnie was having a really bad evening, it was a Gary Historical Society meeting night but I still got dressed to go. Nathan laid into me that they; he laid into me in ways I won't say, but you can imagine and I ended up staying at home."

"And that's why he treats Aunt Tee the way he does."

"I think so," Pulaski replied as we entered Porter County.

"Where do we go from here?" I asked.

"Make a right at the light and then stay on that road. I'll tell you when to turn again."

I thought about what Pulaski had told me about Aunt Tee as I turned the corner and crossed some old railroad tracks. "So are you trying to tell me you had feelings for my aunt?"

"I did have feelings for her." Pulaski admitted. "I guess I still do." He dusted off his hands. "But nothing came of it. I never said anything to her because I didn't know how she would take it, my being a married, white man and all. I don't know if she even realized how I felt." He paused. "And over the years my respect for Teresa continued to grow. Then when my father died... after feeling the way I did about your aunt, I couldn't accept what those men did at that ritual. I couldn't accept the deaths, of course, but I couldn't accept the prejudice either. I couldn't reconcile it." He stroked his head. "I had been a Mason for the majority of my adult life, but that's when I asked myself what did I really know about Freemasonry? Nothing much, I determined. So I started to research it and other spiritual belief systems," Pulaski said. "And you know what I realized? I realized all of the religions were linked in some fashion or another. That they are revamped versions of each other, different rivers leading to the same ocean."

"I think that is probably true," I said.

"I know it is," Pulaski stated. "But there is one thing that really surprised me. When you go back as far as you can go, back before religion as we know it today, I was shocked the trail led to a female figure. What they call a Mother. A dark mother." His voice strengthened. "Finally, after struggling with the answers that came out of my research, I decided what else could there be if it all started in Africa."

I heard the strength of conviction in his voice as we passed a homemade sign that pointed toward the Upp-Wark Indian mounds. "It makes sense, doesn't it?" I replied.

"It does," Pulaski said. "And the proof is there are Black Madonnas in many countries, even a Black Durga, India's oldest goddess, in India," Pulaski continued. "The majority of the historical evidence of female divinity is that she was black."

I wondered what Pulaski was leading up to, but I must say, I had a growing suspicion.

He rubbed the loose skin on his forehead. "Teresa loves this city, Rossi. You have to love it in order to collect and preserve a city's history as we have done over the years." Pulaski inhaled. "And I gave Teresa those photos, and said the things I said because she was born in Gary, because she is a female and because," he hesitated an infinitesimal second, "of her ethnicity."

"In other words, because she is black," I said.

"That's right. Because she is black."

The car went silent.

"I believe the intention of the men who did the ritual that night," Pulaski continued, "was to harvest the energy of the indigenous people of this area, and that it would take someone with indigenous ancestry to put an end to what those men started. Do you understand what I'm saying?"

"As crazy as it may sound to somebody else, I have to say I do," I replied.

Pulaski loosened his seat belt and turned toward me. "And this is not just about Gary, Rossi. You see, Gary was the first. When U.S. Steel created the city of Gary for the corporation, it started a special cycle of the ordinary man being used for corporate gain all over this country. U.S. Steel and its Gary was the largest American dream ever dreamt in the corporate world at that time. So it set into motion a cycle of corporate domination that appeared to be for the highest good of everyone, and only those men in key positions of power knew what was really happening."

"But how could they have known it would turn out like this?" I asked. "They couldn't have known that the pollution would lead to deaths and violent crime."

"They may not have known that specifically," Pulaski replied. "But if they were dealing with the spiritual realm, there is no telling what they knew. I believe they used everything they could," he rushed on. "Astrology is well respected in Mason history and among the Masons who are deeper into spiritual sciences. So they would have known about cosmic cycles and used them to their advantage."

My heart rate increased as I thought of my conversations with Stephanie. "And that's why you believe things can be changed at this time."

"Yes," Pulaski said. "I know there is something to that." He bowed his head as he paused. "I told you I go through bouts of sleeping for long periods of time."

"Yes, I remember something like that."

He pointed. "You see where the white fence ends down there?"

"Um-hmm." I nodded.

"Take a left." Pulaski cleared his throat. "Well, one night I woke up in the middle of the night, and the name of a book I had read, I can't tell you how long ago, was on my mind." He closed his eyes for a moment. "I read that book so long ago, and I don't know where it is now, but somehow the information inside that book was so clear in my mind. It was a book about rituals and how to work with cycles, and how the one hundredth anniversary of a project is like a new beginning; new energies can be evoked. When you break the number one hundred down in numerology, it is the number one. You are at the beginning again."

"And this is Gary's centennial birthday," I said.

"Yes. This time can be a new beginning for Gary and cities like it, because in the beginning of all of this, was Gary, Indiana, and taking advantage of this opening could make a difference all over this country."

"But how?" I asked, feeling the weight of his and Stephanie's words. "What did you expect Aunt Tee to do?"

Pulaski looked down. "I don't know how. If I had known I would have told her. But I definitely didn't expect her to get hurt." He looked out the side window. "I just know because of how I woke up that night, that I believed I was being lead by a higher force and that I could make a difference. And the things I believed, thought and did for the majority of my life before my father died would be cancelled out. That they wouldn't be held against me when I die."

The car went silent again.

"Maybe that's exactly what it was for, at least you're part of it, that is." I said, almost to myself.

"Do you think so?" His tone vibrated a quiet desperation.

I glanced into his aged, hopeful eyes then focused on the road again. "I think I do," I said.

Pulaski guided me to his house from there.

"Well." Pulaski took a couple of breaths. "This is it." He looked at a car parked in the driveway. "And Nathan's here. That's his car."

I looked at the nondescript silver sedan as Pulaski placed his hand on the door handle. "Now I hope you understand why I told Teresa the things I told her." He looked into my eyes. "But it wasn't until this moment that I truly believed it is my fault that Teresa's in the hospital."

"No, Mr. Pulaski," I said. "Don't put that on yourself. It's not that simple."

But his body was heavy with blame.

"Well…." He looked at me. "Good-bye, Rossi. Let me know when Teresa takes a turn for the better. I know she will."

"You'll be one of the first to know," I replied. "And you take care of yourself, Mr. Pulaski."

It took some time but he managed to open the car door. Pulaski got out and I noticed Nathan standing in the doorway. I turned on the car and watched Pulaski take a few steps up the sidewalk . Abruptly, as if something happened, Pulaski turned and looked at me. He raised his arm as if to stop, but he collapsed on the ground.

I jumped out of the car and ran up the walkway. Nathan reached him before I did. As I stooped down beside them, as his face twisted, Pulaski looked as if he was trying to say something.

"He's having a stroke," I said. "We've got to call 911."

"I think you have done enough," Nathan grappled with his cell phone. "My father never should have gone out alone. It is because of you people that he is doing all this crazy stuff." His eyes blazed with deep concern and anger as he dialed.

At a lost for words I continued to stoop beside them, transfixed by the situation.

"I need an ambulance," he spoke hurriedly. "My father has had a stroke. Yes. Yes." He gave an address and said., "Thank you," before he closed his cell phone.

I hesitated, but I had to ask, "Is there anything I can do?"

"Yes," Nathan replied. "You can leave my father alone. That's what you can do."

I stood up. "I'm sorry." Nathan's vehemence was

palpable. "He asked me to—"

"You can leave now."

"I—"

"Leave." His eyes glared.

I did as Nathan asked. I got in my car and drove away. Tears fell as I passed an ambulance. I knew it was for Pulaski.

CHAPTER 38

Pulaski's stroke forced me to think about how fragile we are, all of us, or should I say how fragile we can be in old age. It's just a matter of areas and degrees. Will it be our body or our mind? I also thought of Aunt Tee, so I returned to Methodist Hospital. When I walked into her room things were still the same. But I was near a breaking point in the midst of the quiet hum of hospital machines and Aunt Tee's deathly silence.

I pulled my chair close to her bed as I had done from the first time I visited her in ICU, and I took Aunt Tee's hand in mine. It was cool, and the veins seemed nearer to the surface than I had ever noticed.

"Aunt Tee. Aunt Tee" I stared at her unnaturally blank face. "I've got some things to tell you." I looked around the room. "This first one is really difficult to say but, I know you would want to know. I just left Pulaski, your Gary Historical Society buddy... well, he had a stroke." I held her hand because I needed it. "I can't say I know how he's doing right now because Nathan was very angry at me. He blamed us for his father's problems and, I know when you love someone you don't want anyone to hurt them." I looked at her bandaged head. "So all I can say is that I pray that he will be okay." I paused. "Pulaski and I had a very interesting conversation on the way to his house. I knew you were always the kind of woman who could make an impression, well, you definitely made one on him. I don't think you know how big of an impression you made."

"But if you knew or not, one thing I believe you did was wake Pulaski out of a kind of racist slumber, because basically he told me he was a very prejudiced man before he met you, and you helped him see people of color in a different light." I studied her features. "A black Goddess is what he saw when he saw you, Aunt Tee. Yeeees. I think you took Pulaski all the way there."

I cried as I continued to hold her hand.

"You've had the same effect on me all my life." I wiped at the tears. "When I was a child the sun rose and set if my Aunt Tee said so. And now I realize that's because you saw me, Aunt Tee. I felt, you really saw me, and you allowed me to be a little child without the judgments. I think my mother was aware of that." I stroked Aunt Tee's hand. "And Mama didn't know how to do that, Aunt Tee. Perhaps if she had known, she would have. I've got to give her the benefit of the doubt. And now I even think she was a little jealous of our relationship, which made things worse between the two of you." I paused. "But things are going to be better. Mama and I had a doozy of a conversation about Grandma Anna Lee, how she had served time in prison and all. I wonder if you knew that. I wonder if you knew and never told me." I looked at the empty off-white walls. "Chances are you didn't. You wouldn't have gotten it out of Grandma Anna Lee and I know how secretive Mama can be. And I'm sure she told Daddy he'd better not tell you." I sighed. "But Mama and I have agreed all the secrecy is out the window. We're going to be up front with each other, and we're signing a new

Gwyn McGee

lease when it comes to the relationships between the women in this family. And that includes your relationship with Mama."

I smoothed her hospital gown and made it lay neatly around her neck. Beneath it her chest rose and fell evenly.

"We've got to stick together now that we've got something to fight for." I fought back new tears. "But how will we do it? And it is *we* because concussion or not you are not going to leave us in this alone," I ordered. "We need you, Aunt Tee. I know exactly what Pulaski was talking about when he said you are so full of life. How you believe if there's a problem there's got to be a solution. We need your enthusiasm. We need it so badly, right now. I know I do." I sniffed. "Because I finally realize there is something I'm supposed to do. And I think it's connected with the plan you intended. Somehow I'm supposed to help you get the word out about what's happening in Gary. And it's obvious you can't do anything right now, no matter how much I wish you could. But I've got to accept that, and time is of the essence." I placed her hand back on the bed. "I can't go on ignoring all these signs around me. And now I ask myself, why would I want to? Why would I want to, Aunt Tee? Am I afraid that they're going to hurt me? They've already done this to you, and I won't take that lying down. I won't." I pushed my fear aside. "I, we, have a responsibility to this city. Every citizen who has ever been born here does. And Gary has a responsibility to the rest of the country, because, according to Pulaski, Gary was the first major city purely planned for industrial reasons. We were the first, so we have the responsibility of making the rest of the country aware of

274

the slippery slope: big business gave us homes and big business can take them away.

I rested my elbows on my knees. "And now about some other things, Aunt Tee, I know you don't understand. Even if you were conscious and I started talking about the spiritual connotations of this stuff, I know you would listen quietly and probably say 'Rossi, I don't quite understand what you're telling me, but if you believe it with all your heart, then I believe it for you.' And that's all I need from you in that department, is your support. Because I know with every breath, we all signed up for this job before we got here. I mean, we signed up for it on the other side before we incarnated in these bodies. We made plans to do this very job as family. I guess we must have looked at it like killing two birds with one stone, that's what Daddy would have called it." I laughed a little. "I can see us promising to do our own personal healing, so we could open the way to help Gary heal. Grand ideas, Aunt Tee. Such grand ideas." I closed my eyes and nodded my head, slowly. "Well, we are well down the road of personal healing, and now we've got to do something for Gary, and that's what we're going to do."

I reached out and lightly stroked the area where the IV was inserted in her hand.

"I think the best way to go about this, Aunt Tee, is to set it up just like a multilevel marketing program. You can't get more grassroots than that. One person commits to telling say, five movers and shakers or five organizations, and they commit to do the same thing. Yes," my thoughts started churning. "We'll start with that plan." I thought for a moment. "Now, I'm going to have to go through your files and get a list of your contacts. Of course, you probably had the majority of them with you when you planned to meet Thomas at the library." I looked at the closet. "I wonder what they did with your things."

I got up and looked inside. None of Aunt Tee's belongings were there. It was basically a storage area for hospital supplies.

"What are you looking for, Rossi?" Aunt Tee's weak, raspy voice startled me.

I turned around, and unbelievable as it was she looked as if she had just awakened from a long, restful sleep.

"Aunt Tee! You're awake!" I went over to her bed.

"What am I...." She attempted to raise the arm with the caste, but when that didn't work she raised the hand with the IV to her throat. "My voice sounds horrible. What am I doing in the hospital?"

I touched her hand. At first I didn't know what to tell her. "Obviously, getting better." I said. "But I think I need to let the nurse know that you are awake." I didn't want her to see my eyes fill with tears.

"Wait." Her grasp was weak. "Did I have some kind of surgery?"

"No, Aunt Tee," I assured at her. "You didn't have any surgery. Just save your strength to talk to the nurse." I kissed her cheek. "I'll be right back."

I stayed around as long as they permitted, but once I informed the nurse at the nurse's station that Aunt Tee was conscious, it seemed nurses, doctors and specialists from a medley of departments descended on her room. Finally, I had no choice but to get out of the way. So I told Aunt Tee that Mama and I would come see her later that evening, but when we arrived she was being rolled out on a gurney for more tests. Still Aunt Tee was glad to see us, and Mama even patted her on the shoulder and told her it wouldn't be long before she would be able to come home.

I hadn't talked to Stephanie since Aunt Tee's attack and based on the positive turn of events, I felt I owed her a telephone call.

"Hello."

"Hello, Girlfriend." I said; glad to hear her voice.

"Hello," she replied. "You sound tired."

"I am tired." Her acknowledgment gave me permission to go deeper into my fatigue. "Aunt Tee is in the hospital."

"Oh no. What happened?"

"She was attacked in a library parking lot in few nights ago. She was unconscious but she came out of it this afternoon."

"My goodness, you must feel an overwhelming relief," Stephanie said.

"Relief doesn't come close to how I feel. You know Aunt Tee is like a second mother to me."

"I know," she said. What did they want? Did they take her purse?"

"That's just it, Stephanie. They didn't take anything." I sighed. "We think it's tied to an article that appeared in the paper where Aunt Tee said she was going to launch a nationwide information campaign about what's happening in industrial cities like Gary, when it comes to pollution and all that it means."

"In order for someone to attack her, somebody must think your aunt has a lot of influence," Stephanie replied.

"Aunt Tee doesn't, but she knows some really

powerful, influential people. It wasn't something she set out to do, it just happened through the years. She met a lot of them when Hatcher was mayor. Aunt Tee was involved with all kinds of civic groups, and all kinds of people were coming to Gary; black people who ended up in places of power in this country. People like Vernon Jordan. Colin Powell. Of course, they didn't have the power back then that they have now. Yes, Aunt Tee knows some powerful people. But there may be some other forces at work, Stephanie. I don't know why they might want to hurt us."

"Hurt us? What you mean, us?" Stephanie asked.

I hesitated. "Those of us who are shedding light on what could be underlying reasons for Gary's problems."

The line went quiet.

"Shedding light in dark places always brings on attack of some kind, Rossi. So you be careful because danger was—"

"I know," I cut her off.

The line went silent again.

"So you say your aunt is conscious now?" Stephanie said.

"Yes." I was grateful for the change in an our conversation. "And Stephanie?"

"Yeah."

"I know why I'm in Gary at this time. It's very clear to me now."

"Really?"

"Yes. I'm going to help my aunt with this campaign; this information campaign about what pollutants can do. I already know how it should be structured."

"Wow. I knew you'd figure it out."

"Well, I think I've figured out part of it. And what you told me you saw in my astrology chart is true. My getting clear about helping my aunt comes at a time when there has been major healing between my mother and me."

"Wow," Stephanie repeated. "You're blowing my mind. That is no coincidence."

"And I am consciously intending as I say this to you, that I am acknowledging the connection between healing my family wounds and Gary's healing. It's important that I say this out loud." I turned my declaration into a powerful prayer. "I understand the connection is real. I will no longer pooh-pooh it or deny it." And I hoped God would be there for me because of it.

"It's part of your soul's purpose."

"Yes, it is," I said softly.

"I've got to tell you," Stephanie said, "I got goose bumps when you said it is going to be a nationwide campaign, because after we got off the telephone the other night, I compared Gary's astrology chart to the astrology chart of the United States and I am convinced Gary is simply a microcosm of the macrocosm. That whatever you all do there in Gary will affect the entire country."

"Oh my goodness."

"That's what I saw," Stephanie replied.

"Well, I just wanted to let you know what's going on up here. And to thank you for your skills, and your friendship, even when I'm a little hard to take."

"What can I say? You're my girl, Rossi. You know that."

I smiled. "When I get back to Salt Lake City I'll

tell you the whole story, because there is more, but right now I'm going to go to bed. I'm tired, and we've got a lot of work ahead of us."

CHAPTER 39

The following day Aunt Tee was released from the hospital under medical instructions that included a doctor's visit the next week, but that didn't concern her much. When Aunt Tee found out how she ended up in the hospital; she exhibited the indomitable spirit that we all recognized. True to form Aunt Tee said if they really wanted her to stop they should have killed her, because now she was more inspired than ever to get the word out. But there was one obvious obstacle, Aunt Tee is right-handed, and it was her right arm that was broken, so many of the duties she would have performed herself went to me. But I didn't mind, not making light of Aunt Tee's injury; I felt it was just another way the universe was making room for me to do what I was born to do.

Aunt Tee's house became our unofficial headquarters. I was distinctly aware that since my accident in Merrillville the phone calls had completely stopped. There were no more silent callers. I hoped that meant whoever was behind the calls was no longer interested in what we were doing. I prayed that was true, and with Gary's history all around us we went to work. I was glad when everyone, including Mama, liked my multilevel marketing format. I think Aunt Tee would have praised anything she felt would get the job done because she was determined to launch our plan before Bonner started at Gary Brownfields Initiative.

Pulaski surfaced in our conversation every once in awhile. Aunt Tee called Nathan a couple of times to find out how Pulaski was doing. She left messages, but he never returned her calls.

Thomas and I never told my mother or Aunt Tee, what Pulaski said about the Gary Roundtable. It wasn't a formal decision. After what happened to Aunt Tee, and my mother's ongoing paranoia about the murders in Gary, I guess we separately concluded we didn't want to burden them any further.

The project kept us busy and the day before the launch I was dog tired. Everybody was. We did everything we knew that was humanly possible to insure a successful meeting, and it had been hard work. Hard, satisfying work. The last thing to do on my list was to make some copies at Kinkos in Merrillville. That was it. The next time the four of us would come together would be outside of U.S. Steel.

Before my trip to Kinkos Mama and I decided to take a nap. She had gone to her room and I was in mine. I was on the verge of lying down when my mother tapped on my door.

"Are you decent?" She stuck her head inside my room.

"Yeah. Come on in, Mama," I said, but she was inside before I completed the invitation. "I need a nap," I said. "I need something to shut off my brain." I held my head. "It would be so good if I could."

"Isn't that the truth?" My mother replied. "And I know if I feel that way I can only imagine what you're going through. But I want to give you something before I forget." She approached me and opened her hand. "Here. I want you to have this." Inside was the Tree of Life necklace that had been passed down in my family.

"Mama." Nothing came out but her name.

"I decided I wanted to give this to you now; while I'm alive. I didn't want you to receive it after I dead."

"I don't know what to say." Tears filled my eyes. "I feel so honored to have it." My mother pulled me into her arms. "I know you do. I know you do. And I feel honored giving it to you because I'm proud of you, Rossi."

My heart swelled. "Thank you."

"And I believe I speak for everyone in the family; the members that are still with us, and those who have passed on. We're all very proud of you."

I don't know if I've ever felt the way I felt that afternoon. I know I haven't felt that way since.

Mama started toward the door but then she turned back and looked at me.

"I was straightening up in the sunroom, and I saw some doodling at the top of some of your papers. I saw where you'd written May Scrap and Low Gal; the names of the sisters who were killed." Her forehead creased before she looked down as if she were gathering her thoughts. "Of course that's not their names." She shifted her weight. "I must have called them by their nicknames when I told you about them. Anyway," she continued, "I thought, Rossi is really worried about the murders and everything that is going on around here." She looked up with deep concern in her eyes.

My mother looked as if she expected me to respond but I was stunned into silence.

"You're probably worried about me too and

what's going to happen to me once you leave," my mother continued. "But I don't want you to worry, Rossi. I'm planning on having an alarm system installed next week." She nodded with finality. "Teresa says she has one and it gives her a sense of security nothing else could. So you rest easy. You've got enough on your mind. Okay?"

"Yes, Mama," I said and she walked out of the door. I stood there for a moment thinking about what she'd said, and I knew my mother didn't realize she had never told me the sister's names.

Well I headed straight to the sunroom and I saw a stack of papers on a side table. Sure enough, on the very top of some of my notes Maescrap, Logal and Redman had been included in my doodling. My mother had recognized the first two names as the women that used to be her next-door neighbors. Two women who were murder victims!

That's when it came to me. Maybe the names listed under The Gary Roundtable were not the names of its members, but names of its victims. "Pulaski described a ceremony that ended with the men burying body parts." I whispered to myself. Then another thought surfaced. Was it possible even more people had been killed to fulfill some kind of ceremonial rites? I sank down on the couch at the implications.

This realization shook me. The ceremony was horrible enough but to realize this was not something from the distant past, but a murder that The Gary Roundtable had committed much more recently was extremely frightening.

I jumped when the telephone rang. Out of sheer reflex and knowing there was no phone in my mother's bedroom, I answered it.

"Hello."

"Hello, may I speak to Rossi?" A male voice said.

"This is she," I replied, wondering who the man was.

"This is Nathan Pulaski." He sounded as if he was whispering. "I need to see you, but it must be in private. It's about The Gary Roundtable. You and your family could be in danger."

My body shook as if I had chills. "What you mean?"

"There are some things my father told me but we can't talk about them on the telephone. You've got to come alone, Rossi. No one else must know."

"When do you want to meet?" I asked.

"Can you meet me in an hour?"

"Who is it, Rossi?" My mother called from the bedroom.

I covered the telephone receiver with my hand. "They had the wrong number." I lied then said into the telephone, "Yes, I can. Do you want me to come to your house?"

"No. My father's here." He paused. "I don't want to upset him. There's an old house near Marquette Park's Pavilion. It's west of the building in the wooded area. If you park in the west parking lot near the pavilion, you'll see a sign about the dunes. Next to it is a path. Follow that into the woods and you'll come to a fork. One way says Do Not Enter Private Property. That's where you want to go. It will take you to the house."

"I don't know about this," I said.

"This is a matter of life and death. You must

come."

I could hear him breathing as he waited. "I'll be there," I said.

He hung up.

We'd worked so hard preparing for the press conference, and after everything else I was already physically and somewhat mentally strained, so to receive this phone call, once again, I felt I was on the verge of breaking. But yet and still, feeling like I did, I was not willing to tell my mother. But this was a conscious silence. For if this might be too much for me, how could my mother or my aunt bear it? Maybe some habits, weighing my pain against another's, are anchored in a high cause.

But I did think of Thomas. "I've got to tell Thomas about this. I've got to call him."

I hurried back to my room. Ever since our conversation about his wife and child I had kept my distance. Don't get me wrong, we worked side-by-side preparing for the press conference, and we worked well together. The distance I kept dealt with my emotions. And I must say with Thomas being Thomas, he did not test it.

But this was different. I didn't know what Nathan had to tell me but people had been murdered, and I didn't want to handle this alone.

I sat and waited for Thomas to answer, and my anxiety increased when his system went to voicemail.

"Thomas, this is Rossi. I've discovered something so call me back as soon as you hear this message. It's important, Thomas." I tried to keep the quiver out of my voice. "Nathan Pulaski called me. He's got something he wants to talk to me about but he wants to do it in secret. Can you believe that?" I knew he could probably hear me breathing. "So I'm meeting him in about an hour over at this house that's on private property that's west of Marquette Park Pavilion. This is really serious, Thomas, so don't call my mother's house or Aunt Tee's house. Call my cell phone. I don't want them to know about this."

I gathered my purse and my keys and tapped on my mother's door. When I opened it I could tell she had already fallen asleep.

"I'm sorry," I said from the doorway. "I'm going to make those copies and I wanted to let you know, I'm leaving."

"All right," my mother said sleepily. "Make sure you lock the door," she said. "And I forgot to bring in the mail. Would you bring that in, please, and put it on the kitchen counter?"

"I sure will." I started to close the door.

"Rossi."

I opened it again. "Yes?"

"This is a really good thing that we're doing for Gary. The city has never seen anything like this before and I'm proud to be a part of it." She closed her eyes. "I only wish your father could be here to see. There is so much we didn't get to share. So much I didn't say," she added softly.

Maybe for the first time I caught a glimpse of the special kind of loneliness my mother must have felt being without her lifelong partner. I walked over to the bed and kissed her cheek.

She looked surprised then moisture softened her gaze.

"I'm sure he knows, Mama."

My mother looked into my eyes; as if to make

sure I really believed what I said. When she saw that I did all she could say was, "Be careful out there driving. It's Friday, and every nut in Gary is on the road."

"I will," I said before I left the room.

CHAPTER 40

It didn't take long to get to Marquette Park Pavilion. Although it had been a long time since I'd gone there, the building was easy to find because my father would take my mother and me there quite often when I was younger. For certain it looked different, but the details like the people sitting on benches and those walking on the beach were hazy realities on the peripheral in my mind.

As I parked I thought of the last time I saw Pulaski. He was lying on the sidewalk, his face contorting in a way that was discomforting to remember. Nathan had ordered me to leave. Aunt Tee had been greatly concerned about her friend. I could only imagine the effort his eighty year old body had gone through in its attempt to heal, and the conversations he might have had with his son. I wondered if those talks had anything to do with what Pulaski intended to tell me before he collapsed that day. You see, I'm convinced Pulaski had turned toward my car because he wanted to tell me something. Maybe that something was what Nathan felt he had to share with me, in secret. Either way I was certain, whatever Nathan wanted to tell me was important enough, perhaps even dangerous enough, that he would go through all of this for us to be alone. But now, I no longer doubted The Gary Roundtable was dangerous, and it still existed. They had murdered at least four people for their own ritualistic purposes, I didn't want any of my family to be added to that list.

I opened my car door and my cell phone rang. I fumbled inside my purse, hoping it was Thomas. The telephone number in the display window showed I was right.

"Thomas!" I quickly said, but the connection cut out. I couldn't hear his response.
"Thomas! Can you hear me?"

"I—" The bad connection swallowed his words until I heard, "Where are you now?"

"I'm parked outside Marquette Park Pavilion. Did you hear my message?"

I knew he was talking but I couldn't understand him. "This connection is horrible. I can't understand you," I said, frustrated.

"Nathan called—" Thomas's words came through.

"Yes. Yes, Nathan called. He's got something important to tell me and he set it up for us to meet here."

I tried to understand Thomas's response but it was impossible. "Thomas. Can you hear me? I can't understand a word you're saying!"

"… on my way."

"You're coming here?" I said, excited.

"Yes. I'm going to—"

The feeble connection snapped. "Thomas? Thomas?" I said, but it was completely gone.

I looked at my cell phone. There were no signal bars. I was out of my network range, but I knew Thomas was on his way and that helped a lot. Nathan would just have to deal with it.

To say my thoughts were scattered as I climbed out of my car and began to walk would be a gross understatement. I was also nervous; scared would be a better term. Although there had been no more phone calls since the accident in Merrillville I still wondered if I was being watched as the policeman had said. That's a difficult thing to get over, knowing you're being watched by strangers. It's virtually impossible. It had also been a very difficult to keep to myself.

At the beginning of the path I stopped to see if anyone was watching. When I was satisfied that wasn't, I entered the woods. It was absolutely frightening walking in those woods alone, especially with a small voice inside asking if I was doing the right thing. But I felt I was. "This could be a matter of life and death," I said, as I continued.

A minute degree of trepidation subsided when I arrived at the fork in the road and saw the Do Not Enter/ Private Property sign Nathan had mentioned; I continued onto that property as he instructed. Perhaps I had walked three or four minutes before the house, nestled deeply within the trees, came into view. The structure was two stories and larger than I anticipated. For some reason I had pictured a small, dilapidated building in need of repair, but it was obvious even as I approached this building was well kept, and so was the solid privacy fence that enclosed a large area behind it.

There were no cars that I could see on the property, and I assumed that Nathan, like me, had parked at the pavilion or perhaps behind the fence. As I knocked on the front door I couldn't help but speculate on the value of the property. It wasn't cheap. It had to be worth a handsome sum situated as it was close to the dunes, just outside the national preserve. These were the kinds of things that ran through my mind as I knocked again and someone inside said, "Is that you, Rossi?"

"Yes," I replied.

"Hurry up and come in." I heard footsteps cross a wooden floor. "I'll be right there. I need to close the back door."

Uncertain, I opened it. "Nathan?" I said, as I took several steps into a softly lit room. Electric candles were mounted like sconces above a number of chairs which sat against the walls. In a corner, I also noticed a small table covered with a purple cloth. It had several objects on it.

Once I was inside the house, it was at that moment, that a clear voice inside my head said, "This is not what you think it is". I did not hear this is not what I think it is; I heard the word you and I knew I was in trouble, but an outside key turned in the front door lock, and I was locked in.

Frightened out of my wits ... oh my God. The feeling of being trapped... trapped like an animal is inexpressible. Sheer instinct made me try to open the door although I knew it was locked, and is I had had claws, I believe I would have tried to claw my way out. But instead, like antenna, the hairs on my arms stood up when I heard, but I also felt, several people enter the room. What I saw when I turned around. What I saw....

As ill timed as this may seem to you I must ask, why do men with cowardly hearts hide beneath masks and hoods? Because that's what I saw. Four men wearing black hoods over their faces in black suits and gloves.

I knew I was standing face to face with the Gary Roundtable. I knew they intended to do me harm, and something inside of me, ignited perhaps, by their cowardly effort to hide their identities, fueled by their subterfuge, angered me.

"Laes Rossi," one of them said.

I realized the policeman at the scene of the accident had called me the same thing. "That's not my name," I said. "Where is Nathan Pulaski?"

The men ignored my question, and in ceremonial fashion each one of them went to the table and chose an object. One of the objects was a syringe. "Laes Rossi, you have come to seal this–"

"Are you crazy? I haven't come to do anything. You tricked me into coming here." I surveyed the peculiarly shaped room to see if there was any way I could get out, but there was only one other door that lead out of that room, and it was behind the men. "And you must be crazy if you think you can get away with this in this day and time."

I looked at the bizarre scene in front of me and my logical mind could not reconcile what it knew was happening. Then from a place deep within my gut a question materialized. *Is this the way I'm going to die*? Equally amazing things flashed through my mind as if a core part of me was drilling for strength. Twenty years Grandma Anna Lee endured a federal penitentiary in southern Alabama. My father and all the men who lived through working in blast furnaces. My confrontations with the men who wanted to rape me. Grandpa Eli's belief in the power of his bloodline and the Spirits.

From that same place in my gut, from my solar

plexus, an energy gushed up, and pure rage joined with the injustice of what these men stood for, and I heard that click in my head. That click. And suddenly, I felt, as illogical as it is, that I could kill them.

"All of you are going to have to hold me down to inject me with whatever's in that needle." I didn't recognize my own voice. It was raspy and raw. "And somebody besides me will be hurt. I promised that."

The voice that came out of me stunned one of the men. He stopped and looked at me, causing the man behind him to stop abruptly as well.

"The Gary Roundtable." There was venom in my tone. "Is nothing but a group of cowards... parasites who have been feeding off the poor. That's what you are."

"Go on," the man who'd been forced to stop directed the other. The two other men began to chant something. What? I had no clue, but the words continued to spill out of me.

"You are lower than any of the people you've ever taken advantage of," I taunted. "If Malthusian eugenics is the code you live by, know that you are the slaves in this equation. You are a slave to your greed and your lust for power. So no matter what you tell yourselves, know the truth about who you are."

One of the men who had begun to chant stopped walking and turned toward me. "You seem to know quite a bit. That makes you a very worthy component for ending what was initiated a hundred years ago." His speech was cultured and crisp.

I focused on him. "I know enough to know you are worthless human beings, and that only insane men would think they have the power over generations and generations of people. No one has that kind of power. All of that is in God's hands and it's certainly not in yours, or your ancestors."

"You speak as if we are the only ones who are part of this Roundtable. They're members like us, all across this nation and in other countries," he said, and I heard pride in his tone. "You, Laes Rossi, are nothing in the large scheme of things, only a tiny means to an end."

"Let's get on with this," the shortest man said. "You are allowing her to aggravate you. She is only mimicking what she has heard from others."

"Others like who?" I said. "Like Charles Pulaski? Or Nathan? Maybe one of you is Nathan Pulaski hiding behind those ugly ass hoods. You are pathetic." My fear fought its way to the surface again.

"Nathan Pulaski is a stupid man; openly asking high degree Masons if they knew about us. Lucky for him, we were able to find out what he was up to before he did any harm. He does not have the bloodline to be apart of the Gary Roundtable," the same man said. "But he was the one who informed us that you had found out about us. Nathan has always wanted to be a part of the inner circle and he thought telling us that you knew about the Gary Roundtable would win him some clout. There is not enough clout in the world that would allow a Pulaski to become a part of us, Laes Rossi."

To hear Nathan was partly responsible for my being there struck hard. I felt short of breath. "That's not my name."

"But it is, " another man, cut me off. "You can say whatever you like but you will seal this ceremony." He began to chant again.

"Your mumbo-jumbo doesn't impress me." My

fight instinct quelled. "How can you be proud of a group who kills defenseless old ladies like Mae Scrap and Lo Gal? And don't think if you kill me nobody else will know what I know," I bluffed. "I've made sure that won't happen."

They continued in formation, chanting.

As I stood there my emotions were all over the board. I'd gone from feeling as if I could kill to talking for my life. "I knew you would be here." I continued to bluff. "I just wanted to see how far you would take this insanity. Do you think I didn't suspect that this was a set-up?"

Those words triggered something in the man who had spoken the most because his tone changed.

"They served their purpose in our cause. Just as all of them did. Just as you will."

"Don't talk to her," the member with the syringe said. "Just do what we came here to do." His free hand rubbed his neck beneath the hood. "I didn't want to be a part of this anyway. Let's get it over with."

"Just stay calm," the most outspoken man said as they positioned themselves at four points of a square around me. "It is time," he announced.

"Redman is as to open," they began in a lagging unison. "Featherstone is as to enter." This continued as each man took turns at the points of the four directions. "Maescrap is as to gather. It is formed through Logal, and Rossi will seal it all."

The man with the syringe stumbled over the words and the one I surmise was the spokesman continued alone. "After this day the energy of what has been set down in this city of Gary, Indiana one hundred years ago through the blood of its original inhabitants will flow forever. It is spiritual law. Nepo... Open. Retne...Enter. Rehtag...Gather. Demrof... Formed. Laes...Seal."

It was a bad movie playing out in front of me. I couldn't believe it and I couldn't keep quiet. "Chant the names of your murder victims all you want. You won't get away with it this time. You told me to come alone but I didn't do that. I'm not stupid."

The member with the syringe stopped again. "How does she know what we're saying? How does she know?"

"That's not all I know." I worked on their weakest link. "I know your names too. And if you don't stop what you are doing... if you don't back off from me and my family, I will expose you and anyone else that has been associated with The Gary Roundtable."

"I don't like this. What if she's telling the truth?" He looked around the room. "What if there is somebody waiting to come in here? Maybe they're waiting for when we are about to inject her. They could prosecute us."

"Don't listen to her," the spokesman said. "You," he pointed to the man beside him. "Help me hold her," he said, as they started toward me. "We've said the main words. Let's inject her. We can do the remainder of the rites once we have the body."

But the man with the syringe started backing up. "I don't know about this. I don't know. I think we've been setup."

"You have," I lied for my life as I backed away. "You're going to be caught in the act." I prayed with everything I had that Thomas would show up at any moment. "Everybody's going to know about you. They are waiting outside right now, aware of everything you're doing in here."

"See there," the unnerved member said.

"If there was anybody outside our lookout would have warned us by now," the leader barked.

"They're just waiting for the right moment," I said.

The spokesman grabbed my arm. "You shut up!"

"Let go of me!" I shouted and tried to break free.

I don't exactly remember but I began to struggle with that man, and my strength must have been unnaturally strong because he could not keep a hold on me. But I do recall feeling obsessed about knowing who was beneath that hood. I wanted to see the face of my enemy; so I grabbed it with both hands and tried to snatch it off, but he held on.

A shout from outside broke the drama inside the house.

"There's someone coming!" Someone yelled.

"I told you!" The man with syringe said. "I've had enough of this," he declared as he ran toward the back door.

I saw another man take off behind him.

The third man, the one who had been ordered to hold me said as he left the room, "You can do what you want to do but I will not be implicated in this archaic mess. It's over."

The spokesman hesitated for a split-second, and to this day I remember, the glint of his eyes, shining through the holes and a hood.

"This is one tiny battle in an ongoing war. You remember that," he said before he left, and my knees went weak.

"Rossi!" Thomas yelled from outside.

I was able to make it to the front door as he unlocked it , somehow.

"Thomas!" I wrapped my arms around him, overwhelmed by the moment. Glad to see him. Glad to be alive.

"Are you okay?" He held onto me.

"I'm okay. More scared than I've ever been in my life but okay," I said. That's when I noticed he was alone. They're also three younger men. A moment before there had been no one but Thomas. The mind is a funny thing, especially when it's been strained to its limit.

"Is there anybody in there?" The man with a red hooded sweatshirt and pants hanging low on his hips asked.

I let go of Thomas and shook my head as I looked at him, then the other two. "No."
"When we were coming up I saw somebody run around the back," another one said. "You want Taz and me to go back there, Attorney Bates? We'll go get them."

"No." Thomas looked at him. "We're not here to start a fight. I didn't know what we were going to find when we got here so I just wanted you to have my back in case I needed you."

"You sure you're not hurt? Your clothes are torn," the last young man said.

I looked down. My sleeve was torn, and when I raised my hands to my head my hair was a mess. More out of habit than anything else, I tried to fix it. "I don't think I am," I replied, before I looked at Thomas. "How did you know I was in trouble?"

"Right before I called you, I had dropped by Ms.

Tee's. Nathan Pulaski called and started telling her how Mr. Charles was doing. I knew right then whoever called you could not have been him. So I left her talking on the telephone and contacted Ali." He pointed toward one of the men. "He pulled together some of his friends and... here we are."

Out of the blue, what I had just experienced came down on me, and I completely felt exhausted. "I need to sit down," I said before I sat down right there.

Thomas' forehead creased. "We can't stay here, Rossi."

I knew he was right. I knew it made no sense for me to sit there, on the porch of that house, but right then nothing made much sense to me.

"Come on. I'll help you," Thomas said as he placed his arm around my waist.

I soaked up the compassion in his touch.

We started down the path with the three men behind us.

"What happened in there?" Thomas said.

"The Gary Roundtable. The Gary Roundtable," I repeated, and I sounded out of breath although I wasn't. "I told them to leave my family alone or I would expose them. I told them..." I could barely talk. I guess it was my nerves and I knew I was beginning to be difficult to understand, but I wanted Thomas to know. "I lied and told them I knew their names. I knew all about them." I swallowed hard.

"We could hear you yelling as we came up."

I turned around, and the one Thomas had said was Ali continued to talk. "I think you must've been getting the best of them because somebody in there hollered, "This woman is crazy. She has flipped out."

"They sure did," Taz said. "And then that man ran to the back."

I looked at Thomas. "I don't remember. I don't—"

"Don't talk right now, Rossi," Thomas said. "Don't talk."

I was glad he said that, because my voice was gone. I couldn't say another thing, if someone had paid me.

CHAPTER 41

I was in some kind of shock. Thomas offered to drive me to my mother's house but I didn't want to go there. Not in the state I was in. I didn't want to leave the rental car either. So I trailed Thomas to his house where I called my mother. I told her, on the spur of the moment, Thomas and I decided to have dinner because I was scheduled to leave Gary in two days; one day after the press conference. I'd been gone from Salt Lake for so long I had to get back. But never in my wildest dreams did I imagine what had just happened would ever have occurred two days before.

I was spent; so wasted that when Thomas offered me his bed, I climbed into it. I lay there on the second floor of his home, looking out his bedroom window and closing my eyes; listening to the unfamiliar sounds of his house. Marguerite was not home which made it much easier, but I thought I heard sounds coming from Thomas's kitchen through the open windows. I knew my observations were correct when Thomas showed up with a tray, some soup, crackers and apple juice.

"I know this isn't much but I thought you might want something to eat," Thomas said. "It's chicken noodle soup." He knelt in front of the bed.

I couldn't help but smile a bit. This was another sight I could never have envisioned when I first met

Thomas Bates. "Thanks," I replied. "But I'm not hungry."

"Maybe later," he said, his eyes soft with concern.

I closed my eyes. "Maybe." When I opened them again Thomas was sitting in a brown leather Lazy Boy chair with concern and consternation etched in his lean face.

"Don't look so somber, Thomas. At least I have my voice back." I made light of the situation.

With his fingers interlocked, he leaned forward and rested his elbows on his knees. "What they planned to do to you is unacceptable," he spoke through clenched teeth. I mean— out of the blue they—"

"It wasn't out of the blue," I closed my eyes again. "About a week and a half ago, they faked an accident with a policeman and everything. They threatened me... us actually. My mother, Aunt Tee and me."

Thomas just looked at me. "But you never said anything about it."

"I was going to tell you the day you returned after Aunt Tee had been assaulted, but you told me about your daughter," my voice softened. "And your wife.... After that I felt like I needed to handle it alone."

"You didn't tell me because I have a family," Thomas said. "But what does that have to do with anything."

I looked at him and glanced away. "I'm not going to make excuses for myself," I said. "At the time it felt like the right thing to do." I spoke to him directly. "You have to understand, I didn't want to share my vulnerability, to place my confidence, in a man that I didn't feel could really be there. No matter the relationship. I don't choose that for myself anymore. "Hey." I shrugged. "What can I say? I've got baggage. I'm working on it, but I do."

Thomas released in loud sigh. "Don't we all?"

The room went silent.

"There had also been phone calls," I said. After facing what I had faced at that house there was nothing I was unwilling to talk about. "Whenever I first arrived somewhere; my mother's house, Aunt Tee's or come over here, the telephone would ring, but no one would say anything."

Thomas rested on the arm of the chair. "I remember that happening," he said.

"It happened a lot, because they were watching us. Then after the accident," I quotation marks with my fingers, "the phone calls stopped and I convinced myself they were satisfied with threatening us." I rubbed my eyes. "So when I got a phone call from 'Nathan', I didn't suspect a thing. I really didn't." I hung my head. "My God, they could have killed me," I said softly.

"What actually happened in there, Rossi?" Thomas asked.

"What happened?" I sighed. "The Gary Roundtable had chosen me as their last ritual victim. That's what happened."

"What?" Thomas looked stunned.

"Yes." I looked down at his comforter. "Yes. That's what they had decided. Four men with black hoods." I took a deep breath. "Chanting things I didn't understand, along with the names of their previous victims, and my name, Laes Rossi." My voice trembled. "They had a syringe, Thomas. I guess they were going to inject me with something and then do whatever they had planned with my body." I looked into his eyes. "It's all so unreal." I paused. "Some of it I really don't remember, although I was there, living it." That seemed impossible to me. "Even now as I talk about it, it seems unreal." I looked out the window, then back at Thomas. "Those names that were imprinted on the photograph were imprinted along with what their deaths meant to the ritual. Retne. Enter. Laes. Seal," I said. "It was the name of the victim along with what that person's death stood for.... but it was coded spelling. It was spelled backwards."

Thomas turned into a calculating attorney. "Could you identify any of these men if you had to, Rossi? Did you see any of their faces? Do you remember anything that might help identify just one of them?"

Faint memories of trying to rip off one of their hoods drifted through my mind. But that was all. "No," I said. "Nothing."

"Don't answer so quickly because I want you to think about it. It is so important," Thomas said. "I'm not trying to badger you. I just wish we had some physical evidence."

I looked at him. "I told them we did." I was certain of that. "I told them we knew who they were right after I said I had help waiting right outside, and if they ever threatened to harm anybody else I would expose them. It was—." My memory faded again. "I don't know what else I said but then you showed up."

Thomas nodded, slowly. "That was smart. Threatening exposure is a substantial weapon in a situation like this. Possibly the only one we have to keep them from trying something like this again."

Tears stung the back of my eyes. "The truth is I don't exactly remember what happened in there." I fingered my torn sleeve. "But I remember the last man who left out of that room said 'This is one tiny battle in an ongoing war'. That was the last thing he said, Thomas." I searched his eye. "In other words, even if we won that battle it was absolutely nothing in the bigger picture."

We sat with the implications in silence.

"What we do tomorrow can make a difference in the bigger picture." Thomas looked out the window. "But it would have much bigger impact on television, or in a newspaper photo, if we had some physical proof to back up our allegations that secrets are being kept. Because I'm certain in some people's minds we might look like a bunch of black folks just making a lot of noise. And I don't want what we are trying to do reduced to that."

I understood Thomas's concerns.

"It would make a big difference," I replied. "People believe what they see." If we only had some proof. I thought.

Suddenly, Sally and Francis popped into my mind, and the Native American artifacts they had in their home. I sat up slowly. "Thomas, there is something," I said. "There is something and I'm sure they will allow us to use them."

"What is it?" Thomas asked.

"We are going to have plenty of proof for the cameras," I said excited. "Proof that U.S. Steel was built on land sacred to Native Americans, and that it was known and kept secret. And" I clapped, "if U.S. Steel was built on land like that, it wouldn't be a far stretch that many corporations across this nation were as well."

"I see where you're going," Thomas said. "Sacred Native American land is a hot potato. And you know where these artifacts are?

"I most certainly do," I said. "But we've got to go and get them this evening." I swung my legs off the bed and on to the floor. "I saw a lot of them, Thomas, and Frances told me that there are so many of them that they're all down in the basement." I could feel my-self becoming over-stimulated, but I couldn't stop. "So there's no telling how much prove we can have for the cameras."

Thomas got up from the chair and sat beside me. "This is great, Rossi. Absolutely, great. We want those artifacts on that platform tomorrow, but I think you should rest a little more." He placed his hand on top of mine. "I don't think you're up to this right now."

I looked into his eyes. His concern was front and center. I took a couple of deep breaths. "I may not be, but I don't have a choice. This is too important. And maybe you'll need to take your car and I'll need to take mine because we want to make sure that we—"

"Look." His tone was strong and final. "We've got time. You lay down for a few more minutes," he thumbed toward the soup, "eat a little chicken noodle soup, and in a reasonable amount of time I will take you wherever you want to go. But you've been through a lot, Rossi. Give yourself a little more time."

I looked down. "Okay." Tears came to my eyes again, and I gave him a small kiss. "You're a good man, Thomas Bates," I whispered.

"I am." He squeezed my hand. "And Rossi, if I ever come to the point where I bring legal closure to my," he hesitated, "situation, I'm going to make a trip out to Salt Lake City and you'll be the first to know."

I nodded. "It's a deal," I said softly. But intuitively, I didn't feel it would ever happen.

That night I dreamed, all night. I was fighting off demons with wands of light, and when I triumphed, a band of angels headed by Thomas asked me to join them.

CHAPTER 42

The next day, outside in the open, as near to the U.S Steel plant as we could legally get, the Gary Historical Society held a combination meeting/ press conference. It was obvious our hard work combined with Aunt Tee's and Thomas's local contacts had paid off. My mother stood with Aunt Tee, Thomas and I before our chosen backdrop, the enormous U.S. Steel parking lot, and the mill behind it.

"How many people do you think are here?" Aunt Tee asked as she stood in front of the microphone.

I scanned the crowd that stood under a hazy blue sky. "At least two hundred," I said.

"And we've got media," she said proudly.

"We sure do," my mother said. "I saw are a couple of vans belonging to TV stations."

"Yeah, I checked them out," Thomas said. "They are out of Chicago, and one of the reporters is a freelancer for CNN."

"Great." Aunt Tee looked down at her watch. "Is everybody ready?"

We answered affirmatively.

"Good, because it's time to start." She turned on the microphone. "I want to thank everyone for coming today. They say sometimes you can tell how a journey is going to end by how it begins. If the turnout today, and we've only been at this for two weeks, is an indication of the kind of support this movement can garner in this city, and across this country."

There was random applause.

"I'd like to introduce myself as Teresa Collins, a lifelong resident of Gary, Indiana, although I know the majority of you know me as Ms. Tee, the librarian. As a longtime librarian, civic group organizer, and a member of the Gary Historical Society, my life has been spent cataloging and gathering information. And it is information that will make the difference in this effort. Knowledge *is* power. That is key. Once you know a situation, then you can do something about it, and that is what this is about today. I want you all to be aware that Gary Brownfields Initiative, the name of the organization over the Brownfields project in this area, will be taking on a new executive director next week. We called this meeting/ press conference today because we wanted to be proactive. We didn't want to wait until we got a notice in the mail that your street," she pointed at a woman in the crowd. "Or my street had been selected for redevelopment, and that we were going to lose our houses as result of it. We want to band together now, before the bombshell drops, because there's always strength in numbers. We don't want to be like the people in New Orleans after Hurricane Katrina who tried to fight big business after they had *already* determined what was going to happen. And we don't want any other city to be in that predicament. Detroit. Richmond. Pittsburgh, Pennsylvania. We all want to be ready before the bomb drops. And together, if we link up across this country, we might create the opportunity to even stop the bomb from falling."

"Yes." A woman shouted in the crowd.

"Now, I want to introduce some and thank some others who have worked very closely with me in order to bring this meeting about. My sister-in-law, Pearl Collins. Esteemed Attorney Thomas Bates." Aunt Tee searched the crowd. "A gentleman who couldn't be here today, but who was a major motivating force for this entire thing, Charles Pulaski. And last but not least, my niece Rossi Collins." She looked at me. "Now Rossi doesn't live in Gary anymore, but she was born and raised here and without her none of this could've been done." Aunt Tee pointed at her cast. "Most of you know that I was attacked in the library parking lot, well, I guess when I fell this arm hit the asphalt first. I call it my good arm because I'm right-handed. Have you ever tried to write or do anything with your left-hand when you're right-handed?"

There was some laughter.

"Need I say more? So I am going to turn the microphone over to my niece, Rossi. And she will explain to you the program that we've come up with." Aunt Tee leaned closer to the microphone. "Actually, the entire format was Rossi's idea and I am extremely grateful to her for being my hands, my arms and my legs during this time of recovery." She touched my back with her left hand. "Rossi Collins, everybody."

I stepped up to the microphone and looked the crowd over. "Good morning. First, I want to tell you, I'm a little nervous," I said. "But when I remind myself that we are not the first citizens to attempt a course of action against corporate giants, I feel a little better. As a matter of fact," I looked down at my notes. "Back in February of 1971, based on some information that the Environmental Protection Agency supplied to the United States Justice Department, a civil lawsuit was filed in federal court in Hammond, Indiana by a group called, Independent Citizens Water Pollution Research, Inc., against U.S. Steel Corporation and the Dupont Corporation for alleged pollution of Lake Michigan and the Grand Calumet River. Now they took their fight to court, and that can be, and has been an effective tool, but today we are going to fight this fight with information. An informed public is a powerful public, and as a result of that we have come up with a program called M.A.P.P.S., Mothers Aware of the Power of Pollutants on Society."

Thomas removed a long sheet of brown butcher's paper and revealed our banner.

"Now, before anybody out there starts feeling excluded, when I say mothers I don't mean you have to have birthed a child in order to be included in this group. Or that you must be a female. Our definition of mother is anyone who cares and wants to take care of someone or some thing. Those are the mothers that we are seeking to be a part of this program."

At that moment as fate would have it, I spotted Frances and Sally walking across the grass to join us.

"The woman who shared this definition of a mother with me, Frances Weaver, is here, and I am proud to say her wisdom helped us to come up with the name for this initiative.

"Our plan is as simple as the name of this program." I looked down at the banner. "M.A.P.P.S. There will be a map of this country created from information about pollutants that has been gathered by concerned individuals, organizations and groups. It will be a grassroots effort, where each individual or group commits to telling at least five individuals or groups. Each time that commitment <u>must</u> be made." I emphasized. "And this will be the method we will use to spread the word about M.A.P.P.S. Once five citizens or groups from the same area have submitted their information and it has been posted with M.A.P.P.S., that city or town will be shown on the main map. It will be recognized as a city whose citizens are becoming aware that pollutants like lead and manganese contribute as heavily to violent crime as poverty does." I cleared my throat. "All a city or town needs is five committed individuals or organizations, because we understand that means each one of them will reach out to five more citizens or organizations." I held up five fingers and scanned them across the crowd as a gust of wind blew a candy wrapper onto the platform. "Once that is done, the main map that I mentioned earlier will be featured on the home page of a website available to all on the Internet. Now, I know a lot of you out here don't go on the Internet. You may not have a computer. Or, you may not know anything about computers. But that's okay. The information is still available to you because you can always go to your local library."

"You sure can," Aunt Tee said.

"Because in order to make a stand in this fight we've got to be able to get the information out the most effective, cost efficient way that we can, and today that means the Internet."

Feedback vibrated from the inexpensive microphone.

"We will use our website, You Tube and Google," I said. "Remember—"

The mike did it again. I looked over at Thomas who quickly knelt down to adjust the system.

"Remember, the important thing is for you to know there is a place where the information is being gathered and stored. What kind of information is being stored? Information that will empower the individual, because you will realize others in your community or city are facing similar situations that you may be facing. Ask for some help at your local library. Tell them you want M.A.P.P.S., the one that was started right here in Gary, Indiana, because people all over the country will be doing the same thing. And we the people of Gary, Indiana can be proud of that. We've got to admit our image across this country has been horrible, and we need something to remind ourselves and others that there is worth in this city." I announced passionately. "Gary was a great inspiration for this country when it incorporated one hundred years ago, this year, and it can be an inspiration for this country again."

Applause rang out.

I drew a deep breath. "At this time, I want to share something with you. Something about Gary Indiana and the surrounding area that we all need to acknowledge. You know, there's a belief in our culture that you must get to the root of things in order to know what kind of tree will grow. What kind of plant will manifest itself as a result of the seed that was planted. Look at the parents and you will see the child. It's general knowledge that in the beginning the land here, in the United States of America, belonged to Native Americans; and that was still true when corporations, huge corporations like U.S. Steel were built." A woman in front of me folded her arms. "It's a sensitive subject.

People don't want to point the finger when it comes to this. They don't want to speculate about what might have happened in the past and what kind of results it may have created here in the future; especially when some of those actions were cruel, inhumane and self-centered. Actions that were taken to benefit a few." I paused. "Now we can ask ourselves were those past actions committed with full knowledge of the harm they were doing?" I shook my head slowly. "That is for the people who laid down the roots of corporation like U.S. Steel to grapple with. It is for them to address that issue within their hearts and within the hearts of those who have come knowingly followed in their footsteps, and are still reaping the benefits. Now I'm coming to the end of this." I displayed my palms. "I know I've taken you around the bend and back again. But if we want to do anything here today we want to tell others here in the city of Gary, people in the state of Indiana and in this country of the United States of America, that if U.S. Steel was the model for many other corporations of its type, corporations of like mind, we want to say what the old folks used to say. 'What is done in the dark will come to the light.' We know what you have done. And we know who you are," I threatened The Gary Roundtable." And 'You must reap what you have sown.'"

Aunt Tee stepped aside as Thomas and my mother pulled back an old quilt and unveiled a plethora of Native American artifacts.

"We must acknowledge the atrocities of the past. It is the only way to reconcile them."

Applause erupted again.

I wanted to launch M.A.P.P.S. with heartfelt enthusiasm and I believed I was hitting my mark. Definitely, I felt more at ease with the crowd. I knew the people who had come to the meeting wanted to be proud of themselves, to be proud of their city, and I felt I was giving them a brand new reason. "The map can be found on the website www.MAPPSnetwork.org, and it has already been created. We want this site to be a rich source of information for individuals who are looking for others in their community, who are facing similar problems that they believe are associated with pollutants. I'm talking rare diseases. Respiratory problems. Mental or emotional problems."

CHAPTER 43

I thought I heard a Native American chant. Then I noticed Sally had made her way to the front of the crowd. I couldn't ignore her because she was quite a distraction; but I took a deep breath and attempted to remain focused.

"Right now, if one of you believed pollutants were the reason someone in your family was suffering from a particular condition, and you went to the authorities as an individual with your problem." I shrugged. "You probably wouldn't get very far. But if there is a source of information where individuals have inputted their individual cases, and you find it at www.MAPPSnetwork.org, and you say, 'My goodness. They live in my area, and they are facing medical problems similar to ours, even though we were *told* they are extremely rare. So what could you do? You could band together and address your problems. Find out if your suspicions are valid. There is power in those numbers. That's why class action lawsuits are so effective, because of the numbers."

I motioned for a bottle of water. My throat felt scratchy. Perhaps I was too excited or trying too hard to get my point across. Whatever the reason I hoped the water would help.

"Take your time," a male voice yelled.

My mother passed an open bottle to me. I took several swallows before I began again.

"In the name M.A.P.P.S., Mothers Aware of the Power of Pollutants on Society. We left those double P's in there because we wanted to emphasize the power of pollutants. We could have said Mothers Aware of Pollutants in Society. And it would have spelled the word *maps* perfectly. But we didn't want to do that. No. Because the power pollutants have on society does not only affect our bodies and our minds, the power of pollutants give big business the ability to come in and say, 'we have the money to do an environmental cleanup, and we have the money to redevelop this part of the city that is tainted by pollutants. We have the money to do this thing that is good for the city as a whole,' although many much poorer individuals will lose their homes in the process." I paused for emphasis. "The power of pollutants gives big business the ability to cry eminent domain. So M.A.P.P.S. wants to empower the individual, the underdog so to speak. We want you to know you are not alone. That your dilemma is not a silent one. That others are aware, they know, and because of that knowledge, perhaps, just perhaps, we can band together and make a difference."

By now, Sally's chant couldn't be ignored. It was loud, and Frances had come up front to try and quiet her. A few people were complaining, but it didn't matter to Sally, she just continued to sing her song, and it didn't seem as if she was planning to stop. At first I didn't know what to do, but then I decided before things turned ugly, that I had no choice but to acknowledge her.

"Some of you people in the back can't hear this,

but we're being serenaded up here," I said.

"We can hear it all right." One man yelled. "Who in the world is it?"

"I'd like to introduce you to someone." I stretched out my arm. "Come here, Sally," I said. "You want to come up here and join me?"

Sally continued to chant as she looked into my eyes. I knew the instant she recognized me. Silently, she came forward and stood beside me.

"Earlier, I explained my definition of mother, and I mentioned there was a woman who brought me into that understanding. Her name was Frances Weaver." I pointed to Frances. "Well, this is her good friend, Sally. And I have to say they were both friends of my grandmother who passed away recently. Anna Lee Featherstone."

I smiled at my mother and Sally began a new song, America the Beautiful.

I spoke a little louder. "You know, Sally is the woman who was taken to jail for making an altar on U.S. Steel's property about a month and a half ago. Frances told me that Sally probably knows how to get onto the property because of the hobos who still jump the trains and fish back there. She probably took trespassing notes from them."

There was more laughter.

I watched what I thought was a hawk fly over the crowd, and turned serious. "But some people like Sally here believe that U.S. Steel was built on land sacred to Native Americans." I swept my arm over the Native American artifacts. "That somewhere on this vast three thousand acre property there were Pottawatomie burial grounds and perhaps, burial grounds of other people native to this land. And these people believe, any time land like this is not honored, when the spirit of the ancestors, the spirit of this land is not honored, there is going to be trouble down the road." I paused. "Well, here is the proof that there are Native American burial grounds beneath this steel plant." I pointed toward the mill. "And we can definitely say we are down the road, and there is trouble. There is trouble in this little city of Gary, which has held the dubious title of murder capital of America for nine years straight until New Orleans took the crown after Katrina.

"Now, how do we address, appease if you will, those spirits?" I shrugged. "Perhaps Sally has the answer. For centuries, for thousands of years, indigenous people have done just what she is doing. They have sung songs. Perhaps singing is a way we can honor the people and the land from our hearts, letting them know they are not forgotten."

Sally completed the first verse of America the Beautiful and started singing it again. It was an awkward moment for me until I was drawn in by the sincerity in her voice. There was something about the child-like innocence of her elderly face that deeply moved me, and I decided to join Sally, drawing on the memory of my grade school music classes at Ernie Pyle Elementary. We sang the stanza together.

"Oh, beautiful, for spacious skies, for amber waves of grain. For purple mountains majesty, above the fruitful plane. America! America! God shed his grace on thee. And a crown thy good with brotherhood, from sea to shining sea."

When Sally began again, my mother came and

stood by my side, and Aunt Tee stood beside her. I glanced down and there was Thomas at the very end. I could tell they weren't certain of the words, but we sang anyway. The next thing I knew voices in the crowd had joined in. People, who I am sure like me, probably had not sung that song since they were children.

It was strangely moving to sing that particular song, America the Beautiful; because it made me reflect on how beautiful the land must have been when it was honored by the Native Americans before they were forced to leave their homes across the country. My thoughts bounced from one thing to another as I watched the crowd. I thought about what happened in that house near Marquette Park and the ritual Pulaski had described to Thomas and me, and I thought about racism and the beauty of the Indiana Dunes. But when we all sang 'And crown thy good with brotherhood' I thought about how unbrotherly it was when poor people could lose their homes in the name of progress.

Yet over all, I thought about how good it felt to sing at that moment. To sing with these people who had united for what I felt was a high cause, a cause that Sally believed in, just as Grandpa Eli did.

The singing and the artifacts were obviously news footage gold to the cameramen because they were filming people, especially Sally, up close and from far away. And that's how the meeting ended, with us singing. Although after everyone else had stopped Sally, in her three girlish braids, and a faded floral dress continued her song, her aged voice embraced by the wind.

CHAPTER 44

After the meeting one of the reporters approached me and asked for an interview. I agreed just as Thomas whispered, "You did a great job," in my ear.

"Thank you," I said as I hugged him.

As I walked with the reporter away from the crowd, I was surprised to see Pulaski, sitting in a wheelchair with Nathan, of all people, standing behind him.

"Could you give me a moment please," I said to the reporter.

"Certainly," he replied.

I could feel his curious gaze as it followed me.

"Mr. Pulaski," I said as I went and stood beside him. I glanced at Nathan. "You made it."

"Raw-ee." He replied, his eyes unusually bright.

Pulaski couldn't say my name. I felt bad as I reached down and shook his motionless hand, but I was extremely aware of Nathan standing behind him. I couldn't believe he had shown up at the press conference.

"The stroke affected his speech," he said. "Basically, his entire body."

My body stiffened at the sound of his voice. I knelt beside the wheelchair.

"Oh, Mr. Pulaski, we've been through so much."

"Is this the Charles Pulaski your aunt said was

a motivating force behind M.A.P.P.S.?" The reporter asked.

I nodded, and I saw him motion to the cameramen to start shooting. Somehow I didn't feel it was the proper thing to do, but Nathan didn't say anything so I didn't either. I leaned closer to Pulaski. "Did you get to hear any of the program?"

"Yaw," the reply forced its way through.

"That's good," I said but I couldn't smile. "You should be proud today, Mr. Pulaski." A lump formed in my throat. "This couldn't have happened without you." I touched his hand again.

I stood up and looked at Nathan. He looked so innocent, as if he hadn't a clue as to what had happened. And it dawned on me, perhaps Nathan didn't know. But I couldn't walk away without enlightening him to some degree. So I got close enough to Nathan so no one else would hear.

"You better be careful about who you talk to," I said. "You and your father aren't safe either. You nearly got me killed."

For a moment his gaze clouded with confusion, then a frightened disbelief took over.

"I didn't know," he mumbled. "I was upset because when I got to my father after he collapsed in the yard, he said your name and something about The Gary Roundtable being powerful Masons, and something about danger." He swallowed. "I— I was angry because I felt you brought on his stroke."

I glanced at the reporter who was watching us intently. I knew Nathan was telling the truth, and I let go of a deep sigh.

"You just be careful, Nathan. And take care of

your father."

I bent over Pulaski. "Aunt Tee and Thomas will be glad to see you."

Pulaski's gaze misted with tears, before some of the moisture escaped from the corner of his eye.

"You will make sure that they get to see him, won't you?" I looked at Nathan.

We locked gazes.

He nodded before he said, "Yes, I'll make sure."

"Good," I replied. I touched Pulaski's arm once again. "Good-bye, Mr. Charles."

Pulaski looked down at his lap and didn't look up again.

The reporter and I walked past another reporter who was taping his introduction that included something about singing and Steel Mill Sally. All this made me nervous. It was my first interview, and for it to be on camera only added to my discomfort. But at last, the interview was short and sweet and I was glad when it was over.

We were saying our goodbyes when a woman with a determined stride approached. She acknowledged me but her eyes were on the reporter

"My name is Kathy Johnson," she said, offering her hand. "I gave birth to three sons, right here in Gary. Two of them ended up murdering somebody and the third one was killed by another boy. I always felt there was something wrong with that." Her voice shook. "Now I choose to believe those things didn't happen just because my sons were evil. Or that boy was evil."

I had started to walk away but I lingered after hearing her introduction. At that moment it seemed the sun broke through the hazy weather, and because of

the pain in her voice, I felt the elements were acknowledging what people like this woman had been through,
and what we had set out to do about it.

"I'm not saying they were saints, but for me to
lose all three of them to murder." She pointed toward
the mill. "When my children were little and it was
warm outside, I used to go fishing in the Little Calumet River almost every day to feed my family because
that was the easiest way to keep food on the table. I
could smell there was something in that water, but we
didn't have any money, and I convinced myself that it
was okay because we weren't the only ones. There were
plenty of families feeding themselves from the Little
Calumet." The woman shook her head. "But it wasn't
okay. It wasn't." She shook her head again. "I always
knew something was wrong." She continued to speak
as she walked away. "Now, you put that on the news."

For approximately an hour various people came
up and spoke with me. We chatted and they thanked
me for what we were doing. They thanked me for
providing a voice for regular citizens like them. Over
and over again I told them, although I no longer lived
there, Gary was my hometown, and in doing something
for Gary and in doing something for them, I was doing
something for myself. And you know what? I knew it
was true.

CHAPTER 45

The following day Aunt Tee came to my mother's house. She had never set foot in my parent's home although they had lived there over twenty-five years. When my father died she attended the wake and the funeral, but she did not join the small group of family and friends who came to the house to eat after the services. I knew healing had begun within and between the women of my family when she rang the doorbell. My first instinct was to answer the door myself, but I held back and allowed my mother to welcome her.

"Hello, Teresa," she said. Come on in."

"Why thank you. Thank you," Aunt Tee replied as she entered. She looked around. "My goodness. Look at what I have been missing all these years. Look at this place."

"Hey, Aunt Tee." I walked over and gave her a hug.

"Rossi." Her eyes twinkled.

"Come on, Te—" My mother looked toward the kitchen when the telephone rang.

"You two go ahead, Mama." I walked over to the phone. "I'll get it."

"All right," she said. "Come on back to the sunroom, Teresa," my mother continued. "We were back there looking at television."

"This is one pretty place, Pearl, and I mean it," I

heard Aunt Tee say before I said, "Hello," into the receiver, but there was only silence.

My stomach did a strange flip. I waited and said, "Hello," again as déjà vu surfaced.

Still no answer.

Scared and angry I said out of desperation, "Remember we know who you are. You just remember that. And you'd better make this your last phone call or your names will be in the newspaper tomorrow."

To my utter shock a deep voice said. "No matter what you do the plan will go on. You remember that."

The line went dead.

"Is it for you, Rossi?" My mother called from the sunroom.

"Yes." I said quickly. "Yes, it's for me." I replaced the receiver. "I'll be there in a minute."

After I hung up the telephone I couldn't go into the sunroom, so I went to the bathroom, and I just stood there. Finally, I sat on the edge of the bathtub and I thought about what the man had said. The more I thought about it, the more I was certain, that phone call was a kind of last hoorah. You know, when the bully has to have the last word or the last lick even though they know it's over, and you got the best of them? I knew that's what that phone call was, and I accepted that for my truth. So I got myself together, and I joined my mother and my aunt in the sun room.

"I love the way you arranged things in here," I heard Aunt Tee say as I approached.

"Benjamin liked this room too." My mother glanced at me before she continued. "Your brother always had great taste."

"Always did." Aunt Tee said, standing by a pine plant that was nearly five feet tall. "And your plants, they grow so well in here."

"Don't they though?" My mother smiled. "I've had some of these plants for as long as I've been in this house."

I listened to my mother and my aunt's verbal dance; an acknowledgment of my mother's womanly skills and Aunt Tee's ability to see them. After that, the conversation focused on the press conference, the media coverage, and the article in the Gary Post Tribune.

"That was a large article and a big picture of us," my mother said. "I was kind of surprised." She looked down, but it was plain to see she was bursting with pride. "I didn't think they'd put such a big article and picture in that paper."

"It was a good article," Aunt Tee said, "but there was another article that was just as interesting on the same page."

"I saw that," I said. "It was about some of the old buildings downtown being turned into condominiums for people who might be displaced by the Brownfields projects."

Aunt Tee smacked her hands and laughed. "That's it. That's it." She chuckled some more. "I think we scared somebody. Because I've never heard of that before."

My mother made a face. "I think they were trying to steal some of our thunder, if you ask me. Putting it on the same page and everything. Somebody pulled some strings because we got too much attention yesterday."

I caught myself examining a car that drove by, through the large windows. "We got somebody's attention. That's for sure," I said as I thought about The Gary Roundtable.

"You're probably right, Pearl," Aunt Tee said. "Because they also wrote about property tax break incentives in that article. I think it said something like, if your house is in a designated Brownfields Project zone, until they break ground, according to your income, you might pay little to no property taxes. I guess the businessmen behind it must pick up the rest of the bill. Can you believe it?"

"It was all those media folks, we had there," my mother said. "Those news people did a good job. They had it on two television stations yesterday evening, and one of my friends called and told me it was in the Indianapolis paper this morning. Wasn't it, Rossi?"

"That's what she said," I replied." I sat forward. "I wonder if it was on CNN."

"It was on CNN," Aunt Tee said. "We got national coverage yesterday. International, maybe. CNN is seen all over the world." She bragged.

"Wow." My mother sat back. "This is really something."

It is, I thought, and I knew we had struck a meaningful blow in our own little way.

"So you have cable, Teresa?" My mother asked.

"Mm-hmm. I've been getting it now for years," Aunt Tee replied. "It's really not that expensive."

"Oh really," my mother replied.

I felt the chill of comparisons descend in the room, as my mother began to flip through her television channels.

"Wait, Pearl," Aunt Tee said, suddenly. "Go back. Go back."

"What is it?" My mother pressed the remote again.

"I'm sorry. I know this isn't my house but I thought I saw a—". Right there." She pointed. "It's Etta James."

"It sure is," my mother said.

Etta sang a few notes.

"Now that's music I can relate to," my mother declared. "I'ma be honest. I don't understand that rap music at all."

"You and me both," Aunt Tee replied.

Mama leaned forward. "This must be some kind of TV special because usually they don't play this kind of thing in the middle of the day. You might see it on public broadcasting or something during the evening. But I don't recall seeing anything like this during the daytime."

"Etta looks mighty young," Aunt Tee said. "She takes me back. Wa-ay back."

"She sure does." My mother agreed. "It looks like she's in a nightclub or something, and I could swear I had a dress just like the one she's wearing."

Aunt Tee began to sway. "She's one of my favorites. Always has been. Always will be."

"Mm-hmm." My mother replied.

I quietly thanked the music and television gods for their intervention as Etta started a new song, Something's Got a Hold on Me.

"Ohhh, now. This is my favorite." Aunt Tee got up. "You all have to excuse me, but I just can't sit down when I hear this song. My arm may be in a cast, but I still have my feet." She began to dance in front of her chair.

"Move over there, Teresa." Mama pointed to an open space on the floor. "You'll have more room over there."

I watched in silence, and I'm certain my mother's request had more to do with her concern over Aunt Tee hitting her favorite plant than my aunt having adequate dancing space.

"I'll go on one condition," Aunt Tee said.

Mama's brow lined. "What's that?"

"You two have to join me."

I got up immediately. "You don't have to ask me twice," I said. "Come on, Mama. It'll be our celebration dance."

"I am not up for no dancin'." She leaned back in her chair.

"Why not?" Aunt Tee asked. "You and Ben used to cut up on the dance floor. And I never could do the fox-trot like you."

My mother waved her hand. "Go on now."

Aunt Tee put her good hand on her hip. "You know I couldn't. Come on over here and show me how you do it."

My mother chuckled. "Your brother used to have me out on that dance floor doing all kinds of things. We could dance, now." Slowly, she got up. "Let me see what you two are doing over here." She chuckled again. "I haven't danced in I don't know when."

So there we were. Aunt Tee, Mama and me, lined up together doing the foxtrot.

I watched Aunt Tee as she allowed my mother to

be her teacher. I knew that's what she was doing because I had seen Aunt Tee do the foxtrot many times before.

As we danced, kidded and laughed, gently, like a soft breeze, the last thing Sally said to me when I left her and Frances' house that day, surfaced in my mind. "Don't be scared," she said. "You'll make a difference and she'll be okay."

I don't know why it came to me then, but instantly, I knew Sally was referring to everything that had happened, and maybe would happen. I don't know if she knew the details but I was convinced Sally had known about The Gary Roundtable and what Aunt Tee and I would face. That singer of songs had known, just as she had known my destiny as a Daughter of Mabel was connected with Gary's destiny.

That touched me in a way that I can still feel right now. But at that moment, before I realized it, out loud, I said, "She knew."

"What?" My mother looked at me but continued to step.

"Who knew?" Aunt Tee smiled as she fox-trotted.. "What are you talking about, Rossi?"

Sally knew! I shouted inside myself. But when I looked at my mother and at Aunt Tee, I simply waved my hand, smiled and said, "Don't pay me any attention. I'm just having a good time over here."

You see, telling them what Sally really knew would mean I'd have to tell them everything, and I had no intention of doing that.

Then, a more subtle message crept into my thoughts. What Sally said also referred to Gary. That those of us connected with Gary, Indiana need not worry about our city. That Gary would be okay.

Epilogue

2008

Perhaps Sally's words meant none of those things. Perhaps after everything that happened in Gary I'd been stretched to the point of reading something where there was absolutely nothing. Perhaps Sally was just another woman whose pain had forced her into her own reality.

Or maybe there **was** something else. Maybe Sally's pain opened her to the ultimate reality. The world of Spirit and intuition, a place my Grandpa Eli knew well and my Grandma Anna Lee feared. You see, knowing what many believe is impossible to know yields diverse results in the knower. Like in my case, I knew Thomas and I would never be together, and I felt a sad resignation when he reunited with his family a year ago.

But I have come to treasure some things. Conscious silence, words never spoken because they may cause pain, is a noble thing. My mother knew a lot about conscious silence.

I will never regret not telling my mother and

Aunt Tee about what happened with The Gary Round-table. They did their best to protect me when I was young; I'll continue to do the same for them as they age. The rewards are great. For instance, I cherish the peace in their voices when we talk about the subtle bloom on Gary's cheeks. Impeccable humane tactics by The Brownfields Project and powerful organizations speaking out on the link between pollutants and violent crime, have something to do with that infantile glow.

I've realized something. I've decided Gary, Indiana is female. How else would she stir such passion, and birth all that has come from her? Such love for Gary in her youthful days, and such disdain after her infamous tumble from grace. America's dream city. America's murder capital. And now, perhaps, America's redemption.

To tell the truth, as I sit here two years later, it's difficult to accept what happened in that house actually occurred. Remember, I'm the person who believes in the goodness of humanity, and even after The Gary Roundtable I still do. For me there is no other choice.

But it is rather amazing, isn't it? Because it also means, once again, an astrologist was right. It means, I, through healing my deepest pain, am the wounded healer who initiated a healing for Gary. It means Gary, through initiating M.A.P.P.S and addressing the core of her own sorrows, will be the wounded healer for U.S. cities suffering the same fate Gary has suffered.

But there's something else. I think my father, and others who worked in the bowels of industrial, corporate machines like U.S. Steel, and all the people who toiled and lived on Gary's soil are inseparable from our victory, just like the metals that remain in Gary's air and water. And I do mean victory, be it a battle or the war, because I believe the Master Astrologist set it up that way.

That's what I choose to believe. Now, you may choose otherwise, and, that is your right.

Made in the USA
Columbia, SC
05 April 2020